Kale to the Queen

Center Point
Large Print

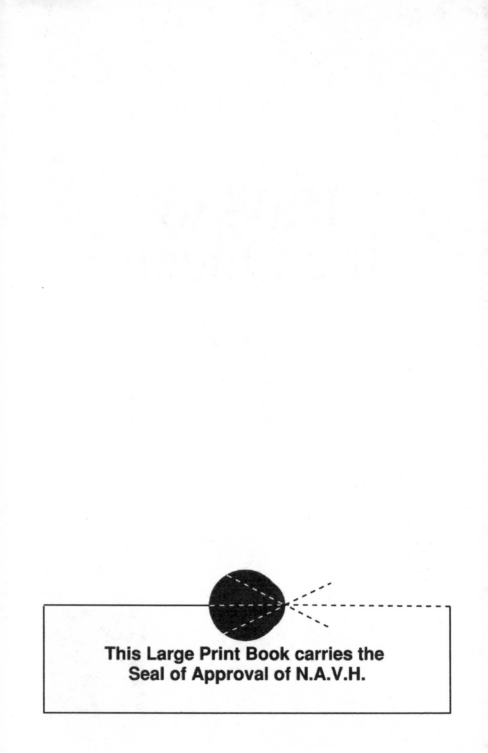

**This Large Print Book carries the
Seal of Approval of N.A.V.H.**

Kale
to the
Queen

A KENSINGTON PALACE CHEF MYSTERY

Nell Hampton

CENTER POINT LARGE PRINT
THORNDIKE, MAINE

This Center Point Large Print edition
is published in the year 2017 by arrangement with
Crooked Lane Books, an imprint of
The Quick Brown Fox & Company LLC.

The text of this Large Print edition is unabridged.
In other aspects, this book may vary
from the original edition.
Printed in the United States of America
on permanent paper.
Set in 16-point Times New Roman type.

ISBN: 978-1-68324-415-8

Library of Congress Cataloging-in-Publication Data
Names: Hampton, Nell (Mystery author) author.
Title: Kale to the queen : a Kensington Palace chef mystery /
    Nell Hampton.
Description: Center Point Large Print edition. | Thorndike, Maine : Cen-
ter Point Large Print, [2017]
Identifiers: LCCN 2017010248 | ISBN 9781683244158
    (hardcover : alk. paper)
Subjects: LCSH: Cooks—England—London—Fiction. | Americans—
England—London—Fiction. | Kensington Palace (London, England)—
Fiction. | Large type books. | GSAFD: Mystery fiction.
Classification: LCC PS3608.A695965 H36 2017 | DDC 813/.6—dc23
LC record available at https://lccn.loc.gov/2017010248

This story is for my dad,
who loves all things British. Love you!

Chapter 1

Kensington Palace. It was older than any building I'd ever seen before. It was glamorous and magnificent, and I was going to work there.

It was crazy to think that I, Carrie Ann Cole, a simple Midwestern girl, was in London, standing in the rain, staring up at the gates of Kensington Palace. My belongings were packed in two suitcases in my hands. What little else I had was in storage or still with my boyfriend of six years, John.

The whole thing was a piece of luck, really. I had graduated culinary school three years ago and worked in a Michelin-star restaurant in Chicago. A friend of mine, who catered events in New York City, got sick the day she was supposed to cater a charity event for the duke and duchess of Cambridge. So she asked me to fly in and take her place. The duchess was so impressed she asked to see me. We chatted, and a week later I got the call. Would I come to London and be the family chef for the duke and duchess and their children?

How do you say no to that?

Now I stood in front of the palace, in a place chock-full of history, to begin a career I hoped would last for many years. The excitement of it had me practically skipping as I gave the guards my credentials and got directions to where I should be. The entire time I soaked in all the sites as if I were Alice first stepping into Wonderland. It didn't matter that the light but constant rain ensured I was damp through and through.

"Leave your bags and come this way, please." The woman who met me was thin and very proper in a black skirt and cream sweater set. Her hair was a perfect gray shoulder-length bob. She turned on her one-inch heels and walked away. "Don't dawdle. You are not on a sightseeing tour."

Jet-lagged, I dropped my overstuffed tote beside my battered suitcase and followed after her. I could barely believe I was actually inside Kensington Palace. Not in the tourist part, but in the royal apartments where, well, the royals lived. I tried not to gawk.

"I am Mrs. Worth, the household manager for the duke and duchess of Cambridge," she said in a crisp British accent. "You are late."

"I couldn't get a cab, so I took the subway," I said as I hurried behind her.

"It's the tube, not the subway. Learn the language, Miss Cole."

"Yes, ma'am." Language wasn't the only thing I had to learn. I knew I wasn't properly dressed. I'd just lost an entire night flying across the Atlantic from Chicago to London. My head was a bit fuzzy. Thankfully, I'd taken some time to brush

8

my teeth and put my hair up on the airplane. But that didn't matter much, as the rain had my bangs curling like a demon around my face.

"You will find, Miss Cole, that I do not have the time or patience for tardiness." Mrs. Worth shot me a look of disapproval over her shoulder.

"It won't happen again." I took off my wet jacket and slung it over my arm as I followed behind her. Thankfully I'd decided to wear black slacks and a white polo for the plane ride. It was evening when I'd left Chicago but midmorning when I'd arrived in London. As a chef, I usually was more concerned with food than time. Luckily my best friend Lucy had calculated the time and figured out that my ticket left me less than an hour to arrive at my new place of employment.

She loved all things British and informed me that it wouldn't do to show up in jeans and a T-shirt. My wet slip-on black shoes were probably not appropriate, but hey, I did just get off a plane.

"The duke and duchess's apartment is two floors up," Mrs. Worth said. "Your room is in the north wing. I've asked Reginald to take your bags there. Now, as the family's personal chef, you will be working in the family kitchen and occasionally in the apartment kitchen itself. The larger event kitchen is run by the palace's head chef, Jeffery Butterbottom. Chef Butterbottom is a world-renowned chef with years of degrees and certificates behind him. While he is not your supervisor, you will defer to him in matters of proper dietary guidelines. That said, you will have a prep and a sous chef and are entirely responsible for what happens in your own kitchen."

"Yes, ma'am," I said. We moved along at a brisk pace as she pointed out various offices. I had the presence of mind to take notes on my smart phone so that I wouldn't be too lost once I was on my own. It boggled my mind that so many people worked here. Everyone had their own station and everything had to be spotless. I watched in awe as a simple nod or frown from Mrs. Worth had people scurrying.

"We are meeting with the duchess now," Mrs. Worth said as she stopped outside the apartment's servants' entrance. She studied me and shook her head. "Your appearance is not as professional as I had hoped. But it will have to do. The duchess is on a schedule, as well."

"It was raining," I said and pressed down my bangs. They were damp and had a tendency to curl inappropriately. My hair was pulled back into a twist; otherwise, it would have been a mass of frizz.

Mrs. Worth's mouth was a tight line of disapproval. Her brown gaze was far from welcoming, but then I supposed that when you had so many employees to deal with, you probably wouldn't be the warm and welcoming type. "When you see the duchess, speak only when spoken to and shake her hand only if she offers hers."

"Okay," I said. "Do I curtsy?"

She heaved a long sigh and opened the doors. The apartments were light and airy. I had read that the duke and duchess had taken over Princess Elsa's apartment in the palace. They had had it completely renovated into a modern style that still echoed the long history of the building.

From what I could see from the servants' hallway, the apartment was as tasteful as the duchess's wardrobe. We passed open doors, and I sneaked a look. One room was clearly a little girl's nursery done in shades of pink and white. The next room was a huge playroom filled with toys and a child-size table with four chairs. The next room was a boy's nursery decorated in playful blues and reds. It was clear to see from the décor that the little prince was a couple years older than his sister.

"Come along," Mrs. Worth said, and I realized I had stopped walking. Mrs. Worth never looked as if she were rushing, but I had to practically run to keep up as she moved down the corridor. The hall itself was well lit, with old wood floors and pale blue walls. She stopped and knocked on a door a few yards from the nurseries.

The door was answered by a woman in her mid- to late twenties. She was pretty, with a round face, friendly smile, bright-blue eyes, and long blonde hair. She wore a simple shift dress and cardigan in matching blush. "Ah, Mrs. Worth, yes, the duchess is waiting for you. Please come in."

"Miss Nethercott, this is Miss Carrie Ann Cole, the new personal chef," Mrs. Worth formally introduced me. "Miss Penelope Nethercott is the duchess's personal secretary."

"Hello, Miss Cole. It's a pleasure to meet you," Miss Nethercott said.

"It's a pleasure to meet you, as well," I said with a smile and a firm handshake. "Please excuse my appearance. I got caught in the rain." I reached up and pressed my curly bangs down.

"You're fine," Miss Nethercott said with a wink. "In time, you'll learn to always carry an umbrella." Then she leaned in close. "You may call me Penny when we aren't in the duchess's salon."

"Thank you," I said. "I'm Carrie Ann."

"Miss Nethercott! We do not want to keep the duchess waiting," Mrs. Worth said with a scolding tone.

"No, certainly not," Penny said and opened the door wide. "Please do come in."

The room was large and bright with windows across one wall. There was a fireplace to the left, and above it was a family picture of the duke and duchess and their children. To one side was a large slender desk that appeared to be an antique. Behind the desk was the duchess, with her perfect brown hair pulled back out of the way. She wore a navy pencil skirt and silk chiffon blouse with a blue-and-white fleur-de-lis pattern. She looked exactly like her pictures. This was the second time I had spoken to her in person, and I still could not get over how lovely she was.

Beside her, the little prince played with a wooden helicopter. He wore red knee-length pants and a red-and-white pullover top, knee socks, and black walking shoes. A woman who appeared to be in her late forties stood watch over him. She wore a gray-and-white outfit and sensible shoes. Her hair was short and tightly curled. Her face was as round as her figure and her cheeks were apple-red, her eyes a sparkling blue. I pegged her as his nanny and sent her a smile and a nod. She nodded at me and then concentrated on her charge.

On the opposite side of the desk, a younger woman held the baby princess in her arms. The little girl was dressed in a blue-and-white dress with a Peter Pan collar and ruffled skirt. Her feet were encased in white ankle socks and soft white shoes. She sucked on her first two fingers, and the nurse wiped drool from the toddler's hand with a white cloth.

"Your Highness, Mrs. Worth and Miss Cole," Penny said and stepped to the side.

"Mrs. Worth, you are on time as usual," the duchess said and looked up at me. "Miss Cole, it's a pleasure to see you again."

"The pleasure is all mine," I said and gave an

awkward curtsy. I felt the heat of a blush rush up my cheeks as everyone patently ignored my faux pas.

"Please forgive the rush. I realize you must have just gotten off the plane."

I smiled but didn't answer.

"As you may know, we have a bit of a snafu," the duchess continued. "We are in need of a chef for this evening's get-together. It is just family, but my cousin is arriving with her best friend and family in tow. It seems that Miss Anderson, the friend, is bringing her son, and today is his first birthday. We must, of course, prepare a small birthday party for the children, and as you know, my previous chef had a family emergency and has left our employ. I would ask the main kitchen to cook up something for the party, but I'm afraid they have already been contracted to run a state dinner with the visiting son of the president of Limberta." She smiled her perfect smile and circled her right hand over the planners and digital tablet on her desk. "Scheduling is everything in a household this size."

"Yes, ma'am," I muttered, "um, er, your Royal Highness . . ." Mrs. Worth gave me a withering side-glance. I bit my bottom lip to remind myself not to speak unless asked a question.

"The party is at seven PM because the children are at bed by nine," the duchess said. "We will need the following menu made up." She handed a sheet of linen paper to Mrs. Worth, who handed it to me. "Can you do it?"

I glanced at the seven courses listed. "Certainly," I answered. This was my first day and my first assignment, and I wasn't about to say no.

"Perfect," the duchess said. "Thank you. Penelope, show Miss Cole to the kitchens and her quarters. I need to speak to Mrs. Worth."

"Yes, ma'am," Penny said and, with a polite nod, pointed toward the door.

I would have to work at not saying good-bye. It was clear I was dismissed and that while everyone was cordial, I was not expected to be a friend. Penny walked me back to the servants' hallway and closed the door behind us.

"Come this way," she said. Her two-inch heels clicked rhythmically on the wooden floor. "Welcome to the household," Penny said with a smile. "There is always something going on. Now, have you been to the offices of staffing yet to get your badge and fill out your employment papers?"

"No," I said. "I literally got off the plane, took the subway—"

"You mean the tube," she corrected me.

"Yes, the tube," I said.

"How did you find it?"

"I'm sorry? I thought everyone knew that there's an entrance from the airport."

"No," Penny said and laughed at me. "What were your thoughts about the tube?"

"Oh, it was awfully crowded," I said. "I barely squeezed myself and my luggage on."

"Hmmm, rush hour," Penny said. "Well, you will be avoiding that from now on, as you will have rooms here so that you will be available to the family six days a week. Your day off is Monday, as weekends are usually the biggest event times for the family."

"Of course," I said. "It was in my contract."

The door at the far end of the hall opened, and a tall man in a black suit, blue tie, white dress shirt, and well-polished shoes strode into the hallway. He walked with the pure confidence of an athlete. I judged him to be in his early thirties, but without the soft face of a man who sat at a desk all day long.

Penny and I stopped as he came up to us.

"Who do we have here?" he asked with a slight Scottish brogue in his deep voice.

"Miss Carrie Ann Cole," Penny said. I noticed how she flushed in his presence. "She's the new family chef for the duke and duchess. Miss Cole, this is Ian Gordon, head of security at Kensington Palace."

"Ah, the American," he said and turned his gorgeous deep-blue eyes on me. He had long black eyelashes and thick black hair cut short in a neat military style. His nose was straight and fit his square jaw, dimpled chin, and slight smile.

"Hello," I said, surprised by how low and hoarse the word came out. I cleared my throat.

"How are you finding England?" he asked, lifting one of his dark eyebrows with the question.

"Good, fine, and you?" I asked, feeling rather stupid for asking.

"Well, that's a question to be discussed over a drink," he said, and his smile turned up a bit. It hit me then who he looked like: he reminded me of a young Sean Connery in the old James Bond movies. "But we don't have time for that now. I've an appointment with the duchess." He glanced at my visitor badge. "You need to ensure you get a proper badge with access to the doors. We take security here very seriously."

"She just got off the plane," Penny said and put her hand on my arm. "The duchess asked her to step in on tonight's birthday party for the children."

"Right," he said, and I was once again uncomfortable under his searching gaze. "I suppose that will have to do for now. Miss Cole, please ensure that Mrs. Worth has her secretary give you an orientation schedule so that they can get you a proper badge."

"Okay," I said.

"Good day, ladies," he said and walked down the hall to the duchess's office. He gave a short knock before entering.

"Wow," I said and stared after him as if he might rematerialize at any moment.

"Ha!" Penny said with a knowing smile. She put her arm through mine and turned me back to our walk down the hallway. "Don't get your hopes up there. Ian Gordon is a decorated soldier and one of the queen's favorites. He takes the rules very seriously."

"Okay . . ."

"One of those rules is no fraternizing between staff," Penny said with a sad sigh. "If you work here, he won't do anything more than tip his hat in your direction."

"Oh," I said, "that's okay. I have a boyfriend. We've been dating for six years and have lived together for three."

"That's a long time."

"I know. John wants to take a break, but I secretly hope we can work out a long-distance relationship. Or, even better, that he'll follow me to London. There is so much more to see and do here, and the international exposure would be great for him."

"Did he suggest the break?"

"Yes," I said with a sigh. "I'm not going to lie. It hurt. But he didn't really mean it. I mean, he was cooking at the time, and I mentioned how hard a long-distance relationship can be for some couples. Then I told him how great London was and how he should move here."

"That's when he mentioned the break?"

"Yes, he said, 'Or we could take a break. It might not hurt to concentrate on our careers for a while.' "

"Did you agree to the break?"

"I might have," I said with a shrug, "but I really think we could do the long-distance thing."

"So are you on a break or aren't you? I'm getting confused."

"I suppose we are, but I'm hoping he'll miss me and relocate to London."

"Really," Penny said. "What does he do that he could relocate?"

"He's a chef, too, in Chicago," I replied. My sleep-deprived thoughts turned to John. He'd come to me the night before and said he thought we should use my time away to take a break from our relationship. I had been devastated. I asked him if there was another woman, but he said no; his work was too important to him to juggle me and another woman. John was a gifted chef whose star was on the rise. It meant long nights at the restaurant, mornings spent at markets in search of fresh foods, afternoons spent on creating new dishes. He wanted to one day be a Michelin-star chef. That meant that his entire being was involved in the food world. He knew every critic and every top-shelf customer by name.

While John was a powerhouse, I didn't want to ride his coat tails. I wanted a career of my own.

It had been a strain on our relationship. While he wanted me to work with him, I wanted to be a personal chef for celebrities. Figuring out the person, the family, and their wants and needs and nourishing them so that they could do their art or their charities or whatever was a goal close to my heart. I didn't want to be a celebrity like John did; I wanted to help them.

But I had fallen into working with John. It was easy to get caught up in his excitement. Somewhere along the way, I got lost in the sea of sous chefs and prep personnel who worked for him, but I wanted to be more.

Perhaps getting his attention was part of the reason I took this job—I mean, besides the obvious glamour of working for the royal family. I felt it was time I took my life into my own hands. So when this incredible opportunity presented itself, I took it. Of course we'd talked about it, and he'd said I should do what I wanted. I was hoping the distance would nudge him enough to see that after six years, I needed to be able to move forward with my own dreams or move on from our relationship. Forward being the choice for me. I tried not to think about what would happen if we ended up moving on. I knew it was cliché, but John was my first and only love.

Nudging him by moving to London for a year was the right thing to do. So why did I suddenly feel as though I had jumped off a cliff into a dark abyss with nothing but my résumé and degree from the culinary institute to use as my parachute?

Here's hoping I learned how to fly—or, at the very least, figured out how to keep from crashing to the ground in a ball of flames.

Chapter 2

I have to get back to work," Penny said. "This is your room, number two-twenty-two. Someone will be by soon to show you to your work space."

"Thanks for showing me the way," I said and opened the door.

I was surprised to find a small suite with a living area and a tiny kitchenette with a door to what I supposed was the bedroom.

Undecorated, the living area appeared to be freshly painted in a neutral beige shade. Thankfully it was a bit brighter than the beige in the servants' hallway. The tiny kitchen had a white subway-tile backsplash, a porcelain sink, and a plug-in two-burner stovetop with a stainless steel tea kettle on top and a dorm-sized refrigerator below. There were open shelves above the sink that held two teacups, saucers, plates, and bowls made out of white porcelain. There were two cabinets with double doors that I assumed held the minimal amount of pots and pans. The eating area consisted of a tiled breakfast bar and two brown stools.

Beyond that was a small couch with a matching end table and coffee table. On the opposite wall was a stand with a small old television set on top and a small winged-back chair. While the couch was striped pink-and-white, the chair had cabbage roses in the same pink. It was a bit like going back into the 1980s.

This must be modern for a palace this old, I thought.

Across from me was a window with white curtains. I walked over to see what view I had. My room overlooked a small alleyway and the rooftops of the kitchens and other buildings in the complex.

The view wasn't much, but it reminded me that I was truly in England, as the rooftops and parking areas looked Victorian. The good news was that the sill was large and flat, so I could put out a few pots of herbs and bring some life to the room.

The place was clean, if plain. I supposed it would be up to me to decorate. I had a box of things coming. I had shipped it here a week ago, but it had to go through customs. I didn't pack much—just a few pictures of my family and some of my favorite old cookbooks.

You could find pretty much any recipe online these days, but there was something about the old cookbooks that drew me in. I think it was because I found comfort in the long line of chefs that had come before me. The older the cookbook, the better.

I imagined that I would put the cookbooks on the empty shelves above the sink. Perhaps a collage of frames over the striped sofa. My best glossy-pictured cookbooks would go on the wooden coffee table.

I stepped into the bedroom. My suitcases were nowhere to be found. I frowned in confusion. Perhaps Reginald put them in the closet? The closet was actually a double-doored wall unit with dark wood varnish and antique handles. I opened the wardrobe and discovered that my suitcases had been unpacked. My clothes were hung up on the appropriate hangers. Starting with my five chef jackets on the left, the closet was carefully arranged in order from my five pairs of black utilitarian pants, six white polo shirts, and the few other things I owned. There were two drawers under the hanging area. I opened them to find my underthings, folded and placed in order.

My cheeks burned when I thought of a complete stranger unpacking my things. Even my toiletries were unpacked and arranged in the tiny bathroom. Still, it was all there. My few pairs of shoes rested between the drawers and my hung clothes. I had packed light, thinking I could buy clothes in London after I had been here a while.

This was my new home for the next year, as per my contract. It was kind of cute in its economy of size and utilitarian mission. I glanced at my wrist watch. I had fifteen minutes to shower and get dressed before Mrs. Worth, or whomever she sent, showed up to continue my orientation.

"You wanted a glamorous adventure," I told

myself as I got into a lukewarm shower. "You got it."

Within minutes of my getting dressed, there was a knock from the hallway. I grabbed a chef jacket and hurried to answer the door. A second impatient knock came before I reached it. "I'm coming," I said.

When I opened the door, it wasn't Mrs. Worth who greeted me.

"There you are," an older woman said. "I'm Mary Perkins, Mrs. Worth's secretary. I'll be completing today's orientation. You are Chef Cole?"

"Yes, hello," I said and slipped on my jacket.

"Good," she said in a matter-of-fact tone. "Button up, as we have a tight schedule. I've brought your complete orientation agenda for the next couple of days. This includes your security badge and key card. I trust you have the key to your room?"

"Oh, yes," I said and snagged the single key on a small key ring that sat on top of the breakfast bar. Under it was a room inspection list.

"By now you should have inspected your room," Mrs. Perkins said. "The maintenance room inspection is provided for you. Please sign it and bring it with you tomorrow when you attend orientation. There is no copying of room keys. If you lose it, you will be docked twenty-five pounds from your salary. Lose it twice and the price goes up to fifty pounds, three times to seventy-five pounds, et cetera. I'm sure you see the importance of keeping your key safe."

"Yes, ma'am," I said.

"Well, lock your door, and let's get on with it." She moved her hands in a small sweeping gesture as if to push me away.

I locked the door, pocketed my key, and followed after her while I buttoned my coat.

"You will keep a clean chef coat every day for kitchen use and a second clean coat for when you are meeting with Mrs. Worth or the duchess. Never wear the coat you are cooking in outside of the kitchen. Am I clear?"

"Yes, ma'am."

"Very good, then," Mary replied. "These are the rules: you are not to be seen in a dirty chef coat outside your kitchen, and an apron will never be worn outside the kitchen."

She was a formidable woman in her late fifties. She was shorter than I was, but then most people were since I was five foot nine inches tall. I would have to look up what that was in metric units now that I was in England. There were a lot of things I would have to do differently. Luckily I adapted well.

Growing up, my family had moved a lot. I had gone to nine different schools. If I could survive that, I could survive this.

As the secretary to the household manager, it

was clear to me that Mrs. Perkins took her duties very seriously. She dressed in a plain wool skirt that appeared to reach exactly two inches below the knees and a camel cardigan sweater set along with hose and flat brown loafers. Her gray hair was pulled back into a low ponytail at the base of her neck, and a pair of reading glasses dangled from a beaded eyeglass holder around her neck. She wore little makeup. There were small pearl earrings at her ears and a wedding band on her left ring finger. All this combined with her constant stern expression lead me to believe she was a very serious woman.

"The duke and duchess's apartment has twenty-one rooms," she said. "The family's living and entertaining areas and three kitchens. You are not to enter any of the apartment rooms without being asked to do so by the duchess or her representative. There is absolutely no snooping. The duke and duchess are a young couple, and they should feel as if their home is their sacred space. Am I clear?"

"Yes, ma'am."

"Good. Your room is near the private kitchen and is accessed only through the servants' hallway. There are no gentlemen callers allowed in the palace and especially in your room without express permission. The doors close at midnight and do not open again until six AM. If you do not arrive in time, you must find accommodations for the night, and you will not be compensated. Security for the royal family is of far more importance than your comfort."

"Okay," I said. The rules were a bit dorm-like, but it wasn't as if I went out clubbing every night, either.

"Your ID badge is also a key card and allows you access to this hallway, the staff entrance, and the family's private kitchen." She swiped her ID card. "There is no parking for the staff. If you need a ride, there is plenty of public transportation available."

"Great, I like to walk."

She didn't seem affected by my agreeableness in the least.

"As I said, there are three kitchens in the apartment. The first is the family kitchen, where the duchess likes to cook whenever she can. The other two are staff kitchens, which include your kitchen and the main kitchen. Caterers use the main kitchen as well for large events. You are not to set foot in that kitchen unless given permission, and even then, Chef Butterbottom is the boss. You must do what he says."

"He sounds like a regular Gordon Ramsey," I said.

"It is not uncommon for head chefs to be— shall we say—perfectionists. Now, you are the manager of the family kitchen." We turned right, went down a flight of stairs, walked through a short hall, and entered a small, square kitchen. "This is your station. You will have two assistants, Francis Deems and Michael Haregrove." She waved her hand and two men stood from the small table where they sat. They both wore white shirts, white pants, and white athletic shoes. One was short and bald. He wore an apron around his waist and carried a chef hat in his hand.

"Hi, I'm Chef Cole," I said and held out my hand.

"Francis Deems," the bald one said, his blue eyes clear. "It's a pleasure to meet you, Chef." He leaned in with a stage whisper. "You can call me Frank."

"Thank you, I will." I turned to the taller of the two men. This one was thin with a gaunt face and brown hair and eyes. His skin tone was olive. "I assume you are Chef Haregrove?" I held out my hand.

"We are not chefs," he said and shook my hand. "We are assistants to the personal chef, which is you, Miss."

"Not chefs?" I turned to Mrs. Perkins.

"The duchess is not frivolous with the household budget," Mary Perkins said. "One personal chef is enough for her small family."

"But tonight's menu—"

"Is unusual, as the duchess said. She is confident you will manage it. And, while they are not chefs, Mr. Deems is an expert in meats and butchering," Mrs. Perkins said, "and Mr. Haregrove is your food prep assistant."

"I'm good at fast chopping, Miss, er, Chef," Haregrove said.

I swallowed the sudden rush of nervous energy that went through me at the thought of creating a seven-course meal for twenty-two people by myself.

Unconcerned by what must have been a sudden look of panic that crossed my face, Mrs. Perkins continued, "The kitchen has everything you need. You will be expected to create a weekly menu and send it to Mrs. Worth to be approved. Once approved, you can go shopping for anything you need. The list of preferred grocers is in your welcome packet. There is also a small green-house stocked with fresh vegetables and herbs." She walked through the kitchen to a wall made out of glass and pushed open the door. I followed her out into a beautiful Victorian greenhouse. Inside were waist-high raised beds of herbs and vegetables, and in the corners, fruit trees came up from large pots set in the ground.

"This is wonderful," I said as I looked around.

"Jasper Fedman is the head greenhouse gardener. He will send you a list of what is ripe. Mark what you want to use and he will ensure it is harvested and cleaned for you."

"Great!" I replied.

"This is the extent of your area of the palace.

As I have said, the other apartments and family spaces are all off limits. We have a temporary identification card printed up for you. You will wear it at all times. Tomorrow after breakfast is finished, you will report to the office of human services, and they will replace the temporary identification with a real one. There will be a photo and a copy of your fingerprint on it. There are regular tours at Kensington Palace. It is our duty as staff to ensure tourists never enter the private areas."

"I understand."

"Security is tight in the palace," she said. "You may have noticed that there are mesh screens on all the windows. Do not open them. They help prevent any glass from being blown inside in case of an attack. There are also several emergency procedures. Those are covered in the welcome packet in your room. Also, we conduct quarterly drills. We expect you to participate and sign off on them. It's part of your contract."

"Yes, ma'am," I said and followed her back into the kitchen.

"Also there are cameras in all of the hallways to allow for the safety of the royals."

"Are there cameras in the kitchen?"

"Not inside the rooms, as privacy is still maintained in good measure. Well, that's it then. Do you have any questions?"

I clipped the temporary badge on the pocket of

my jacket. "Yes—who unpacked my clothes and where are my suitcases?"

"Reginald put the suitcases in your room. It is your chambermaid's job to take care of such errands so that you have time to devote to properly prepare the menus the duchess gives you."

"Oh," was all I could say in answer. "I've never had a chambermaid before."

"I'm sure that you will meet her soon." Mrs. Perkins sent me a frown. "If you have any further questions, they can be answered tomorrow. Now, tonight's menu for the children's birthday party is set. I presume you brought it with you. Is there anything on the menu that you can't do in a professional manner?"

"I've prepared everything on the menu the duchess gave me before and should have no issues."

"Should?"

"The meal will be perfectly prepared with fresh ingredients and served on the duchess's time-line."

"Good," she said and gave a short nod. "My office is connected to Mrs. Worth's office. We're located up two floors, the second door on the right. I will expect you to be prompt with all your meals, as the duchess and her family have busy schedules. The duchess prefers good English home cooking with fresh organic foods that are locally sourced and contain no antibiotics or

GMOs. I'm certain you know that we must cook only the best for the growing family. There will be none of your American chicken nuggets and that dreadful macaroni dish."

"Mac and cheese?" I asked.

"Exactly," she said with a shiver of disapproval.

"Yes, ma'am," I said. "I specialize in fresh and seasonal cooking. What about desserts?"

"They are expected and traditional. Tonight we are expecting a birthday cake that will appeal to a toddler. Along with ice cream that pairs perfectly with the cake."

"Are there any foods that the family does not like?"

"No. The duchess does not allow the children to be finicky. They must learn to eat whatever is put in front of them. They will spend a lifetime being served food from all parts of the world. They must learn from the start that they are not to offend. Now, since it's late May, there are many delightful vegetables available. Again, I expect you to consult with the gardener." She glanced at her watch. "Are there any more questions? I'm running late for my next meeting."

"No, no more questions," I assured her.

"Good," she said and turned on her heel. "We expect nothing but perfection. See that you give it, and we won't need to take any disciplinary action against you."

"Right," I said and gave a soft sigh. Then I realized that Michael and Frank stood behind me. I pasted a brave smile on my face and turned to my staff.

"Well, let's get started," I said with an authority I didn't feel and pulled out the menu. "We'll start with warm cheese puffs and shrimp cocktails. Frank, I need sixty-six jumbo shrimp shelled and deveined. Michael, please shred me two cups of Leicester Cheddar, chop rosemary for inside, and leave some uncut for a garnish. Also I will need freshly ground horseradish, fresh tomatoes for paste, and a lemon."

I put on the apron. "Any questions?"

"No, Chef," they said in unison. They looked at me with trust in their gazes.

Let's hope I lived up to it.

Chapter 3

First order of business: we had to prepare a light lunch for the children and their nanny. Next was tea for the children and the duchess. Last was the impromptu party for the children.

"The duchess usually prefers to eat lunch with the children, but she has a charity luncheon to attend today," Michael informed me. "The nanny oversees lunch with the children to teach them proper table manners, otherwise she eats with the staff."

"What about dinner?" I asked. "There is only a menu for the children."

"Nanny watches them eat at dinner as well, but she does not eat with them," Michael continued. "This way, she can correct them."

"I see," I said and looked at my staff. "What about you? Do you eat with the staff?"

"No, Chef," Michael said. "We eat with you in the kitchen. Well, I will eat supper with you. Frank has a family. He eats supper with them after the kitchen is cleared and you let us go for the night."

"You have a family?" I asked Frank.

"Yes, Chef," he said. His eyes lit up with pride and his chest puffed up. "I have two boys in grammar school."

"Oh, how nice," I said. "I understand raising boys is a lot of work. Let me know if you need extra time for school functions or whatever comes up."

"Yes, Chef," Frank said. "Thank you."

"Mr. Haregrove, do you live in the palace?"

"No ma'am, I live just down the street from Mr. Deems in my mum's house. She had to go into a nursing facility last year, and so I keep her place up for her."

"I'm so sorry to hear that," I said and opened one of the two refrigerators to take out the produce that was meant for the children's lunch. "You must be very busy between your mother, her house, and work."

"Oh, no, Chef," he said and took the carrots and asparagus from me to cut and prep them. "My mum actually likes the nursing home. She orders people about as if she were the queen herself." He laughed. "My job is to stay out of the way and say, 'Yes, Mum, that's fine with me.' "

The three of us laughed. I felt that things might just work out with this staff.

The lunch menu consisted of blanched carrots and asparagus in a mild white sauce, slices of lean beef with mashed cauliflower, warm rolls, and stewed apples for dessert. Each was to be cut small enough for little forks and knives to handle. It made me smile, as back home my nephews would be eating with their fingers at this age.

Not because they couldn't eat with a fork, but because my sister was too overwhelmed to think about teaching table manners to three-year-olds.

The day flew by. For the birthday party, we needed courses that appealed to children but were sophisticated enough for adults. Shrimp cocktails were first. I made fresh pea soup for the second course. Next was a salad. For the adults, I planned a sophisticated mixed green and onion salad with vinaigrette.

Frank came in from the greenhouse with a frown on his face and a bowl of freshly cut greens in his hands.

"What's the matter?" I asked.

"Nothing."

"You look angry," I stated as he dumped the greens into the sink to be washed and sorted.

"It's that Jasper Fedman," Frank said as he washed the greens, placed them on a linen towel, and dried them. "He thinks that because he is in charge of the greenhouse, we have to do whatever he says."

"What did he say?" I drew my brows together. The last thing I needed was to alienate a member of the household staff on my first day.

"Never you mind about that," Frank said and mixed the salad. "I set him straight, I did."

I glanced out toward the greenhouse but didn't see anyone.

"I should go talk to him. I don't want anyone giving my staff a hard time."

"No worries, Chef," Frank said. "I took care of it."

"Frank and Jasper get on each other's nerves," Michael said in a low voice beside me. "They have been fighting over the smallest things since Frank worked for Chef Butterbottom. I wouldn't let it concern you."

I watched as Frank plated the salads for the adults and frowned.

"I don't like people bullying my staff," I said. "I'll have a talk with Jasper first thing in the morning." Right now, I had to get this dinner ready.

The next course for the children was a pretty plate of cucumber and carrot with a buttermilk drizzle. Then came a lemon sorbet. After that was fish. The children had finger filets in a cracker crust, while the adults had seared mahi-mahi. The meat course was grilled lamb chops. I made a banana cake with vanilla bean frosting and fresh strawberry filling for dessert. The cake was something children would love but had sophisticated flavors for the adults. When it was all taken up to be served, I wiped my hands on a towel and looked around with relief. I'd done it. I'd completed my first day. It was a bit like running a marathon, but I was satisfied with all the dishes.

I glanced out to the greenhouse. What I didn't like was a greenhouse bully. It was nearly ten at night and Mr. Fedman was long gone. I made a mental note to talk to him tomorrow. If nothing else, he needed to know that I took care of my staff.

Penny came by with a note from the duchess. I had let Frank and Michael go home and was just finishing cleaning the kitchen myself.

"Well, someone has gotten off to a good start," Penny said and handed me a piece of official stationery.

I opened it to see a simple note of thanks from the duchess. It was handwritten. I slowly looked at Penny, who was munching a carrot stick and trying but failing to look bored. "She wrote this?"

"That's her signature," Penny said and sat down at the small kitchen table near the greenhouse entrance. "You made a very good impression."

I sat down as well, stunned to have the note. "Wow. It was a good first day."

"Until Chef Butterbottom finds out. He thinks he should be cooking for the family as well. In fact, he took his complaints to the queen herself, but she told him it was the duchess's household, and if she wanted a private chef, then she would have one."

"I didn't think I was so controversial," I said and unbuttoned my chef's coat. "You look tired. Would you like a cup of tea?"

"American tea or British tea?" Penny asked with a twinkle in her eye.

"British, of course," I said and stood. "I spent a week learning how to make proper tea from Mrs. Warwick at the Chicago Tea Room."

"Chicago offers proper tea?"

I smiled. "Mrs. Warwick is from London. She worked for the prime minister in the seventies."

"Whatever is she doing in Chicago?"

"She followed her daughter to America to see her grandchildren grow up." I started a kettle of fresh water and spooned tea leaves into a sterling tea ball. I turned to face my new friend. "She went straight to the tea room and gave them a good talking to about how to make tea. The owner hired her on the spot. Mrs. Warwick has worked there ever since."

Penny laughed. "You tell a good story."

"You should have seen her," I said. "She was quite insistent that I get all the details of proper tea making correct. Slapped my hand a couple of times."

"Oh, dear, she makes us seem rather uptight, doesn't she?"

I smiled and put the ball in the teapot and poured the boiling water gently over it. Then I put the lid on the pot and wrapped it in a cozy. "I've met a couple just like her today."

"Ah, Mrs. Worth is one of them, I imagine."

I got out two teacups and saucers and placed

them on the table along with a small pitcher of cream and a pot of sugar cubes. "And her secretary, Mrs. Perkins."

"Right," Penny said and leaned back in her chair. "Of course, they are traditionalists. The duchess keeps plenty of that sort about to please the queen. It might be the twenty-first century, but there are still proper ways of doing things."

I placed the teapot on the table and sat down. "May I pour?"

"Sure."

"Do you like cream and sugar? I understand the cream should be poured before the tea."

"Very good," Penny said. "Yes, cream and one lump of sugar, please."

I added only cream to mine, poured the cups, and then took a sip. There was something about the British way of making tea that added flavor I hadn't noticed before. "How'd I do?"

"Perfect," Penny said.

The clock on the wall struck eleven PM.

"Are you always working so late?" I asked.

"I have the room next to yours," she explained. "I work late most days. That way I'm available to the duchess if she needs me."

"Did you grow up in London?"

Penny smiled. "I grew up in Yorkshire, actually. My father is a doctor and my mother an accountant."

"How did you end up here?"

"I met the duchess at school," Penny said and sipped her tea. "She was a year ahead of me. We had a few classes together and started hanging out."

My eyes widened. "So you were there for the entire romance?"

Penny put her cup down. "I'm sworn to secrecy on all of that." She leaned in close. "They have so little privacy, and she's my friend."

"Everyone here is quite protective of the duke and duchess," I said and sighed. "I can't imagine it's easy to live such a public life."

"The duchess works very hard to see that the children get as normal of a childhood as possible. It's why she hired you, actually. She wants the family to eat fresh and healthy foods, which is not quite the standard British fare."

"I've been studying classic English dishes," I said. "When I interviewed, she told me that she hoped to have the children eat traditional foods at home, only without the fat and heavy sauces."

"She brought you in to bring English foods into the new millennium?"

"Yes," I sat back. "At the culinary institute, I specialized in recreating traditional foods in a modern way."

"Oh, Chef Butterbottom is going to really dislike you." Penny tapped her perfectly mani-cured fingernails on her teacup. "He thinks you should never mess with true English recipes. Traditions matter."

"Oh, boy." I sat back. "I can't wait to meet him."

"Don't worry—you most likely won't meet him. He likes to stick to his domain."

"Perfect." I picked up the tea set, rinsed the cups and saucers, and put them in one of the two dishwashers. Adding soap, I closed it up and hit the start button. "So, do you mind helping me find my room again?"

Penny stood. "Sure thing." She linked her arm in mine and we headed toward the door. "That's what friends are for."

"Wait," I said, "I forgot to take off my chef jacket. I was told no jacket outside of the kitchen unless the dinner guests request to see me." I hung the jacket on a line of hooks just inside the door. "Now we can go."

I put my arm back through Penny's and we headed toward our rooms. The door at the top of the stairs was locked. "Really? I didn't even know there was a door here," I said.

Penny pulled off her identification badge and swiped it. "It's locked from eleven PM until six AM to ensure security for the family. The family is a target for kidnappers and such."

"Wow, I never thought of the downside of being royal."

She stepped through the door and stopped me. "You need to swipe your badge as well. There is

43

a security camera above the door." She pointed it out for my benefit. "It is household policy that everyone swipes their cards before they enter. They double check. The first time you forget, you are docked a week's pay. The second time, you are escorted out of the household for good."

"It wouldn't do to lose a full week's pay on my first day," I said and swiped my card. "I really want to keep this job."

"That's why the consequences are so steep," she said as the door closed behind her. She leaned in close. "There are cameras in all the hallways. Security wanted them in the nurseries, but the duchess put her foot down. There was quite the argument that the cameras would keep the babies safer, but with so many hackers, the duchess was afraid someone would steal pictures of her children playing or sleeping. Tabloids pay huge sums for that kind of thing."

"Poor things," I said. "I can't imagine."

"With great wealth and power comes great responsibility," she said. "Well, this is my door. Room two-twenty-six. Feel free to knock any time. Once you get settled, I'd love to take you around town."

"Sounds perfect. Thanks, Penny."

"You're welcome," she said and unlocked her door. "Oh, and pay no attention to the ghosts."

"Ghosts?"

"It's an old palace," she said with a wink. "There

are bound to be all manner of spirits around. I generally give them a wide berth and just go about my day."

"I'll keep that in mind," I said, unafraid of such silliness. "Good night."

"Sleep tight," she said and disappeared inside her rooms. I got to my door, inserted the key, and unlocked it. I suppose modernizing the servants' apartments with swipe key cards was too expensive. It was a big household, and they had to cut costs somewhere.

I turned on a light and headed straight for bed. Jet lag had taken its toll. I laid down fully clothed, only taking the time to slip off my shoes and pull a throw over me. I figured I'd get up in an hour or two to shower, change into pajamas, and check my e-mails.

I closed my eyes. I thought I heard footsteps in the hallway, and the last thing I thought of before falling asleep was Ian Gordon standing in front of me, unsure of what to do with an American chef in Kensington Palace.

Chapter 4

Jet lag had me wide awake at four AM, and I realized that my tiny kitchen didn't have a coffeepot or any coffee. I stumbled around in my clothes with my hair at a funky angle from sleeping on the bed without combing it out.

If I wanted coffee, I would have to go to the family kitchen. I knew there was a pot there. It was a twenty-five cup peculator, but at this point, I didn't care. I stripped off my clothes, leaving them in a pile, making a note to buy a hamper. Then I walked into the bathroom to find the duchess's thank you card stuck to my right cheek by sweat and drool. I peeled it off and saw that any value it might have had was now lost; her signature had transferred to my skin.

Hopefully a shower would fix that. *Right.* All the scrubbing in the world would not budge the ink. I looked as if I had asked her to autograph my face. Not exactly proper etiquette. I sighed.

By then it was four thirty AM, and I was dressed for work. This time I carried two chef jackets. One was on a hanger to be cleaned and pressed if I was ever called out to the dining room. The other would be one of the two I would keep in the kitchen to wear while I prepared meals.

Going down the hall, I was thankful that my

shoes had thick soles and were therefore silent on the wooden floor. I swiped my card at each door and went down to the kitchen without seeing anyone. I turned on the kitchen light and took a deep breath. The room smelled of herbs and spices, with the lingering scent of banana cake.

Alone in my kitchen for the first time, I glanced around to take everything in. The black-and-|white linoleum floors were old but clean. The tall white cabinets had porcelain pulls. There were two ovens and a gorgeous Viking six-burner stove and grill along with two refrigerators, a vegetable washing station, and, blessing of all blessings, a French press I hadn't noticed yesterday. I wouldn't have to use the giant perc.

A window over the sink looked out onto the black morning. There was a light on a nearby building corner that illuminated the parking lot. I chuckled as I put water in the kettle and put it on to boil. I had before me all the glamour of working in the royal household. Scooping out coffee beans, I poured them into the grinder and ground them coarse for the French press. I had picked up the habit of making French press coffee in college when I couldn't afford one of those K-Cup machines. There was something about grinding beans; adding boiled, filtered water; and letting it steep like good English tea that made me happy.

The time in the kitchen was my own. My

assistants wouldn't arrive until six AM to help make a fresh but simple breakfast for the family. I pulled out my cell phone, plugged in earbuds, and turned on my favorite music.

As I sipped my coffee with cream, I went through the menus for the rest of the week. I had been given lists of the family's favorite breakfast, lunch, tea, and dinner foods. There was a list of fresh vegetables and fruits available from the greenhouse garden along with the arrival times for the daily deliveries of meat, fish, seafood, and dairy products.

My favorite song came on, and I started dancing to the music. I pored over the details I would need to create a varied, colorful menu for the week as I shuffled and shook to the beat.

Someone tapped me on the shoulder. Startled, I screamed, turned, and kicked without thought. That someone was Ian Gordon, who rubbed his shin and yelled something. I pulled out my earbuds.

"You shouldn't sneak up on people," I said. "You scared me." I could still feel the rush of adrenaline and hear my music pouring out of the earbuds at a high level.

"You kicked me," he grumbled.

"It could have been worse," I said. "My usual startle reflex is to hit the person in the nose with the flat of my hand, knee them in the groin, and push them away. Lucky for you, my reflexes are off due to jet lag."

"Are all Americans so vicious?" he asked as he straightened.

"Beats me," I said and shrugged. "What are you doing here?"

"Morning security checks," he replied and crossed his well-muscled arms across his broad chest. "Saw a light on in the kitchen and came down to see what was going on."

"Nothing to see here," I said and picked up my mug of coffee. "Just a jet-lagged chef putting together a weekly menu."

"Looked more like you thought you were at a disco." He lifted one of his dark eyebrows.

I felt the heat of a blush rush over my cheeks. "I thought I was alone."

"Were you singing? What was that song?"

"Nothing," I said. Uncomfortable, I glanced around to see if there was anything I could do to get his mind off my singing. I'd always been told I should only sing in the shower. My dance moves were on par with my singing. Crud, he'd seen those, too. "Do you want a cup of coffee? Freshly made." I pointed at the half-empty French press. Then I frowned. "Or do you prefer tea?"

"Coffee will do, thank you," he said.

I put my cup down and grabbed a thick white mug for him and poured in the coffee, careful to hide the trembling in my hand. It was all his fault. He was the one who had startled me. "How do you take it?"

"Black," he answered.

I turned to find him close. The heat of his body radiated off of him. He smelled like spice and man. I closed my eyes and remembered how John's brown hair fell over his eyes in that cute way I liked.

"I'll take that." Ian lifted the mug from my hand.

I grabbed my own cup and moved away to stand by the table. "You might want to strain it with your teeth," I warned. "I like it thick."

"I'm sure I'll manage without any trouble." He took a sip, swallowed, and nodded. "This is very good coffee."

"Thanks," I said.

"It would be better with some whiskey in it."

"It's always five o'clock somewhere," I blurted.

His right eyebrow rose even higher. "Indeed."

There was an awkward silence, the kind of uncomfortable situation that always made me blurt out stuff. I racked my brain to come up with something that didn't sound too idiotic. "Okay, well, I've got more work to do."

There, that wasn't too bad.

Except the man didn't take the hint. He simply studied me and sipped his coffee.

Fine. I made a show of putting my earbuds back in and turning back to my lists and menu-making. He kept watching me. I finally pulled out one earbud and turned back to him. "What?"

He shrugged. "I was waiting to see if there

would be any more dancing." His dark eyes twinkled.

"No," I said. "No more dancing. I'm sure you have other rooms to check on."

"I do."

Again he didn't move.

I put my earbuds back in and did my best to ignore him. I hoped that eventually he'd go away. I concentrated on my menu and decided on pancetta and greens frittata for today's breakfast. It would be simple and super healthy. Thankfully eggs were on the duchess's good list. Frank had said last night that all the eggs came fresh from the palace's own chickens and were kept on the countertop. The greens and leeks would be in the greenhouse.

Oddly, when I looked up, Ian was gone. His mug of coffee was drained and sitting near the sink. I had to admit that I was attracted to him. Who wouldn't be? But Penny said he didn't date the household staff. Unlike most women, I didn't take this as a challenge; I took it as a fact. Besides, I was in a relationship—even if we were on a break. It was why Ian studying me had been so awkward. I wasn't used to it.

I put on a white apron and slipped my phone into the front pocket. The greenhouse was still dark. I glanced at my watch. It was only five AM. Before turning on the lights, I noted that the sky had lightened a tiny bit. Dawn would come soon.

I gave a quick flip of the light switch and waited a few seconds as the fluorescent lights warmed up to the task at hand.

It smelled loamy, earthy, and, well, green, due to the fresh herbs and salad greens. I stepped farther in to find the kale, spinach, radicchio, and mustard greens I would need for the frittata.

I hummed to myself as I picked radicchio. The kale was in the far corner. I did my best not to dance my way over. Someone somewhere in the palace might be watching. I wasn't sure what kind of impression I was making.

What I saw next stopped me in my tracks. A sharp electric jolt of fear rushed down my spine, and I dropped the greens on the floor. I opened my mouth but nothing came out.

There, crumpled under the kale bed, was Francis Deems. He was so pale it was as if all the blood had rushed out of his body. He wore the same clothes he'd had on when he had left the night before. His mouth hung open, and his eyes were blank. There was a pool of blood seeping out from under his shirt, staining it and the ground rusty red.

I started to get lightheaded and realized I wasn't breathing. After taking a deep breath, I could taste the metallic scent of blood for the first time. With oxygen flowing into my lungs again, I sprang into action.

"Mr. Deems." I went over, crouched down,

and shook him on the shoulder like I was taught to do in CPR class. He was cold to the touch.

His blank gaze was creepy, but I soldiered on. I felt for a pulse. He had none. Swallowing hard, I leaned back on my heels.

I'd never found a dead person before. He was cold and had no heartbeat. There was a lot of blood. It was pretty clear that CPR would not be needed.

Swallowing back the fear in my throat, I stood. What did I do now? How did I call security? What were the emergency procedures? Darn it, I hadn't had time to go through orientation.

I stumbled back through the greenhouse. My legs felt rubbery. There was a phone in the kitchen near the door where I entered. I stopped at the sink and took a moment to get a grip. Fearing that I wouldn't be able to speak, I clung to the sink and closed my eyes a moment. My heart was in my throat and racing so fast my hands trembled. I opened my eyes, turned on the water, and washed my hands. There was bottled water in the refrigerator nearest the door. I opened it, grabbed one, twisted off the top, and gulped down half the bottle.

My stomach protested for a brief second, but I forced myself toward the phone and picked it up. Pasted inside the body of the slim phone was a list of extensions. One was marked "Emergency." I punched the numbers.

"Operator, what is your emergency?"

"Francis Deems is dead." The words came out of my mouth in a raspy whisper.

"I'm sorry, what did you say?"

I cleared my throat and took a deep breath. "My assistant Francis Deems is dead."

"Right," the female voice said. "How do you know this? Has his wife called you?"

"No," I said and cleared my throat again. "I found him in the duke and duchess's private kitchen greenhouse." That was a mouthful, but I didn't know how else to explain where he was.

"I see," the operator said. Her tone was careful. "Are you in danger?"

I glanced around, suddenly realizing that a killer might be in my kitchen. "I don't think so." I fought a new wave of fresh fear.

"But you are not sure."

"I'm not sure," I said, retreating until my back was against the cool wall. "Please send help."

"I've already done that," she said. "With whom am I speaking?"

"Oh, right, my name is Carrie Ann Cole. I'm the new family chef for the duke and duchess of Cambridge."

"One moment."

I heard her breathing and kept my eyes on the surrounding kitchen, trying not to panic. If the killer was here, I was not about to let him sneak up on me.

"I found you in the system," she said. "I see you have not gone through orientation yet."

"No," I said. "It's scheduled for later today. Is someone coming?"

"Yes, security is on the way."

At that moment, Ian stormed through the door with two men I'd never seen before following behind him. All three had guns in their hands. It was one thing to see men with guns in their hands on television and another to be faced with them in real life.

"What happened?" he barked.

I dropped the phone and pointed to the greenhouse. "It's Frank. I think he's dead."

"Stay where you are, and don't touch anything," he ordered.

I wrapped my arms around my waist as the three men quickly searched the kitchen and then entered the greenhouse.

"Hello?" a disembodied voice called. The phone receiver twisted on its cord. "Hello? Are you there, Chef?"

"Yes," I said after I had picked up the receiver. The word came out in a strangled whisper.

"Chef?"

Clearing my throat, I tried again. "Yes, I'm here. So is security. I didn't think you carried guns in England."

"They are protectors of the duke and duchess and have the right to kill, if necessary."

I thought for a moment that Ian would make a good 007 agent and giggled.

"Are you all right, Chef?"

"Yes," I said.

"Then I will hang up now."

"Thank you," I said and hung up the phone. I kept my back to the cold wall. I looked out the window and noted the sun had finally risen.

The talking in the greenhouse was muffled. I tried not to think about what was inside. Michael came in through the same door as I had.

"Good morning, Chef," he said and then paused as he studied me. "Are you quite all right? You look a little green."

"No," I said with a shake of my head. "Don't come in any farther." I held my hands up. "Frank is dead."

"What? Frank Deems is dead?" His eyes grew large.

"I'm pretty sure," I said. "I found him in the greenhouse under the kale bed."

"My God," Michael said and sat down at the table. "Not Frank." He looked at me, his eyes tearing up. "He was my best friend. That is tough news. Tough news indeed. Whatever shall we do?"

"Nothing yet," I said. "Security is inside the greenhouse now. They asked me to stay put. I haven't moved an inch. If he was murdered, then the killer might still be close by."

Michael swallowed hard. "I see."

I took a deep breath and the clock struck six. "Oh, dear, the duchess is expecting breakfast for her family in an hour."

"What shall we do?"

"Make it, I suppose," I said. "Are you up to working?"

"Yes," he said and rose. "What is the plan?"

"Pancetta and greens frittata." I winced. "We won't be serving anything out of the greenhouse for some time, I think. Would it be possible for you to run to a market and get fresh leeks and greens?"

"Certainly, Chef," he said, his gaze filled with concern. "You look as if you are still in shock. Are you able to do this?"

"The family has to eat," I said, trying to be as practical as I could. I wrote down the greens I needed and handed him the paper list. "Please hurry."

"Yes, Chef," he said. "Do you want me to check with Chef Butterbottom first?"

"No," I said. "I'm sure there will be enough fodder for the entire kitchen today. No need to bring him in as if we can't handle things. Go to the market. Hurry, please, we only have fifty minutes left."

"I won't let you down," he said, his hands tracing the brim of his chef cap. "And you're sure it was Mr. Deems?"

"I'm sorry," I said. "It must be hard. We can talk about it after breakfast is served."

"Right." He plopped his cap on his head. He glanced at me, his brown eyes filled with tears. "I can't believe my friend is gone."

"I know," I said and patted his arm. "Please, don't tell anyone. I'm sure security would be very upset to hear about it on the news before they even get into their investigation."

"Mum's the word." Michael blew out a long breath, pulled a tissue out of his pocket, blew his nose, wiped his eyes, and headed out.

I kept my place against the wall. There wasn't much else to do until he got back. Raspberries, blackberries, and blueberries would be put in crystal fruit cups and given a dollop of yogurt on top. I could start that now, I supposed, but then I figured I'd stay where I was until Ian gave the all clear.

My knees weakened and I slid down to the floor. Hugging myself, I wondered what else could possibly go wrong.

"The kitchen and greenhouse are clear," Ian said when he finally stepped out. "I've called the medical examiner and an ambulance to pick up the body. Once they are finished, I'll need a statement from you."

I stood. "I need to make breakfast for the family."

He frowned. "This kitchen is too close to a

crime scene. You will have to go to Chef Butterbottom's kitchen and work there."

"Won't I get in his way?"

"He doesn't make breakfast. As long as you are in and out and clean up after yourself, I'm certain it'll be okay."

Michael came in through the door with a grocery bag in hand. He stopped short and pulled the cap off his head. "Mr. Gordon, how are you, sir?"

"What's in the bag?" Ian asked.

Michael handed it to him. "I bought greens for Chef Cole to use in the frittata."

Ian reached in and pulled out one of each type of green and tasted a corner of it. "This will do," he said as he handed back the bag. "I told Chef Cole that you will have to make breakfast in Chef Butterbottom's kitchen this morning while we complete our investigation."

"But—"

"There is no *but,* Mr. Haregrove," Ian said. "If Chef Butterbottom has any problems with the situation, have him call me. Is that clear?"

"Yes, sir."

"Good," Ian said and turned his hard gaze on me. "Take what you need from the other kitchen. We can't take the chance that things were disturbed in your area."

"Yes, sir," I said and turned to follow Michael out.

"Oh, and Chef Cole," Ian said.

"Yes?"

"I still will need a statement from you and Mr. Haregrove. Please return to this area after breakfast to answer a few questions."

"Okay," I agreed and grabbed my chef coat off the hanger and my menu tablet off the counter and followed Michael.

"I hope you know where you're going," I said, "because Chef Butterbottom's kitchen was not on my tour."

"Certainly, Chef," Michael said. "Both Mr. Deems and I worked there for two years before we got promoted to the duke and duchess's private kitchen."

"How was it, working for him?" I asked. I wondered if Michael would be happier working for me or in the big kitchen.

"Frank and Chef Butterbottom didn't get along. But then, Chef rarely gets along with anyone. He's always in a snit these days. Rumor is he thinks only he should be cooking for the future kings."

"But before me, the duchess did all the work. Surely he understands that a personal chef is less important than the estate chef."

"Apparently it doesn't matter much to him," Michael said with a shrug. "He's a bit of a petty despot."

I laughed at the description. "Aren't we all when it comes to our work space."

We hurried through winding servants' hallways,

up and down staircases. The palace was a hive of work spaces tucked in behind the elegant apartments and tourist places. There were security guards everywhere. Some walked the halls; others stood at the top or bottom of staircases. All of them checked our badges and frowned at my visitor badge. They had handheld scanners and scanned the badges so that security practically followed us all through the palace.

"Is it always like this?" I asked.

"Never, Chef." Michael wrinkled his forehead. "It must be because of your finding Mr. Deems."

"Right." I kept walking, trying not to gawk at the muscular men in black suits, white shirts, and navy ties.

"This is it," Michael said and opened a door. A flick of a switch brought the room into full view.

"Wow," was all I could say as I stepped inside and looked around.

The kitchen was huge. In fact, you could probably put four of my kitchens inside of it. Everything was either stainless steel or black-and-white. Pots hung from pot racks located over vegetable sinks. There were four Viking stoves with six burners each. The stoves had wide ovens under them, but there was also a proofing box the size of my old apartment refrigerator, three different areas with double ovens in the walls, four double-door subzero refrigerators, butcher-block counter tops, and marble pastry counter-tops.

The entire room sparkled as if a million cleaning ladies had spent the entire night wiping away all the kitchen grease and grime. I had a thought that I should take my shoes off before I left a mark on the black-and-white tiled floor. The entire back wall was windowed to let in natural light. The windows overlooked the Orangery, an adjacent building where tourists came to have tea. Clearly Chef Butterbottom must be a true master to be given this palatial kitchen.

"Over here, Chef," Michael called to me. "This is the best spot to get our meal made without bothering Chef Butterbottom."

"Okay." I walked to the oven in the farthest corner from the door and the lovely windows. "Let's get started then." I put on my chef coat and Michael put on his apron. "I need the greens thoroughly washed and then finely chopped. Also, make a percolator of coffee and a pot of breakfast tea. Prep the sugar and creamer."

"Yes, Chef." He went straight to work as if his life depended on it.

A quick glance at the clock above the sink told me we now had forty minutes to get our meal cooked, plated, and then back to our part of the palace while it was still warm. It was good to have a problem to solve to keep me from thinking about what had happened to my staff member.

"We'll need a serving cart and some warmers to keep everything fresh until it gets to the dining room," I said.

"I've already got a plan for that," Michael said.

We worked quickly in tandem silence. The heat from the stove rose up and curled my hair under my hat. I put the frittata in the oven and pulled out six crystal fruit cups. I sliced banana, oranges, and fresh coconut strips and then tossed them in a yogurt vinaigrette, placed them in the cups, wrapped them in plastic wrap, and placed them in the refrigerator. I made some fresh blueberry and ginger scones. We had five minutes to get it all to the family's dining room.

The duke and duchess ate breakfast buffet style. The complete menu included oatmeal porridge, the fruit salads, hard boiled eggs, the frittata, and breakfast sausages. The duchess had asked that any breakfast sausage be locally sourced, low fat, and low sodium. Luckily there were some made with turkey purchased just before I arrived. I made a mental note to order more that afternoon.

We placed the food on two serving pushcarts, one for hot food and one for cold, and I quickly changed chef jackets. We raced out of the kitchen and down the hall to a staff elevator. Then down another hall to the apartment door and the back of the dining area. We had two minutes to set up the buffet. Luckily Mrs. Perkins was waiting for us at the door.

"Where have you been? We barely have time to set things up." She scowled at me.

"There was a security incident in the kitchen greenhouse. We had to scramble to purchase new ingredients and then take over a portion of Chef Butterbottom's kitchen to get this done."

"We will talk about this after we set up," Mrs. Perkins said. "This is a very serious problem."

"Yes, ma'am," I said.

She opened the door for us and practically thrust us inside. I had never moved so quickly and carefully in my life.

The dining room was large and bright. Curtains had been pulled back to let the morning light come in. There was a large wooden buffet covered with crisp white linen. We carefully placed our warming dishes at one end, the cold dishes at the other, and the scones in between. The chambermaids had already set the silver- and drinkware on the table. Plates rested at one end of the buffet in a small pile. A pot of fresh flowers sat in the middle of our buffet. It matched the flowers in the centerpiece on the dining table.

I had a thought that it must be someone's job to buy fresh flowers for all the rooms. Perhaps a palace florist?

"All right, out, out." Mrs. Perkins scooted us and our trays out of the room.

The door closed hard on the back of my heel. The sting brought tears to my eyes and I bit my tongue to not make a sound. I looked at Michael and he at me.

"I'm afraid you'll have to show me the way back," I said and slumped my shoulders.

"It's not so bad," Michael said. "Despite everything—including missing poor Mr. Deems—we made the breakfast on time. That is quite a feat."

"I suppose." I followed him back down the hall. Once out of the apartments, we were once again scrutinized and our badges scanned at every turn. I really needed a map to the palace so that if anything happened to Mr. Haregrove, I would be able to do this on my own. "Please don't quit or die on me, Mr. Haregrove. I don't think I'd live to see another day. I'd most likely get lost in the corridors, never to be found again."

He laughed. It was a warm and hearty sound that filled the cold spots in my heart. "Chef, you are funny. Did we not just pass eight security men in the hall? You are a woman. I'm certain you would be willing to stop and ask directions."

I smiled. "Yes, come to think of it, I would."

"You have nothing to worry about."

"But that doesn't mean I want you dead." I was serious. "Please take care of yourself."

"Do you think what happened to Mr. Deems might also happen to us?"

"I have no idea," I said and shrugged. "I was the

one who found him. There was a lot of blood, but I didn't see any obvious wounds."

"That's not good, not good at all." He opened Chef Butterbottom's door and I pushed my cart through first, only to be confronted by a very big man with a bald head and beady eyes.

"What in bloody hell do you think you're doing in *my* kitchen?"

His words blasted through me like dragon fire. His cheeks were red. He narrowed his eyes, and I noticed that his fists were clenched. He was a bit like a massive toddler having a tantrum.

I decided to remain calm, like when confronted by a big angry dog. I put my hand out in a stop sign. "We were instructed to use this space for the duke and duchess's breakfast."

He took a threatening step forward. "Who told you that you could mess with my space? Look at the dishes you left. Dirty counters, dirty sink, dirty floors."

"Ian Gordon, the head of security, told us to use your kitchen. We had little time. The food had to be served in the apartments. There was no time to clean until we got back. Which is now." I kept my shoulders back, my chin up, and my tone firm.

"Chef Butterbottom," Michael stepped up and held his hands up like a policeman at a traffic stop. "May I introduce Chef Cole. Chef Cole, this is Chef Butterbottom, head chef for Kensington Palace."

"It's a pleasure to finally meet you," I said. "I've heard a lot about you."

"If that's true, then you should have known that no one—no one—dares enter *my* kitchen without my permission. I have rules and expectations. I do not expect to come into my kitchen and discover an unclean space that smells of bad American cooking."

Ouch. "We were ordered to use the space." I tried not to raise my voice, but it might have gone up a little. "We are here to clean up now." I took a step forward to let him know I was not intimidated by his ranting.

That only made things worse. "*I* am *the* boss of this kitchen. I am sure you have been instructed that when you are in this kitchen, you work for me. Have you not?"

I paused. *Darn it, he's right.* "Yes, Mrs. Worth explained that to me. But that has nothing to do with what is happening now."

"It has everything to do with it. I don't like Americans. I don't like American food. And yet I come to my kitchen and discover an American mess made by an overprivileged, undereducated American chef."

"Excuse me, but I was in the top one percent of my culinary class."

"Did you study in Le Cordon Bleu? No? I thought not. You are in my kitchen, Miss America. I have certain expectations. Those expectations are for you to return my kitchen to the manner in which you found it. There are cleaning rags and hand brushes under the sink."

"Excuse me?"

"I expect the floors to be scrubbed by hand and then polished with soft cloths. No chemicals! I won't have anyone slip and fall because someone who does not belong in my kitchen got lazy and used chemicals instead of elbow grease. Am I clear?"

"You are clear."

"Am I clear?" He bellowed again, and I was reminded of one of my culinary instructors who loved to bully his staff.

"Yes, Chef."

"Then get to it. I have a phone call to make to Mr. Gordon. He needs to explain himself." He stormed off. A big man in white T-shirt and white pants, he reminded me of Mr. Clean, or maybe a WWE fighter.

I looked at Michael, and he mouthed, "I'm sorry."

I shrugged, and we went back to our area from earlier. The cuttings had been bagged before we left. The pots and pans and baking sheets were all rinsed and sitting in the sink, ready for the dishwasher. Seriously, the place was inspection-level clean. But clearly not clean enough.

I filled one sink with dish soap and another with vinegar water. I used one dish cloth for the soapy water and the other for the vinegar. Michael put the dishes in the dishwasher and ran it. I washed down the counters and the stove and wiped out the oven and the refrigerator with hot soapy water. Then I handed that cloth to Michael to wash down the rolling trays.

While he did that, I set out to rinse everything with cold vinegar water. The vinegar not only disinfected but cleared the soap and deodorized everything. I made sure the oven hood and everything we had touched was wiped clean.

Michael followed behind me with a soft polishing cloth.

I could hear Chef Butterbottom yelling into the phone. It was clear he had gotten ahold of Ian and was pitching a first-class fit about us. He slammed down the phone. By this time, I was drying the pots and pans and returning them to their original places.

Michael had indeed gotten a hand brush out from under the sink and, with a new sink full of hot soapy water, he began to scrub all the edges and crevices in the stove and countertops.

"Those are clean," I said.

"Even so, Chef is watching and expects us to ensure that it is well scrubbed. Trust me. He will come out and inspect everything before he lets us leave."

"What do you mean, 'lets us leave'? I have a schedule to keep. I have to see Mrs. Perkins, Mrs.

Worth, the security office, and Mr. Gordon all before I can fix the children's lunch, which must arrive precisely at noon."

"Then we'd better get started on the floor," Michael said with a sigh.

"I am not cleaning the floor by hand." I crossed my arms in defiance. "Neither should you. They make mops for that."

But he got down on his knees, dragging a bucket of soapy water down along with his brush. "In this kitchen, Chef Butterbottom is the boss. I need my job."

"Please don't tell me we have to clean the entire floor."

"No, no, only the area we used."

"Fine," I said with a sigh. "I'm not using a hand brush, but I'll use a mop. Where does he keep them?"

"They keep the mops in the closet across the hall. It will really be best if you let me clean around the baseboards and feet of the stoves and the counters with the hand brush."

"Fine," I said. "I'm getting a mop."

I took two steps toward the door when it opened suddenly.

"What in bloody hell are you doing?"

I looked up to see Ian Gordon striding into the kitchen. "We're cleaning up."

"With a scrub brush and a rag?"

"I was going to get a mop."

"Chef Butterbottom doesn't want anyone to use a mop in his kitchen. He says you miss things," Michael said.

"Chef Butterbottom is the boss in his kitchen." My tone showed my disgust. I was tired and not happy. A quick look at my watch told me my orientation was now going to have to wait until after the children's lunch was prepared.

"The duchess is not paying you to do scullery maid work," Ian said. "I need you both to come with me."

We stood and, as if on cue, Chef Butterbottom came barreling out of his office. "You are not finished. I have to inspect the cleaning before you can leave."

"I need them both to come with me now," Ian said and widened his stance and crossed his arms.

"They cannot leave my kitchen without completing their work. I won't have it."

"The place looks clean enough to me." Ian raised his right eyebrow in a motion I had begun to expect. "This is official security business."

"That is the excuse you used to let them into my kitchen to begin with," Chef growled. "You may be head of security, but you have no right to allow anyone in my kitchen. Also no right, no right at all, to let them out of their work." He pointed at his chest. "I'm boss here. That means I can and will fire anyone who does not meet my standards or who is disrespectful. There is an important dinner tonight, and I need to have a clean kitchen to start with."

"I need my job," Michael said, loud enough to be heard, but still softly. It was clear he had the least amount of authority. There was no way he was going to get in the middle of this.

"You're not going to get fired," I said.

"I can and will fire whomever I choose in my kitchen," Chef Butterbottom stated, his gaze squarely on me.

"Fine, fire him; I'll hire him back for my kitchen."

"It would take weeks," Chef said. "The paperwork alone will take a day or two to sort out. Maybe it's you I should fire."

"She isn't going anywhere until my investigation is over," Ian said. "I'm taking them both now." He gently took my arm and turned me toward the door.

"If you ever cook in my kitchen again without my permission, I will fire you immediately. I am very serious," Chef said.

"Yes, sir," I said and resisted saluting him.

Ian sent me a look as the kitchen door closed behind us and we stepped out into the hall.

"What?" I asked.

"You are either fearless or quite stupid," Ian replied.

I inhaled sharply. "I'm not stupid."

"Then fearless."

"Maybe," I said. After all, what small-town girl would travel to another country to cook for royalty?

"She is very good at her job," Michael said.

I looked over my shoulder at him. "Thank you."

"You're welcome."

I walked beside Ian. "Thanks for getting us out of that ridiculous situation. Chef Butterbottom must be really insecure to be so controlling."

"You're welcome, but I didn't come to talk about Chef. I need to question you both. Then you will need to see the inspector in charge of the murder case and answer his questions."

"So it wasn't an accident?" I asked. I was hoping there was a chance that Frank had hit his head and bled out. I knew head wounds were messy.

"It wasn't an accident," Ian said grimly.

"What happened? Do you know?"

"I can't say until we question you," Ian said and showed both Michael and me into and out of an elevator. Then down another hallway.

"That's fine, but I have thirty minutes before I need to start lunch for the children," I said.

"This is going to take longer than thirty minutes."

"That won't do." I stopped and planted my feet.

"Respectfully, we're on a deadline, security chief," Michael said.

"Not any longer," he said and took a hold of

my elbow, forcing me forward. "I've explained the situation to Mrs. Worth. She has told the duke and duchess. A murder inside the palace changes everything. The family has been moved to a secret location. Until we know they are safe, they will not be here."

"Then I need to pack and go with them. As their chef, I've been contracted to travel with the family to ensure the quality and consistency of their meals."

"She's right," Michael said, trailing behind me. I appreciated his support.

"You are both under suspicion for Mr. Deems's murder," Ian said bluntly. "You are not going anywhere near the family."

"Wait, wait, what?" I pulled my arm from his grasp and stopped in the hall. Michael stayed behind me. "I didn't kill Frank. I only met him yesterday. What reason would I have to kill him? And Michael is his best friend. Why would he kill him?"

"That's why we need to interview you."

I put my hands on my hips. "Do we need lawyers?"

"You will have a barrister assigned to your case, should you need one."

"I don't have a case," I said. "I didn't do any-thing. Don't you have cameras everywhere? Can't you look at the footage and see that I was nowhere near Frank when he died? And as far as

Mr. Haregrove goes, he wasn't even in the palace at the time. Were you?"

"Let's take this one step at a time," Ian said. "We're going into the security offices, where I will interview you both separately. After that, the inspector will come to interview you, and we will determine if you need a lawyer."

I clenched my hands in frustration and a little fear. "I should be with the family."

"Chef Cole . . ." Michael sounded as if he was going to ask if I was all right. Which I wasn't, but I wasn't going to tell them that. *Don't show fear or weakness,* my father used to tell me. People and animals will sense it, and you will lose control of the situation.

I think I was a little beyond controlling anything by that point, but I soldiered on. "My head hurts."

"I have painkillers in my office," Ian said. "Come on, then. The sooner we get started, the sooner this will be all worked out."

"He's right, Chef," Michael said and carefully took my arm in his. "I'll be right here. Okay?"

I was an alien in a foreign country's royal household and appeared to be considered a suspect for murdering a man and stuffing his body under a kale bed. This was a situation that I thought could only happen in the movies.

I went along quietly, thankful that my phone was in my pocket. At the very least, I would

Google what to do when accused of a crime in England. All I could do was hope that the Internet had the answers I needed before I found myself tossed into a cell somewhere. The palace was old; I wondered perversely if it still had dungeons.

Chapter 5

Here's a water and two NSAIDs for your headache," Ian said as he entered the room.

"Thank you." I tossed down the pills and drank the water. I wished I'd eaten something earlier; I felt a bit lightheaded. Ian took the glass from me and put it to the side of the table.

"If you are going to take my fingerprints, you can save your time," I quipped. "They took a complete set as part of my interview process. They should be on file."

"You watch too many American crime shows," he said. "Real life is very different. Now start from the beginning. Where were you last night?"

"I'm sure your computer system shows that I left the kitchen with Penny after the birthday party was over. We went back to our rooms, where I promptly fell asleep in my clothes because I felt jet lagged."

"Miss Nethercott was with you when you went into your room?"

"No." I fidgeted in my seat. "Her room is before mine. We said good-bye, and I went straight to my room. I know there are cameras in the hallway. You can verify it."

"We are working on that. You fell asleep at what time?"

"I have no idea. I walked in, put my things down on the counter, went straight to bed, and laid down. It was only going to be for a moment, and then I planned to get up and shower and such. But the next thing I knew, it was four AM and I was wide awake."

"Can anyone confirm that?"

I scowled at him. "I certainly hope not. Please tell me you don't have cameras hidden in my room."

"We don't. I know these questions sound ridiculous, but they are the same questions the inspector on the case will have."

My hands trembled, and the room started to spin. I looked at the tabletop in a poor attempt to make it stop.

"Are you all right?" Ian asked.

"I haven't eaten, and I think it's all catching up with me." I looked up. "Do you have a piece of candy or some orange juice?"

"Put your head between your knees," he ordered and stood. "I'll get you something."

I did as he said and concentrated on breathing. I heard him walk out and then come back into the room. He touched my shoulder.

"Here, drink this."

I sat up slowly and took the glass of juice from him. I drank it, all the while feeling a bit like Alice in Wonderland.

"What are you laughing about?" he asked as he sat back down.

" 'Drink this'—like *Alice in Wonderland*. Does that make you the Mad Hatter?"

He studied me as if I had lost my mind. Maybe I had.

"I've asked the main kitchen to make you a sandwich and tea. You should remember to eat," he said.

"Trust me, I'm not in the habit of forgetting to eat," I said and finished off the juice. I put the glass down and pushed it toward him. "Now you can get my DNA as well."

"Don't be an idiot," he said and picked up his pen. "What made you forget to eat today?"

It was my turn to look at him as if he'd lost his mind. "I found a dead guy in my greenhouse and then had to rush into Chef Bumblebottom's kitchen to create a meal in half the time allotted. And then I had to run through the palace to deliver it and return to the kitchen to be treated like a minion in Bumble's little army. Seriously, Haregrove was cleaning the floor by hand. Who does that?"

"It's Chef Butterbottom," he corrected me.

"You say po-tay-to, I say po-tah-to," I replied and waved his concern away with my hand. I noted that the shaking had subsided a bit. I thought I saw the corners of his mouth twitch.

"Where were we? Right, you woke up at four AM . . ."

79

"I showered, changed, and went in search of coffee. There wasn't any in my room."

"I found you making coffee in the family's kitchen at four forty-five AM. That was a pretty quick shower."

"I'm a chef, not a glamourpuss," I replied to his unstated question. "I don't need more than five minutes to get dressed and go." It was something I learned at my internship. I loved my sleep. Since I preferred only basic makeup, I could be ready for work in fifteen minutes. That meant I could still be in bed while others were up blow drying their hair and primping. It's also why my hair was long and pulled back. I didn't have to do much but brush it into a low ponytail and be done.

I was thankful my heart-shaped face was pretty on its own. At least, that's what John would say. Right then I wished I were home with him—even if he had his nose in a new recipe.

"You went straight from your room to the kitchen," Ian continued.

"Yes."

"Did you see Mr. Deems?"

"No. I didn't expect to, as my assistants don't start work until six AM. I went into the kitchen. It was dark, so I turned on the lights and made coffee. I was using the time to go over the duchess's preferred list of dishes and foods to create the day's menu. That's what I was doing when you came in."

"Funny—that's not what I saw." His eyes twinkled. Oh, man, it was hard to resist a man with twinkly eyes. My thoughts went to John and how his eyes had once twinkled. It was part of why I had fallen in love with him.

"Well, it was what I was doing."

"You didn't see or hear anything suspicious?"

"No. Well, except you. What were you doing up at four forty-five AM?"

"My job," he replied. "When did you find the body?"

"I don't know. I didn't check the time. It was before six because my assistants—well, as far as I knew, no one was there yet. I had just sketched out a daily menu. Breakfast was leek and greens pancetta frittata, fruit cups with yogurt, scones, and sausages. I went into the greenhouse to pick the greens for the dish—"

"Why didn't you wait for your assistants to do that?"

I stared at him blankly for a moment, then shrugged. "I'm used to doing things for myself."

"I see. Go on."

"I picked some spinach and radicchio, then headed for the kale when I smelled something metallic—you know, like the blood meal that they sometimes use in gardens. I rounded the bed and stopped short. I have no idea what happened next. I think I dropped the greens I was holding when I saw Mr. Deems lying there. His eyes were open and there was a pool of blood under him. That's where the smell came from, I think."

A security guy knocked and brought in a tray with a club sandwich and chips along with a fork, napkin, and another glass of water.

"Dig in," Ian ordered.

"I'm not sure I can." I swallowed hard, but my stomach grumbled. "I found a dead body. The memory is making me queasy."

"You are queasy because you haven't eaten all day," he countered. "Take a bite of the sandwich."

The last thing I wanted to do today was to get sick in front of a hunky security guy. Even if he thought I was some sort of homicidal maniac.

"Take a bite." He lifted up one triangle of the sandwich and pushed it in front of me.

"Fine," I said and took it from him, all the while sending him a narrow-eyed look. I took a bite. The sandwich gummed up in my mouth. I grabbed for the water and washed it down as best I could. "Done."

"Good." He went back to his pad of legal paper and his pen. "Were you aware of anyone in the greenhouse when you found Mr. Deems?"

"No," I put the sandwich back on the plate and prayed my stomach would settle. "I've had CPR training. They say the first thing to do when you find a person in distress is to call his name, shake him, and see if he responds."

"You shook him?"

I nodded and chewed on my bottom lip. "On his shoulder. He was very cold to the touch. I felt for a pulse but there wasn't one."

"I see."

"The next step is to search the airway to remove any blockages and then start CPR. But I made the decision not to do anything. His eyes were open and lifeless. He was dead." Tears welled up in my eyes. I hadn't realized that I was so worried that I could have somehow saved him, but chose not to do it. "He was dead, wasn't he? I couldn't have saved him. Could I have?"

Ian put his hand on my hand. The heat from his skin warmed my cold fingers. "CPR would not have saved him."

Looking up, I met Ian's eyes and saw comfort for a brief moment before his gaze hardened. He removed his hand. "What happened then?"

"I realized that I don't have any emergency training yet. I didn't quite know what to do. Then I remembered there was a phone near the door of the kitchen. I went inside and called the emergency number listed on the phone."

"That's it?"

"Yes, I was still on the phone when you and your men came through." I picked up one of the French fries—er, chips—and chewed on the end of it. This time the food tasted better. Maybe it was the salt or the heat of the fry that soothed my belly.

"That's it? You never saw another person?"

"That's it." I grabbed another fry and chomped it down. "I don't know why you suspect me of all people. I have no reason to kill Mr. Deems. I'm not even certain how he died."

"The inspector will be in soon." Ian stood. "Eat. It's going to be a very long day for you."

After he left, I picked the bacon out of the sandwich, then the tomato and lettuce. Really I was just pushing the food around while I propped my cheek in my left hand. "This needs ketchup," I said to the air. Sure, other chefs would be horrified at the thought of ketchup on what was once a beautiful plate of food, but ketchup was a comfort food I had grown up eating on my fries. And what I really needed right then was comfort.

I reached into my pocket to get my phone and checked my messages. There was a text from John wishing me sweet dreams and letting me know he'd call today. Did John miss me already? Why did the idea surprise me? Was the better question whether or not I missed him?

My best friend Lucy had e-mailed about her day and asked how I was doing in London. I worried my bottom lip and replied with a few bland words about being fine and settling in. What would my friends think if I got fired on my second day? Or worse, was thrown in jail for the rest of my life for murdering my assistant?

I rubbed my forehead. The pain pills had kicked in, and there was now only a dull ache. I knew I was being overdramatic, but I tended to do that in serious situations.

There was a mirror on the wall that must have been two-way. On my way in, I'd seen a small office behind the mirrored wall. It was furnished with a large desk, a single chair, and a set of three tall file cabinets. There was also a window behind the desk. I had the feeling this was not so much an interrogation room as a conference room. If I had to guess, the office must have belonged to Ian.

When I looked down, I noticed that I had indeed devoured nearly the entire plate of fries. I sat up straight and dusted the salt off my fingers, wiped them clean with the napkin, and pushed the plate away. A glance at my watch told me it was nearly tea time.

So much for my second day at work.

There was a short knock at the door, and I turned to see a short man wearing a suit of fine brown wool, a crisp white shirt, and brown-and-white striped tie. He carried a briefcase and strode to the chair on the other side of the table from me. "Good day, Chef Cole. I am Inspector Garrote. I have a few questions for you."

"Oh," I said. "Hello."

He opened his briefcase and pulled out a recorder and a legal-sized notepad. Then he stopped and looked up at me. His eyes were hidden behind thick horn-rimmed glasses. His hair was light brown and would most likely have been blond when he was younger. His nose was rounded and his jowls soft.

"I understand you have spoken to Security Chief Ian Gordon," he said.

"Yes, he asked me questions."

"Good, good," he said. "Then you won't mind my asking the same."

"No, certainly not," I replied, picking up his accent. It was weird. Like I said, I had moved around a lot as a kid, and that had fostered the annoying habit of taking on whatever accent the person speaking to me had. I read somewhere it was a survival instinct and an attempt to blend in quickly with the locals. But it didn't work as an adult.

"Are you mocking me, Chef Cole? Because there is nothing humorous about murder."

"No, sir." I shook my head and tried my darnedest to be sincere.

"Then I'll begin." He cleared his throat and asked me the exact same questions that Ian had asked, only in a different order. I suppose it was to ensure my story remained the same.

It was indeed a long day. The sun had set before Ian let me go back to my part of the palace. I met Michael in the hallway, and we walked toward the elevator.

"Did they keep you the entire day as well?"

"Yes, Chef," he said. He looked nearly as tired as I felt. I remembered that he had lost a coworker and perhaps a longtime friend today. There was so little I really knew about these men.

I put my hand on his arm in a poor attempt to comfort him. "My condolences on your loss. Did you tell me that you and Mr. Deems were best friends?"

He pushed the elevator button. "We'd worked together for twelve years. I am godfather to his two boys."

"How old are his boys?"

"They are eight and ten years old. I'm going to check on his wife, Meriam. She'll need some help getting through the next few days. Security Chief Gordon told me they won't release the body until a complete autopsy is done. It could be a week before a funeral can be scheduled."

"Please send along my condolences." We stepped into the elevator. "Did you leave with Mr. Deems last night? I know you told me you live fairly close to each other."

"I made the tube, but Frank turned back. He said he left something in the kitchen."

"But I didn't see him return to the kitchen," I said. "I was there late having tea with Penny."

"Maybe he stopped at a pub for a pint," Michael

87

said. "Frank was known to do that from time to time."

"Was he a heavy drinker? I know so very little about you both," I said.

"It's quite expected," he said and patted my shoulder. "You haven't been here long enough to know anyone well. It truly is too bad. I think you would have really liked Frank. Despite his flaws—and we all have them—he was a good egg."

"Who would have wanted to kill him?"

"That's what the inspector and Chief Gordon are going to find out."

The elevator doors opened. There was a security guard at the entrance.

"May I see your badge, please?" he asked. We showed him our identification and he scanned it in his handheld device. "Thank you."

I turned to Michael. "Go to Mrs. Deems. I'm sure this nice security officer can help me find the kitchen."

"Thank you, Chef," he said. "Chief Gordon tells me that the palace has been cleared and the family will return by luncheon tomorrow. I will be in the kitchen by nine AM."

"Good, I'll see you then." I watched as he turned left and hurried down the corridor and out of sight. I turned to the security officer. He was a rather fit man with a square jaw, blue eyes, and blond hair. His name badge said "Jones." "Well, then, Officer Jones, is it too late to get my orientation completed and my real identification badge?"

"I'll check," he said, his voice a comfortable baritone. He spoke into the walkie-talkie that sat on his shoulder. The person on the other end came back with an affirmative. "Mrs. Worth would like you to meet her in the HR offices along with Chief Gordon and the minister of orientation. Follow me."

I patted my pocket to reassure myself that I still had my phone. When this day was done, I was going to call John. I needed a friendly voice in the midst of all this chaos. Maybe, just maybe, he'd realize he needed me and would come rescue me from this madness. But deep in my heart, I knew I couldn't count on it.

Chapter 6

I was a bit disappointed in the way that you handled Chef Butterbottom today," Mrs. Worth said. It sounded as if she was more than disappointed; her tone said she was clearly annoyed. "I expected better from you."

It was late. I had finished orientation and was waiting for my official badge to be laminated. Mrs. Worth sat behind a desk, and I stood in front of it with my hands behind my back. "Finding Mr. Deems's body threw me off my game. I'll try to do better next time."

"See that you do." She scanned papers in front of her, not bothering to look at me. It was a tactic to let me know I was less important than whatever work she had to do at eight PM at night. "For the next month, the family kitchen greenhouse will be off limits. I've set the gardeners on it. They will have to remove all the beds, do a thorough washing, and then regrow everything again." She made it sound as if it were my fault.

I bit my bottom lip to keep from pointing out that she was wrong.

She paused for a moment and then went on. "You will shop for your fresh produce at the approved markets on this list." She handed me a piece of paper. "They open at five AM, so you will have an hour to pick out your day's ingredients."

I took the paper.

"As you may know, the family has been allowed to return. They will be back in time for luncheon tomorrow. I expect you to send a daily and weekly menu to me via my e-mail before midnight tonight so that I can have it approved."

"Yes, ma'am."

She finally looked up. She folded her hands on top of the papers, studying me. "I would suggest that we never have another day like today. Am I clear?"

"Very clear."

"Good," she said and pushed her chair back. "I see Miss Smithson has your identification card ready."

I turned to see the pretty blonde assistant to the minister of orientation come into the room with my badge in hand.

"Be sure to keep it on your person whenever you are in the palace—outside of your room, of course," Mrs. Worth continued. "When you leave the palace, keep it with you in a safe place. We are not happy if it gets stolen. Are we, Chief Gordon?"

"No, ma'am, we are not," Ian Gordon said from his station just outside her door.

"Now, Chef Cole, you must be tired. Chief Gordon will see you back to your rooms. I suggest you get some rest. The family will return in the morning, and I only expect the best from you. Do you have your employee handbook?"

"Yes, ma'am," I said and held up the book with the emergency information and a map of the corridors along with the rules of the palace. "I plan on studying it thoroughly."

"Good. Have a good evening." She looked down at her papers. "You are dismissed."

I turned and left the room, clutching my rule book and my new identification badge. Ian turned and kept pace with me. It was pretty clear I was being closely watched.

"How was your day?" I quipped.

"Unusual," he answered and showed me to another elevator. "Miss Nethercott had a staff dinner plated and sent to your room."

"Thank you."

"Don't thank me, thank her."

"Didn't she go to the safe place with the family?"

"She did." We entered the elevator and he pushed the button to floor two.

"Then how did she think of my dinner?"

"She texted me, asking how you were."

"Aw, that was nice."

"I told her you didn't eat."

I glanced at him as he held the elevator door open, and we stepped out into the hallway just outside the kitchen. "That was nice of you."

"I need you alive if I'm going to solve this case."

"I see," I said. We passed the kitchen and took the hall and stairs up to the family's apartment and my room. He stopped at my door.

"Let me have your key."

"Why?" I asked.

"I want to ensure that your room is still safe."

I handed it to him and he took out his gun.

"Stay put," he commanded.

"Okay." I was so tired that the thought of a killer waiting for me in my room just seemed like another inconvenience in an already crazy day.

He went inside, flipping on the light switch and disappearing into the bedroom. I had the sudden worry that I had left the bed unmade. Had I picked up my dirty clothes? I walked into the living area when my phone buzzed in my pocket.

I pulled my phone out and saw that it was John calling. "Hello?" I said once I picked up.

"Hey, baby, how are you? I wanted to tell you that I've made quite the impression on the *Tribune*'s food critic."

"John, that's great news. When does the review come out?"

"Tomorrow's edition. Matt is stoked. We plan on a full house for the next month."

"You know you can't count on anything until the review comes out. Matt knows that, too." Matt was John's boss and the restaurant's owner.

"It's going to happen," John said with confidence. "Some of the regulars saw his face as he left and have already started reserving entire blocks of tables."

"Oh, well, that's great news," I said.

"How's the personal chef gig?" he asked, surprising me with his interest.

"It's good. It's a once-in-a-lifetime opportunity. I miss you."

"You, too," he said it as if he was distracted.

"I know we're on a break, but you said you would come visit. My day off is Monday—you could fly in Sunday night and we could spend Monday together in London celebrating. I might even be able to introduce you to the duke and duchess of Cambridge."

"London is far away, love. Things are heating up here. Seriously, Matt is popping champagne. There's no way I could take a day off. Why don't you fly back? You can see the packed restaurant, and we can celebrate the review."

"It's a new job. I told you, I can't leave."

"What do you mean you can't leave? Don't you get weekends off?"

"John . . ." I glanced up to see Ian leaning against my bedroom doorjamb, his gun holstered and his arms crossed. "I have to go. We'll talk about this later. Okay? I've had a bad day."

"Sure, baby," he said. "Sure. I'll see you soon." A good review could make a restaurant. A great review could make a chef. John's attention was not focused on me.

"Bye," I said and hung up. I looked at Ian. "Find anything?"

"No, you're clear." He straightened and walked to me. "Who was on the phone?"

"I don't think I have to tell you that," I said. "I get to have some privacy."

He reached up and gently placed his thumb under my chin. "Yes," he said softly. "You do get your privacy. As long as it keeps the family safe."

Our eyes met for a long moment. I finally stepped away. "It was my boyfriend, John," I said. "He's a chef and got reviewed tonight. He's certain it's going to be great and wanted to celebrate."

"Sounds like you wanted him to celebrate here."

"I miss him, but he can't. The restaurant is booked solid for the next three months, which means his days off are few and far between."

"And you're good with that?"

"We're on a bit of a break." I put my hands on my hips. "Why does that matter to you?"

"It doesn't," he said simply as he pushed past me. "Your room is clear. Have a good night, Chef."

I closed the door and flipped the bolt. My life had gotten terribly complicated since my arrival in London. In a fit of emotion, I strode to my room, stripped, and hit the shower. I reminded myself that I wasn't a quitter. It was only my second day. Besides, how much worse could things get?

Chapter 7

Early the next morning, Penny knocked on my apartment door.

"Do you have any biscuits left?" she asked.

"Sure, come on in. I was just making tea. I'm going to cook up a meal for Mrs. Deems."

"Oh, that's nice," Penny said and took a seat on the barstool. I plated some cookies I'd made before everything got crazy. I put the cookies and the tea out on the bar. "I heard that some of the royals are coming back to their apartments already. The duke and duchess can't be far behind."

"Cool," I said. "I hate feeling like I'm not doing my job."

"I heard from Harriet, who is on staff with the prince, that the family is quite upset by this. Ian had to really scramble. He had to explain why something like this could happen in their home when they pay him to ensure it doesn't happen. I heard he got called in front of the queen herself." She stirred sugar in her tea and took a cookie off the plate.

"I would be shaking in my boots," I said and sipped my tea. "I can't imagine. No wonder he was so grumpy yesterday. He treated both me and Michael as if we were suspects."

"No, really?" She seemed surprised. "Why?"

"Because I found the body and Frank was killed in the greenhouse attached to our kitchen."

"That's pretty circumstantial if you ask me," she said.

"That's what I said. He was reaching, I think."

"From the palace gossip, I bet he is reaching. He needs to get this thing solved and solved quickly. The press is having a field day."

"It doesn't make me feel sorry for him," I said stubbornly. "The rest of the staff isn't talking about me, are they?"

"Only that you and Chef Butterbottom had some kind of clash yesterday. Word has it you won that skirmish. Be careful, my friend. No one wins a contest of wills against Chef."

"Yes, well, maybe this time he's met his match."

Penny was silent for a moment.

"What is it?"

"You just reminded me that I heard a rumor about Chef Butterbottom . . . of course, it probably means nothing."

"What did you hear?" I leaned in closer.

"Chef Butterbottom and Mr. Deems were seen in a heated argument the night before Mr. Deems was killed."

"Now that is interesting," I said and sat back. "Frank fought with quite a few people that night. Witnesses said he fought with Michael, Michael said Frank fought with Jasper, and now he may have argued with Chef Butterbottom. That makes Chef Butterbottom and Jasper as much suspects as Michael and myself."

"He does have access to both the kitchen and the greenhouse."

"No one would think twice if they saw either of them leaving the greenhouse that night," I said. "Do you know if Ian knows?"

Penny shrugged. "I wouldn't say anything to him unless I had proof of some sort. You know, a witness to the arguments or someone seeing them leaving your kitchen or the greenhouse late that night."

"There are cameras in the halls," I said. "If I can find out who might have witnessed the argument and prove Chef Butterbottom left the kitchen around the time of the murder, Ian will have to consider a new suspect." I drummed my fingers on my chin. "Can you see if you can hunt down the source of the rumor? We can ask them to come forward with the information. Once we do that, then I imagine I will have enough for Ian or the inspector to take a second look at the hallway cameras."

"Brilliant plan," Penny said and sat up straight. "I kind of like this sleuthing business."

"I'll like it better if we can ensure Michael's innocence," I said. "Finding the witness to the arguments would go a long way to solving this case."

• • •

After Penny left, I finished preparing the meal, put on a brave face, and left the palace to take the tube to see Mrs. Deems and give her my condolences. I made a lasagna, salad, and garlic bread. I placed the easy-to-reheat meal in a carry basket and got the address for the Deemses' home from Miss Smithson in human resources.

"It's in a bit of a dicey area of town," she explained. "Do be careful and watch your purse."

I got on the tube and checked for my connections and my exit point. I thought Michael had told me they both lived just outside of town. But Miss Smithson said it was a dicey part of town. It was all confusing.

The only theory I had was that London was like Chicago. People said they lived in town, but they actually lived in attached suburbs. Still within the metropolitan area, but just outside the town proper.

At least this morning I was leaving town, which meant that the tube was not as cramped as going into town. Not bad for a Friday.

"That basket smells wonderful," an older woman sitting in front of me said.

"I'm sorry, it's right in your face," I said with an apologetic smile. Despite the smaller crowd, I was still standing with one hand on the bar above the seats.

"You won't hear me complain," she replied. "It's

the best smell I've ever had on my way home from work. I smell garlic and tomatoes. Am I right?"

"Yes, it's a lasagna for a friend who just lost her husband."

"How terrible for her, poor dear. Is she very young?"

"She has two boys ages eight and ten," I said. "I thought the meal might help them. Besides, it's kind of a tradition in my family."

"You're American," she stated. "Where from?"

"Most recently Chicago," I said. "Was it the accent that gave me away?"

"That and the clothing," she said. "The jeans and athletic shoes give you away." She paused. "But the smell of that meal is so wonderful that all is forgiven."

"All is forgiven?" I drew my brows together.

She grinned. "We have our fair share of foreigners here. A few bad eggs make us wary of all. Especially in this part of town."

"Oh," I replied, not knowing what to say.

"It's quite all right, though. I think you'll be safe enough with that basket in your hands. As long as you don't have to go too far. It certainly smells good. Someone might pinch it for themselves."

"I don't think I have too far to go," I said.

"Good thing," she replied as the train reached my stop. "Be safe now."

The damp, tiled tunnel of the tube station smelled like an old zoo. I waited for the majority of people to move past me, then trailed behind. There was a short walk through a hall and then a huge crowd waited by two giant service elevators that moved at a snail's pace. It would take at least four trips before I got close enough to squeeze into the elevator.

I saw a sign that pointed toward stairs. I figured that might be faster. After all, I only had so much time before I had to get back to work. Pushing around the crowd, I followed the corridor to the spiral staircase. At the bottom was a warning: "There are two hundred fifty-two steps to the surface."

I mulled over that fact for a moment. How bad could it be? Bad enough that no one else appeared to be taking the stairs. I decided to give them a try. At least it would make for a good workout.

I was out of breath and my legs were trembling by the time I reached the surface. I made a note to myself to only take the stairs *down* from now on. A glance at my watch told me I had better catch my breath again and press on. The elevator doors opened, and a crowd of people spilled out. I walked with the crowd out into the gloom of the street.

It was a cool gray day. I was glad for my jacket as I followed the signs, down one street, left, up two more blocks, and there I was in front of a two-story brick row house. The steps were freshly swept and the door painted brown.

I rang the bell and Michael answered.

"Chef Cole," he said, "this is a surprise." Two boys came running down the stairs to see who was at the door. They had fresh, round faces, short-buzzed blond hair, and cornflower-blue eyes.

"Hello," I said. "I brought a meal." I handed Michael the basket. "I wanted to give my condolences. How is Mrs. Deems doing?"

"She's upstairs with her mother," he said. The boys studied me as if I were an alien creature. "Come on in. Let me take this into the kitchen."

Following him inside, I said hello to the boys.

"These are my godsons, Charlie and John," Michael said. "Boys, this is Chef Cole, the personal chef for the duke and duchess."

"Did you find my da?" The youngest asked, his blue gaze filled with curiosity. "Did he say anything to you?"

"Yes, I did find your father," I said. "But he didn't say anything to me."

"It's because he was dead," the little boy said matter-of-factly.

"Yes," I agreed. "I'm so sorry."

"Are you American?" the older boy, John, asked, his tone solemn.

"Yes."

"I wondered why you have a funny accent. I've never met a real live American before."

"Boys, go on and play now," Michael said.

"Aw," the oldest said and jammed his hands in

his pockets. "I wanted to ask her about America. Is everyone really fat?" He tilted his head and studied me. "You're not fat. Are you sure you're American?"

"I'm sure," I said. "And no, we're not all fat."

"You're not loud either," the littlest said. "Americans are all supposed to be fat and loud."

"Off you go, boys." Michael pushed them out of the kitchen. "Sorry about their manners."

"It's okay," I said as I watched them go up the stairs. "Their dad just died, and I'm a stranger."

"You've come a long way from the palace," Michael said. "To be frank, I'm not sure Meriam is up for visitors."

"I understand," I said with a wave of my hand. "I wanted to bring food. It's what we do in my family. How is everyone holding up?"

"The boys are young, and I don't think it has sunk in yet. I think the little one, Charlie, still thinks his da will come walking through the door and tell his mom to stop blubbering. It's what he would do if he were still with us."

I noted the curtains were drawn in the kitchen and the parlor. The house had the lived-in look of an older home, with a small parlor in front, a tiny dining area, and a kitchen in the back. The house was attached to every other house on the block. There was no yard, only a sidewalk out front. I wondered if they had any yard at all in the back.

"Let me at least make you a cup of tea," Michael said. "If nothing else, I know how to cook. Please, have a seat."

I sat down at the small two-person dinette set and watched Michael work in the kitchen as if it were his own. "You said that you and Frank had known each other a long time."

"Since we were boys, actually," he said. "I got the job at the palace first and he followed. Then he got married and had kids."

"But you didn't?"

He put the kettle on the stove to boil and turned to look at me. "My wife was hit by a drunk driver and died two years after we married."

I felt awful for having stepped into such a touchy subject. "I'm sorry," I said. "I shouldn't have asked that. It really was none of my business. It's just that you seem so at home in this kitchen."

"I guess since Janine died, I've been as much a part of this family as the kids." The kettle whistle blew and he poured the water into the pot and placed the cozy around it to steep. "Do you take cream and sugar?"

"Just cream please," I said. "Thanks."

The house was quiet except for a television playing softly from the empty parlor.

Michael took a seat across from me and poured the tea. "Sorry, no biscuits. I gave the last to the boys."

"Do you want me to run to the store and get some?" I asked. "Surely they will have family and friends stopping by to see how Mrs. Deems is doing."

"No need," he said and handed me my mug of tea. "Frank was the last living soul in his family. He might have some cousins somewhere in Ireland or America. Anyway, they're all too far to travel and too distant to care. Meriam has a sister, Tammy. They had a bit of a falling out, but I expect she'll be here for the funeral."

"He had a small family then."

"Yes, unlike me. I have a brother and three sisters. How about you, Chef? Do you have a big family? What do they think of you living across the pond?"

"My parents divorced when I was young. My dad recently remarried, so he's busy with that, and my mother spends a lot of time out of the country."

"I'm sorry to hear that."

"It's okay." I shrugged. "I have friends and my boyfriend, John."

"You have a boyfriend?"

"Don't sound so amazed."

"Oh," he said and put his hand up like a cop stopping traffic. "I didn't mean you weren't pretty enough to have a boyfriend. I only thought that you were unattached because you moved—"

"Across the pond," I finished for him. "You

know, with the Internet, you can live anywhere in the world and still see each other every day."

"It's still different," he said with a shake of his head. "You need to be able to touch the person. I'm curious. What did he say when you told him you were taking this job?"

" 'Good for you,' " I said and sipped the last of my tea.

"He didn't protest? Not even a little?"

"To be fair, he's a chef—as he puts it, 'a rising star.' His focus has been a bit divided lately. Well, mostly on his career. But he said I should go for it."

"I see."

"And when I packed, he was at the restaurant . . . and when I left, he was preparing for a surprise visit from the local food critic."

"Huh."

"It's a big deal."

"I see."

"Okay then," I said and stood, as the conversation had suddenly gotten very awkward. "Please give Meriam my condolences. Will I see you at work today?"

"Can I be there for the dinner shift?"

"Okay. I've got to go. I've got grocery shopping to do."

"Do you have the list of approved markets?"

"I do," I said. "And I have an appointment with

the head gardener today to see what the timeline is on the greenhouse."

He walked me to the door. "I'll let her know you stopped by."

"One more thing," I said.

"Yes?"

"I heard a rumor that Chef Butterbottom was seen arguing with Frank the night he was murdered. Do you have any idea if it's true or what they might have been arguing about?"

"No," he said with a shake of his hand. "Butterbottom didn't exactly care for Frank. That said, there isn't anyone he really does care for."

"Okay," I said. "It was worth a try."

"Do you think he might be a good suspect?"

I shrugged. "I'm going to have to prove the argument was more than a rumor. Then we have to hope it's a strong enough motive for murder."

We had gotten to the door when I heard a familiar voice call out from upstairs. "Michael, can you bring us some tea?"

I glanced up to see Mrs. Perkins's formidable self rounding the top of the stairs. "Oh, hello," I said.

"Chef Cole, what are you doing here?" she asked.

"She stopped by to bring food," Michael said. "I told her Meriam wasn't up to taking visitors." He lowered his voice for my ears only. "Mrs. Perkins is Meriam's mum."

"Oh," I said. "My condolences for your loss." It made sense now why she was here.

"Right. Good." Her tone softened for the first time since I met her. "Thank you for that, Chef."

"Let me know if you need anything else," I said and went through the doorway.

It seemed that the palace staff were like the residents of a small town; everyone was related. I'd have to be careful who I said what to. I was so glad I hadn't made any comments to Michael about Mrs. Perkins's sternness . . . or had I?

Chapter 8

One of the approved markets was within walking distance of the tube station. Tucked between a sundries shop and an Italian restaurant, the market was unassuming. I picked up a basket and looked through the day's fresh produce.

I assumed the family had gone to stay with the duchess's parents while security had ensured the safety of the household. I know that other royals had moved back into their apartments as early as late last night. Penny was a wealth of palace scuttlebutt. Several members of the family had apartments at Kensington Palace. They each chose whether or not to have a private chef. The reason the duke and duchess had three kitchens was because the duchess liked to cook for her family herself. But with two children and an increasing role in charity events and state dinners, her time was limited, and they had brought me in to give the children a consistent, healthy diet.

Lunch today was for the children only since the duchess had an event she had to attend. I planned parmesan spring chicken slices with fresh snap peas, spinach, and new potatoes. Dinner would be simple: roasted lamb, fresh mint jelly, asparagus, wild rice, and mushroom pilaf, with fresh fruit for dessert.

I studied the pile of snap peas and picked one up, snapped it, and sniffed.

"You aren't going to get fresher peas than those," a gentleman in a grocer's coat said. "The truck brought them in from the country this morning. I think they still have morning dew on them."

"Ha," I laughed. "I think that's from the misters overhead."

"Can't pull anything over you Americans." He was my height, thin, with sparse brown hair, a long sharp nose, and calm gray eyes.

"How did you know I was American?" I glanced down at my outfit. "Are my clothes that odd?"

"It's not the clothes. It's your accent." He held out his hand. "I'm Joe Flannary. This is my market. Well, actually, my great-grandfather's market, but since I'm the last one alive, that makes it my market now, doesn't it?"

"Carrie Ann Cole," I introduced myself.

"Where in America are you from?"

"Chicago."

"What brings a young lady from Chicago into my market on this fine morning?"

"Well, I have it on good authority that this is one of a handful of markets approved by the royal chefs. Is that true?"

"True enough," he said and puffed up his chest, expanding his white apron. "We've been proudly

110

serving them for more than one hundred years."

"Good, because I'm the new family chef for the duke and duchess of Cambridge. I need to pick up a few things for lunch and dinner."

"What's that you say? You're a chef?"

"I'm a chef."

"If you were truly the new chef, you would know they have a fine greenhouse full of fresh veggies and such. Grow their own these days."

"Except that there was a bit of a problem in the greenhouse yesterday, and they are cleaning it all out and starting again. So here I am, grocery list in hand, looking for your freshest spring peas and asparagus."

His gray gaze turned thoughtful, and he stroked his chin. "That's right, I did hear something on the news this morning about the kitchen greenhouse. What was it, a fire? A bad infestation of gnats?"

"I'm not at liberty to say," I replied.

"Indeed." He studied me thoughtfully. "But if you were the real chef, then you would have simply called and had us deliver your order. It has to pass through the security and be tested before it's allowed in. We can't be poisoning the young family."

"You can believe me or not." I shrugged and read from my list. "I need two pounds of your best peas, asparagus, spinach, carrots, some new potatoes, and wild mushrooms."

"We have all of that." He grabbed a plastic sack and chatted with me as he gathered up everything on my list and placed it in my hand cart. "Now, do you need any meats, cheeses, or breads?"

"I have all that in the kitchen," I said. "This will do—wait. I need coffee for my room and some late night crackers and cheese."

"Coffee, crackers, and cheese," he said as I followed him through the aisles. "Who lives on that?"

"I do," I said and pulled what I needed from the shelf. "Don't you have other customers to help?"

"My staff is doing a fine job," he said and looked around. The store was not that busy. Most likely because it was in London in the middle of the morning and most everyone was at their office jobs.

"Are you sure you don't want some tea and biscuits?" he asked.

"I try to stay away from processed sugar," I said. "But you're right, tea would be nice to have for guests."

"In your hotel room?"

"In my apartment. Or do you call it a flat? It's actually a small suite of rooms," I corrected him. "At the palace, where I work. Not all that glamorous."

"Right," he said with a wink.

He rang up my purchases at the register and I paid cash. I had been given a petty cash account

112

for these types of purchases. I knew if I needed something delivered, it would be billed to the duchess and delivered as he described. But sometimes you want to see for yourself where the food comes from—even if it was a grocery shelf.

"Well, Miss Cole—it is Miss, right?"

"Chef," I reminded him and picked up the two paper bags full of fresh ingredients.

"That's right, Chef Cole." His gaze twinkled. "It was nice to meet you. I hope to see you again soon at my humble grocery store."

"Good-bye, Mr. Flannary." I waved as I walked out into the busy London street.

"See you soon, American Chef."

Back in the kitchen, I put the fresh produce in the sink with ice water to crisp up and wash. A little white vinegar helped keep it fresh and wash off any bacteria, dirt, and wax that might linger.

It was difficult not to keep looking at the boarded-off door that led to the greenhouse. Someone had placed a "Do Not Enter" sign on it. As if crossed boards weren't warning enough.

I sent a quick message to Michael to let him know that I didn't need him to come in tonight. It was best he stayed with Mrs. Deems. With only the family to cook for, I figured I could handle two meals by myself. I washed my hands and put on my chef coat. My identification badge was clipped to the hip pocket where it would be accessible at all times but out of the way.

I chopped veggies and sautéed the chicken for the children's lunch. Michael was usually the one who ran the covered meals up to the nursery. I would do it today. It was a good thing I'd become familiar with the pathway from the kitchen to the nursery.

There is something mindful and almost Zen-like when it comes to chopping veggies, making sauces, and adding spices. I was careful to keep the flavors not too extreme. The children were small and their palates were developing. That meant they tasted some things stronger than others.

For a twist, I served the meal in a bento box, placing the chicken fingers and fresh veggies into a square bento-box shape. It was fun and artistic, and I hoped it would delight the children.

Completing the meal with little flourishes of fresh radish roses, I covered the dishes, changed my chef's coat for the clean one, and walked them up the stairs, down the hall, and to the nursery. I knocked once and waited.

The older of the two women I saw attending to the children my first day opened the door. Up close, I noticed that she actually wasn't much older than me. She nodded. "Chef Cole, what a surprise. We expected Mr. Haregrove."

"He is attending to the Widow Deems," I said softly. "I told him I would handle lunch and dinner today by myself." The staff knew about the death of Mr. Deems, but I wasn't sure how much the children knew, and I didn't want them to hear.

"Of course, how kind of you. Please come inside." She opened the door wider, and I walked into the room between the two nurseries. It was big and wide, filled with what my elementary school teachers had called centers when I was young. One corner had tricycles, a rocking horse, and other modes of transportation. Another had a bookshelf and comfy seats for reading. There were art supplies in another space and what appeared to be letter and number learning stations in the far corner. Near the open windows was a tiny table set for lunch. It was perfectly child-size with proper china and silverware. A pot of fresh violets sat in the middle.

"My name is Mrs. Killigan, but you may call me Teresa. I am governess for the prince. This is Miss Lovejoy." Teresa waved her hand toward the younger woman with soft blonde hair who was reading a storybook to the little princess. "She is nanny to the princess."

"So nice to meet you both," I said and took the covers off the plates and set them up on the table.

The little prince came running over. "Hello," he said. "How do you do? Are you a chef?"

"Yes, I am," I replied.

"Where are you from?" he asked as he climbed into his chair.

"I'm from Chicago," I answered.

"Where's that?"

"In the United States." I tucked the tray under my arm and held the dish covers in my hand. "Do you know where that is?"

"Far away," he said and took a sip of his milk.

"Across the Atlantic Ocean," Mrs. Killigan said. "Wait for your sister before you touch anything on the table."

"Have a good day," I said, but the children were already lost in the excitement of lunch.

I heard from Penny that the duchess liked to spend as much time as possible with her children, but like any mother with outside responsibilities, there were many times when she didn't have that luxury. Let's face it, being a part of the royal family meant a great deal of responsibility.

It was nice to get to know other members of the household staff. I wondered if they had known Frank well. But it wasn't a question I could ask in front of the children.

Ian Gordon came around the corner as I headed down the stairs back to the kitchen. "Chef Cole," he said.

"Mr. Gordon."

"Where is Mr. Haregrove? He didn't come to work today."

I stopped beside him on the steps. It was a narrow passageway, made all the narrower by Ian's athletic body. "He's with the Widow Deems," I said. "I told him he could take the day. He'll be back tomorrow. Why?"

"No particular reason," he replied.

"Are you keeping track of us?"

"That's my job," he said, his gaze sincere. "A man died on my watch. It won't happen again."

"Good to know." I chewed on my bottom lip. "Are you any closer to finding the killer?"

"We have our suspects."

"Anyone I know?"

"Perhaps," was all he said, and then he continued up the stairs. "Good day, Chef."

"Right." I went back to the kitchen. It was spooky working alone in a place next to where a man was killed. But then the palace was old, and I figured that Mr. Deems wasn't the first dead man to have been found on the grounds.

Chapter 9

S o glad you decided to come with me," Penny said as we entered a small pub near the palace. "Everyone will be here. There are so many people for you to meet."

"I imagine a wake is not the best place for introductions," I said.

"I think Mr. Deems would approve," Penny said.

Inside, the pub was packed. "A crush" is what Penny aptly called it. Loud music played. People young and old were gathered, talking loudly and trying to be heard. I spotted Mrs. Worth seated near the fireplace, talking with Mrs. Perkins and an older gentleman. Mrs. Killigan and Miss Lovejoy were there as well. Michael stood near Mrs. Perkins, speaking to a young man I didn't know. Even Chef Butterbottom was there. I thought it might be wise to steer clear of him.

"Come on," Penny said and put her arm through mine. "Let's get a drink."

We approached the bar. The interior was old and decorated with dark woods, cream-colored plaster, crossbeams, and such. There was a collection of old smoking pipes hanging from the ceiling, both long and short. Tables were scattered about. People sat on stools and in small clusters of overstuffed chairs. Others stood and tried to weave themselves around the crowd.

There was a sad air to the festivities and yet still one or two groups laughed. Most everyone had a sober expression, a drink in their hand, and a black ribbon pinned to their chest.

"The first thing you should know about this pub is that everything is ordered through the bar, even the food," Penny said as she pulled me through the crowd and up to one of the four bartenders.

"Who do we have here?" a man in his thirties asked Penny. He looked at me with a teasing leer. "Fresh meat?"

"Stop it, Tommy." Penny slapped his hand and then kissed his cheek. "This is Carrie Ann. She's the new family chef for the duke and duchess."

He looked at me carefully. I wore the same outfit I'd worn that morning to visit Mrs. Deems. Considering I only packed two, this was the best I could do. "She looks like an American."

"I can hear you," I said.

"Carrie Ann, this is Thomas Evans."

"Hello," I said.

"How do you do?" he replied.

"Tommy knows everything there is to know about Kensington Palace and what goes on in and around it. Don't you, Tommy?"

"Shush," he said and put his finger to his smiling

lips. "Bartenders don't spill secrets. If we did, then we wouldn't be bartenders long."

"I'll have a pint," Penny said and looked at me.

"Scotch, neat," I said.

"Now there's a girl after my heart." Tommy's eyes lit up. His smile was attractive, and I found myself blushing. He poured out her pint and then my shot. "Wait," he said when I reached for my drink. "You're the one who found Frank, aren't you?"

I pulled my hand back and swallowed. "Yes," I said.

"Wow. That must have been tough." There was sympathy in his gaze.

"It was."

"Were you afraid?"

"Of Frank? No, I liked him. I wanted to help him, but it was too late."

"That must have been terrible," he said and patted my arm. "Here," he said and placed the shot glass in my hand. "Your drinks are on me tonight."

"Thanks," I said with caution.

"No worries." He winked. "Maybe you'll spill some secrets of your own."

"Only if you share as well."

"It's a deal," he said and held out his hand. I shook it.

"Come on, there are people you have to meet," Penny said and dragged me away.

The wake was held at the local pub because it was where the staff from the palace hung out. It was like a big family. I found that after a few drinks, stories were being told in every corner about Francis Deems and the funny things he did, or adventurous things, or things he got away with. The stories could be told now that he was gone.

My head spun, and I realized I'd never remember all the names of the people Penny introduced me to, but I would remember their faces if I saw them in the halls.

I ended up near Mrs. Perkins, who stood in line for the ladies' toilet. "I'm sorry for your loss," I said. "How is your daughter holding up?"

"She wanted to be here, but Charlie got sick," Mrs. Perkins said. It was the first time she had spoken to me without a superior tone. "Thankfully, Frank left her some insurance money. She and the boys will be fine."

"That's good to hear," I said and nursed my scotch. Even though several people had offered to buy me drinks, more than a couple of these and I would have to be escorted home.

"I wanted to say thank you for stopping by this morning," Mrs. Perkins said and tried not to look at me. "It was thoughtful of you. You'd never met Meriam and still you came with a meal."

"Mr. Haregrove told me that Mr. Deems had two children, and I thought having a prepared meal would be helpful in this trying time."

"Yes, well, Michael said you treated Frank with respect and that will be remembered. Here of course, not at the palace. At the palace, there is still a chain of command to be kept. Tradition, you know. Well, I don't expect that you would know since you are American."

"I'll learn," I said.

"Good."

She disappeared into the toilet when the door opened and the room was free. The toilets were down a narrow flight of steps. The walls were painted brick and the floors titled. I thought it must have looked just like this for at least a couple of hundred years. Men came and went quickly, laughing and joking with each other. For the girls there was always a line.

Back upstairs, I made my way to the bar. Maybe Tommy had some secrets he would share.

"Hey, beautiful," he said and leaned on the counter with a bar rag in hand. "Can I get you another drink?"

"Yes, please," I said and put my empty glass down. I was feeling mellow. "Did you know Mr. Deems well?"

"As much as I know anyone on staff," he said and poured me another glass.

"Speaking of the staff, I haven't met Jasper Fedman yet. Is he here?" I looked around the crowd for the greenhouse manager.

"Come to think of it, I haven't seen him," Tommy said and pushed the new glass toward me. "I'm not surprised as he wasn't a big fan of Frank."

"Really?" I leaned my elbow on the bar and rested my chin in my hand. "Why not?"

"Those two went to school together and were like brothers at one point, but they had a falling out of some sort." Tommy shook his head. "It happened years ago, but they haven't done anything but fight over silly things since. I'm guessing he's not here out of respect for Frank's family."

"Huh," I said. "Come to think of it, Michael did say Frank had run into Jasper the night before he was killed."

"Really?"

"Yes, but he didn't think it was a big deal. He said he could handle Jasper."

"I imagine he could," Tommy said. "Only petty squabbles between those two. I suspect Jasper is hurting. It's tough to lose a friend. Even if they were at each other's throats."

"I can only imagine," I said and sipped my drink. Tommy got called over to refill someone's glass, so I left the bar and searched for Penny, only to run into Michael.

"Thanks for coming tonight, Chef Cole," he said and toasted me with his glass of beer. "Thanks for this morning as well. Meriam said the lasagna was spectacular."

"It must be so difficult for her right now," I said. "How are you holding up?"

"I'm okay," he said. "I'm worried about the boys. They don't seem affected at all by their father's death."

"They're young. I'm not sure they understand what death is at that age, do they?"

"I imagine it's just a lot of people being sad," Michael said. "Charlie keeps looking for his dad to come home."

"Who would do such a thing?" I asked. "Leave two boys without a father? Do you have any idea?"

"None," Michael said, his expression grim. "If I get my hands on them, I'll see they hang for it."

"I don't think England has the death penalty anymore. Do they?"

"No, but I would make an exception. Frank was my friend."

"How good of friends were you if you two fought that night?"

"Friends fight," he said and shrugged. "It happens, especially if you're close."

"Fine, I get it. He was your friend. What were you fighting over?"

"It wasn't important. We would have made up the next morning. Frank was like that—always seeing my side of things."

"Hmmm, we still don't know any more about the argument between Chef Butterbottom and

Frank. Do you think they were arguing over something unimportant like you were?"

"Oh, I doubt it was unimportant. Chef Butterbottom could be a real hothead when it came to his opinion. It's his way or the highway."

"Sounds like he could be a suspect. Did you find out anything more about their fight?"

"No. According to the staff, the argument was just a rumor. No one actually saw anything. They only heard them fighting down the hall and then couldn't tell what the fight was about."

"Darn. That makes Butterbottom less of a suspect. Do you know if there was a break-in? I'm too new to know if there was anything of value in the kitchen or greenhouse that would be worth killing Frank over."

"The only thing of value was the entrance to the apartments, but then you have to have a key card, and there are so many cameras and security checkpoints." He shook his head. "There is no way Frank could have stumbled upon someone using the greenhouse to break in."

"Did anyone have a grudge against Frank?"

"Enough to kill him?" Michael shrugged. "I don't see how."

"Mr. Gordon seems to think they have a good suspect. Do you have any idea who it is?"

"No," Michael said and drew his eyebrows together. "I wonder who they're thinking it might be."

"I imagine it had to be an inside job," I said. "Like you said, security wouldn't make it easy for an outsider to get in and out without being noticed. Chef Butterbottom has to be our best suspect."

"Butterbottom is arrogant and capable of a lot of things, but I can't imagine he killed Frank."

"But it would have to be a staff member, right?" I asked. "Or a guest or visitor. Someone who had access to the personal apartment areas."

"A lot of people come and go at the palace. Staff and family members. That means it could have been someone here," Michael said and studied the crowd.

His words made the hair on the back of my neck stand on end. I could be mingling with a murderer. "Still, there doesn't seem to be a motive. People don't kill for no reason at all."

"Unless they are a serial killer, like Jack the Ripper."

"I highly doubt there is a serial killer on the loose in the palace," I said. "I'm sure Ian would have him dispatched forthwith."

Michael laughed at the idea and then spotted someone coming in the door and sobered. "It's Meriam. Please excuse me."

It didn't take a genius to decipher the look in Michael's gaze. He was in love with Frank's widow. Why hadn't I noticed it before?

"She showed up," Penny said as she appeared by my side. We both watched as Michael made his way toward a lovely blonde with pale skin, an oval face, and big green eyes. She wore a long-sleeved black wrap dress, little eye makeup, but red lipstick.

"She looks like a movie actress," I said. "I wouldn't have put her and Mr. Deems together."

"They were teenage sweethearts," Penny said. "She worked for a magazine for a year, and then when she got pregnant, she decided to be a stay-at-home mom."

"Michael is very attached," I said, trying to feel out the situation.

"That's putting it mildly," Penny said and sipped her latest pint. "Everyone knows he's been half in love with her since she and Frank got married."

"But he told me he has a girlfriend," I said. "Isn't she bothered by how much time he's spending with Meriam?"

"Mr. Haregrove has a girlfriend? That's news to me. I'll have to ask around."

I drew my eyebrows together. "I'm pretty sure he told me he had a girlfriend. Oh, no, wait. He told me he was living in his mom's house while she's in nursing care."

"Michael does have a roommate, Felicity. Last I knew, she was off on a model shoot in Africa for two weeks."

"Michael lives with a model and Frank's widow looks like a movie star? I don't—"

"Understand the appeal?" Penny snickered. "I guess it must be surprising. These two are nice enough, but they aren't exactly what you would call alpha male material."

"Right?"

"There is prestige in working at the palace," Penny said. "Besides the money being good, having access—no matter how slight—to the royal family brings on its own kind of fame."

"Then your boyfriend must be stunning," I teased.

"He is," she replied and sipped her beer. "In my dreams." She laughed at me. "Got ya! No, no boyfriend. I'm enjoying being single as long as I can. Besides, it drives my mum crazy that I haven't settled down yet."

"Tommy seems to like you," I pointed out.

"Watch out for that one," she warned me. "He loves the ladies and he loves to leave the ladies, if you know what I mean."

"Oh, I'm not on the market," I said. "I have John, remember?"

"The man who can't remember that you are in London?"

"He can remember; he's just busy. And he misses me."

"Well, maybe you can have him come over for a weekend sometime. I'd love to meet him.

Meanwhile, promise me you'll be my wing-woman at parties."

"I can do it," I said, "if you promise me you'll teach me what it's like to be a Londoner."

"It's a deal," Penny said. "Come on, let's pay our respects to Meriam."

We wound our way through the crowd to the back, where Michael had helped Meriam get a seat next to her mother. The crowd of well-wishers had begun to thin by the time we made it to her side.

"Meriam," Penny said and took her hand. "My sincerest condolences on your loss." She kissed Meriam's cheek. The widow's eyes welled up with tears and she dabbed at them with a hand-kerchief. It suddenly made sense that she wore no eye makeup; it would only run down her face.

"Hello," I said and took her hand. "I'm Carrie Ann Cole. I'm so sorry for your loss."

"You're Chef Cole?"

"Yes." I gave a short nod.

"Thank you for stopping by and bringing the basket of food. It means a lot to me and the kids."

"I didn't know Mr. Deems long at all, but he seemed like a good man."

"He was." She sniffed and touched the tears at the corner of her eyes.

"I'm certain he will be missed," I added and then stepped away to let others more familiar with Meriam and Frank step in and share their tales.

Telling Meriam my condolences was enough for me. The two drinks I had were hitting me harder than I thought. Perhaps because I was still getting used to the change in time. Perhaps it was because the music and crowd were loud. I saw Penny talking into the ear of a tall, handsome man with a bright white smile.

I nudged my way over to her. "I'm going to head back now," I said. "Thanks for bringing me."

"Do you really have to go?" Penny asked in the way that girls do when they are relieved that you are leaving but don't want to sound like it.

"I'm certain. I've got to make the family's breakfast in the morning. Thank you again for introducing me to so many good people." I looked at the handsome young man. "Take care of her, please. She might have had a few drinks."

"I will," he said and put his arm around her back.

"I haven't had that many," Penny said and giggled.

I winked at her. "I'll see you tomorrow."

The pub wasn't that far from the palace. All I needed to do was skirt around the park, as I wasn't sure I wanted to walk through it by myself in the dark. When I turned the corner of the pub, I heard a noise coming from the alley behind it.

Cautiously, I peered into the darkness to see two

guys with their backs to me and one man facing them. Despite being backlit by the lights from the pub, I recognized the man facing my direction as Michael.

"We want our money. We aim to get it—even if we have to take it the hard way," one gruff voice said. It came from a burly man in the shadows. I thought he might be wearing jeans and a biker jacket. Did they have bikers in London?

"I'll get it," Michael said. "There's insurance money."

The second big guy appeared to be bald, and he shoved a fat finger into Michael's chest. "You have forty-eight hours and we're coming for it, funeral or no funeral."

"I'll have it."

"You better." The two men turned and my heart pounded in my chest. I ducked down the block and hid in the doorway of the nearest building. Plastered against the door, I was glad that my coat was dark.

The two men came out of the alley and turned away from me and toward the front entrance of the pub. I waited until they were out of sight before I went back to the alley to check on Michael. But when I got there, he was gone.

There was a tap on my shoulder and I gasped. I jumped and turned around.

"You shouldn't be out here alone," Ian said.

I was never so glad to see someone in my life.

His bulky frame and air of confidence made the fear leave my body.

"I was walking home from the wake," I said.

"It's not safe for a woman alone on the street. Why didn't you take a cab?"

"It's not that far. I figured as long as I stayed on the streets I'd be fine."

"This is London, Chef, not some small American town. The streets are safe enough during the day, but it's best if you don't wander around alone after dark."

"I'm from Chicago, not a small town," I said. "I think I can handle myself."

"Right," he said and pointed toward the way I was going. "I'll walk you to your door, anyway."

"I don't want to keep you from something," I said. "I'll call a cab."

"I'm heading back," he informed me and pointed the way. "I stopped by to give Mrs. Deems my condolences and let her know that I will stop at nothing until I find the person who did this to her husband."

"Wait, I didn't see you at the wake," I said as we walked side by side down the sidewalk. "You were there?" How could anyone miss Ian? He stood out even in a crowd.

"I wasn't there to socialize," he said. "I went in, gave my condolences, and left."

"That seems antisocial. What's the matter?" I

had to ask. "Don't you like the people who work at the palace?"

"I like the staff," he said and stared straight ahead. "I don't have the time to do more than memorialize Mr. Deems with a shot of whiskey and give my condolences to his widow. I've got work to do if I'm going to keep the palace safe."

"It seems we have something in common," I said.

"Why'd you go?"

"Penny said it would be a good way for me to meet more people who worked at the palace. She thinks I'm alone too much."

"What do you think?" he asked.

"I think I have a boyfriend in Chicago and I would rather concentrate on doing a good job for the duchess than party all night."

"Good plan," he said. "It appears you might have a good head on your shoulders after all."

I crossed my arms over my chest and said, "What do you mean I *might* have a good head on my shoulders?"

He didn't answer the question but quickened his pace.

"What do you mean?" I asked again, chasing after him.

He quickly used his badge to gain entrance onto the palace grounds. I had to stop and wait for security to scan my own badge. By the time I made it through security and to the apartments,

Ian had disappeared into the warren that was the palace.

I went to my room, turned on the lights, and kicked off my shoes. Then I grabbed a notebook and wrote down what I could remember about my night.

Three men in an alley, too dark to see anything but the face of Michael Haregrove. The other two were demanding money. Michael said there was insurance money.

They would get their money in forty-eight hours.

"Why are they trying to get money from Michael?" I mused out loud.

Chapter 10

Mr. Haregrove will not be returning to your kitchen," Mrs. Worth said. "I have scheduled four adequately trained assistants for you to interview today. I suggest you pick two."

"Wait," I drew my eyebrows together in confusion. "What happened to Michael? I just saw him last night."

"He has been suspended from his duties," Mrs. Worth said. "That is all I can say about it. We realize that this leaves you with no help and three meals to plan for the family. This is Miss Jones." Mrs. Worth gestured toward a woman standing slightly behind her. "She is on loan to you for the day from Chef Butterbottom. Use her services wisely. Here are the résumés of the assistants you are to interview along with the times of the interviews. I hope you find them convenient. We did our best to work with your schedule. All interviews are conducted in the personnel office. If you have any further questions, Mrs. Perkins will be in the office after noon. Now get to work."

Mrs. Worth turned on her heels and strode out of my kitchen.

I held the papers in my hands and looked at Miss Jones. "Well, then, what do you do best?"

"I am a sous chef, and I specialize in pastries,"

Miss Jones said. She appeared to be my age or slightly older. She had brown hair pulled back against her nape, large brown eyes set wide apart, and very fair skin. She wore a light-blue shirt and black slacks.

"Good. Thank you for your help. We need to make breakfast for the family. We can discuss the rest of the day's meals after."

"Of course," she said. "I'll start with dried fig breakfast muffins topped with seeds and dried cranberries."

"That sounds wonderful," I said. "I'll add poached eggs, sausages, and a fruit compote. That should do for the morning menu. Lunch will be simple, as the children are going out for a small picnic in the park. I'm making cheesy tomato bread. We'll add chunks of sharp cheddar cheese and a fresh spinach salad with strawberries."

"Perfect, I'll get started," Miss Jones said and pulled a chef coat off the hooks near the door.

I added a black apron to my outfit and went to work on the sausages and fruit compote. Today's fruit was warmed in a gentle sauce made with reduced lemon juice and fresh ginger. I placed pears, plums, and kumquat in crystal cups, poured the lemon ginger sauce over them, and let them sit. Next was poaching the eggs, which didn't take long. We plated the meals and put them on the serving cart. Miss Jones took it away for the family.

I washed my hands, dried them on a towel, and took a moment to sit at the table and study the résumés of the people I was to interview. There were two women and two men. All had solid qualifications and most had studied at London's cooking school. It seemed that my choice would boil down to how the interviews went and who I got along with.

My thoughts turned to Michael. Why wasn't he here? Did something happen to him last night? Should I have told Ian about what I saw in the alley? I didn't want to get Michael in trouble. He seemed like a great guy to me, caring about his family and friends.

During orientation, I had been shown how to access a private web portal for the staff at Kensington Palace. I used my phone to access it now. On the intranet was a list of personnel and their phone numbers. I found Michael's number and dialed it.

Miss Jones came back with the serving tray as Michael's phone started to ring. I walked through the kitchen and out into the hallway for privacy.

"Hello?" The person who answered was female.

"Hi, um, I'd like to speak to Michael Haregrove. Is he available?"

"Who's asking?" She sounded belligerent. I wondered if this was his roommate, the model.

"I'm Chef Cole, Mr. Haregrove's new boss," I replied. "May I speak to him?"

"They should have told you that he isn't coming in to work today."

"Mrs. Worth told me," I said. "I assume he's home. May I speak with him?"

"Yeah, well, you assume wrong. Michael's been arrested. I have no idea when or if he'll be back here."

"Arrested? What for?"

"They pinned that murder on him," the woman said. "My brother the murderer. Reporters have been calling all morning. They're hanging out in front of our place. Like I can tell them anything."

"They arrested Michael for the murder of Francis Deems?" My voice went up at the end of the sentence. I couldn't believe what I was hearing. "But they are best friends."

"Were best friends," the woman said. "The coppers think that the best murder suspects are family and friends. So they picked up Michael."

"I'm sorry," I said. "You said he's your brother?"

"I'm his sister," she said, "Rosemary. Michael called me to let me know he'd been arrested. I live in Bath, but I came as fast as I could to look after Mum and the house for him."

"Rosemary, as his sister, you know Michael didn't kill Mr. Deems."

"What I know won't matter in court. I wasn't here that night, so I can't be my brother's alibi. Michael wouldn't let me lie for him, either. He always did have an overly developed sense of right and wrong."

"Do you know anything about Michael owing people money?" I asked.

"No, why?"

"I saw him in an alley last night being pushed around by a couple of burly guys who were demanding money. Does Michael gamble?"

"Naw. Like I said, he has an overly developed sense of right and wrong. He won't even enter an office baby pool."

"Weird."

"Are you sure it was Michael in the alley?"

"I'm sure," I said. "I recognized his voice and then he stepped into the light. I saw his face, and he looked worried."

"Bloody hell, Michael," Rosemary muttered.

"What? Do you know what was going on?"

"My brother," she said with a sigh. "He likes to run to people's rescue. My guess is that he was taking the heat for one of his friends."

"Do you have any idea which one?"

"No," she said. "In this neighborhood, it could be any number of guys."

"What about Francis Deems? Could he have been taking the heat for him?"

"Frank? No, he's dead. The bookies know they can't squeeze money out of a dead man. It's why they rough guys up, not kill them, you know?"

"Yes, I suppose that makes sense."

"Michael is protecting someone. I just don't know who," she said.

"Well, if you think of anyone or hear anything, can you give me a call?"

"Sure," she said and took down my number. "Are you going to go to the coppers with what you know?"

"No," I said and leaned against the hall wall. "Last night probably has nothing to do with the murder or Michael's arrest. I think it's best to keep it between you and me for now. Okay?"

"Okay," she said. We said our good-byes, and I hung up.

"Keep what between yourselves?" Ian asked.

I jumped at the sound of his voice and turned around. He stood at the top of the steps. I put my hand on my heart to try to slow the racing. "You should not sneak up on people," I scolded. "You about gave me a heart attack."

"I wasn't sneaking up on you," he replied and continued down the steps. "You were intent on your conversation and didn't hear me."

"Wait, you're blaming me for being startled?"

"No blame," he said. "But I did tell you to be aware of your surroundings at all times. What if I had been intent on hurting you?"

"I had my back to the wall."

"But all your attention was on your conver-sation," he pointed out. "Or I wouldn't have surprised you. Now, back to my question: what are you keeping to yourself?"

"I'm getting my boyfriend a present for his birthday," I lied. "That was his sister."

"I see," he said and studied me.

I am a terrible liar, and I had to work very hard to remain poker-faced under his scrutiny. "What happened to Mr. Haregrove?" I asked to break the tension. "He seemed fine when I saw him at the wake yesterday. Mrs. Worth said he was out indefinitely. Do you know why?"

"Mr. Haregrove has been arrested for Mr. Deems's murder," Ian said. He crossed his arms. "We're trying to keep the whole thing out of the press."

"I don't understand. Mr. Haregrove is the nicest person. Why would the inspector think that he, of all people, killed Mr. Deems? I mean, don't you need motive, means, and opportunity?"

"Mr. Haregrove is having an affair with Mr. Deems's wife," Ian said.

I gasped at that news. I suppose I shouldn't have been surprised from the way Michael looked at Meriam, but I was. Frank was Michael's best friend. You don't sleep with your best friend's wife. "What makes you think that?"

"We had a witness come forward."

"Who?"

"Mrs. Deems's mother came forward with her suspicions," he said. "The inspector confronted

Mr. Haregrove, and he admitted as much."

I rubbed my temples as a sudden headache appeared. "Mr. Haregrove was sleeping with his best friend's wife? That doesn't make sense. The two were so close. Mr. Haregrove told me that he was Mr. Deems's sons' godfather."

"You'll have to ask Mr. Haregrove why he did it," Ian said. "What I know is that he had motive to get rid of Mr. Deems. That motive was so that he could marry Meriam himself."

"Did he tell you that? Did he confess?"

"No." Ian shook his head. "Mr. Haregrove is maintaining his innocence."

"Well, surely the security logs will show that Mr. Haregrove couldn't have done it. He wasn't in the palace at the time. Aren't the logs precise about who is in the building and where they are going?"

"There was a power glitch that night," he said and scowled. "We suspect someone knew how to get past the system. It came back on an hour after the coroner estimates Mr. Deems died."

"Wait, don't you have redundant systems?"

"We do," he said. "Whoever messed with it took out both. That's why we know it's a palace insider."

"What about the security person who monitors that system?"

"He responded to an emergency call and left his station."

"I don't understand," I said and drew my eye-

142

brows together. "Do you only have one security guy on duty at night?"

"We have several," he said. "Enough for you not to be concerned for your safety."

"Then what was so important that he left his post?"

"A fire broke out in the server room. It was quite a mess."

"So the murderer set up a diversion and then sabotaged the system so that he could kill Mr. Deems."

"That is the prevailing theory."

"But what was Mr. Deems doing in the greenhouse anyway? As far as I knew, he had left for the night. Why return?"

"We're still trying to figure that out."

"And your server room, is that okay?"

"We've had the IT department in there replacing and updating everything for the last two days. This kind of thing won't happen again."

"No wonder you've been busy." I scratched my head. "The fire in the server room means that you had to let firefighters in to stop it, right?"

"Yes."

"Then how do you know someone didn't slip in disguised as a firefighter, kill Mr. Deems, and slip out?"

He chuckled. "That is a bit of a stretch, don't you think? In crime, as in life, the simplest explanation is usually the correct explanation."

"What about Chef Butterbottom?"

"What about him?"

"I understand he and Frank didn't get along. Rumor had it he was arguing with Frank the night he was killed. And so was the greenhouse keeper, Jasper Fedman, for that matter."

"Chef Butterbottom doesn't like anyone," Ian said. "And both arguments are just rumors. No one has come forward as a witness to them."

"But either still could have done it."

"I can't prove it," Ian said. "What I can prove is that Mr. Haregrove had plenty of motive and access to the victim. Now, let's head back into the kitchen. I understand you are interviewing new staff today."

"Yes," I said. "I have four people to speak with. I'll be interviewing them in the conference room where you had me talk to the inspector, right?"

"Yes," he said and opened the kitchen door for me. Miss Jones was inside, cleaning dishes and prepping for the lunch menu. "I see you have help today."

"Yes," I said. "This is Miss Jones. She's on loan from the main kitchen."

"Hello, Mr. Gordon." She smiled and wiped her hands on a towel. "How are you today, sir?"

"I'm well. Thank you for asking." He looked at me. "I thought you might need a map to get to the conference room." He pulled one out of his pocket. "That way you won't get lost."

"Thanks." I took it from him.

"Good day, ladies," he said and left.

I unfolded the map. It was a floor plan of the palace with dotted lines from my kitchen to his conference room.

"He really brought you that?" Miss Jones asked looking over my shoulder. "You know you can ask anyone if you get lost."

"I think he wants me to not wander into places I don't belong." Shaking my head, I put the map in my pocket and got started on the lunch bread. My thoughts turned to Michael as I worked. There was no way he had killed Francis Deems. No way. I'd only known him two days and even I could tell he wasn't capable of the deed.

I paused in kneading the dough. No one had told me how Frank died. I saw a lot of blood, but no gaping wound. That meant he was killed from behind. But if he was killed from behind, why did I find him face up?

"Do you know how Mr. Deems died?" I asked Miss Jones.

"I thought you were the one who found his body."

"I did," I said. "But I didn't get an official cause of death. I thought you might have heard something."

"They say he was gutted with a butcher knife," Miss Jones said as she prepared the side dishes. "That's why they arrested Mr. Haregrove. After all, he is a butcher."

"But I thought it was Mr. Deems who was the butcher," I pointed out. "Mr. Haregrove was the prep chef."

"Oh," she said and shrugged. "All I'm telling you is what I heard. Mr. Deems was gutted with a butcher knife in the greenhouse, and it was a crime of passion. Mr. Haregrove has access to the butcher knife, the greenhouse, and Mr. Deems. Plus, he is having an affair with Meriam. Murder solved, if you ask me. Not that they ask me."

But it all seemed a little too easy to me.

Chapter 11

The duchess decided she wanted to cook dinner for her family. She did that when she could to try to give her children a sense of normalcy. Therefore, I had the evening off.

I went to see Michael. He was out on bail but could not leave his home. The tube ride was crowded with the evening rush hour, but I didn't mind. I kind of liked the crush and the endless announcements of a train approaching and minding the gap as you got on and off.

Climbing the stairs out of the station, I felt a bit virtuous. "No need for a gym here," I said to no one in particular.

Huffing and puffing, I made my way through the turnstile and down the four blocks to Michael's house. I had gotten the address from the palace's intranet. This time I brought a basket full of chocolate chip cookies.

I knocked once and waited. The light in the parlor was on, and I could hear a television somewhere that either Michael or a neighbor was watching. It was hard to tell which because the homes were all connected.

Knocking again, louder this time, I heard someone get up. There was a half-moon transit window in the door and Michael's face popped into view. He opened the door.

"Come in quickly. We just got rid of the reporters, and you don't need your picture in the papers with me."

I entered the home and walked with Michael to the parlor. Inside it was cozy with bookcases filled with books, two wingback chairs, and a fireplace with a fire going. He was listening to music. The air smelled of freshly baked bread.

"Rosemary is upstairs napping, and I don't want to disturb her," Michael said. "I'm sure she'll be disappointed to have missed you."

"Oh, no, I don't want to disturb her rest. I'm sure she needs it. I'm only here to bring you some cookies," I said and handed him the basket.

He opened it and sniffed. "Classic American chocolate chip."

"I had to go to two markets to find everything to make them like we do at home. Only Tollhouse chips will do," I said. "And my secret ingredient."

He snagged a cookie and took a bite. "Cinnamon."

"Yes, that's it."

He stuffed a second cookie in his mouth and tilted his head toward the kitchen. "Come on, I'll make tea."

The kitchen itself was modern and spic and span. Everything was white or silver, even the kitchen curtains on the window over the sink.

You could tell Michael was a cook based on where he placed things in his kitchen. His knives were sharp and well displayed. Pans hung from a hanger over the stove. There were pots of herbs growing in his window.

"Do I smell bread?" I asked.

"Twisted egg," he said. "My sister's favorite." He opened the cupboard to get out a plate and cups. "Please, have a seat."

There was an oblong table with five wooden chairs around it. I sat in a chair that faced the living room. It was an odd home. The foyer was cozy with flowered wallpaper, the parlor thick with books and dark leather chairs, and the kitchen bright and white and simple.

"Have you lived here long?"

"My parents bought it in the fifties," he said. "Mum loved the wallpaper in the hall. Ever since she went into the nursing home three years ago, I can't bring myself to take it down."

"Does your father still live here?" I could imagine him looking rather like Michael, only thinner and stooped.

"No, he lives out in the country now with his new wife."

"His new wife?"

"Yes, he divorced and remarried less than a year after Mum got sick. They left the house to Rosemary and me and took off for Bath. He says he likes the quiet of the country."

"I see." The teapot whistled and he turned off the stove and poured hot water into the tea pot before placing a cozy around it. The way he made tea seemed rote, but I bet it brought him comfort. It was the small rituals that kept us going in hard times. "Are the books yours or his?"

"They started out as his," Michael said and brought over the plate of cookies and sat down. "But I've been adding to them my entire life." He sent me a small smile as he poured the tea. "I guess that means they are mostly mine."

"Real books are treasures, aren't they?"

"Yeah," he said. "I get lost in them."

I chewed on my bottom lip for a moment. "I heard about the arrest. Do you have a good lawyer?"

"Good enough, I suppose," he said and bit into a cookie. "He got me out of jail for now. I have to wear the bracelet, though. They know wherever I go." He stuck out his long leg and pointed to the plastic bracelet around his ankle. "In this neighborhood, it's a bit of a fashion statement, or so Rose tells me."

"Did you do it?" I had to ask.

He looked me straight in the eye. "No. I would never."

"See, I agree. It doesn't make any sense." I sighed. "You were his best friend."

"Frank and I were friends since grammar school. There wasn't much we wouldn't do for each other." He put his elbows on the table and buried his face in his hands. "They won't let me see Meriam and the boys. I don't know how she's coping."

I patted his arm. My heart filled with sadness at the tragedy. "I can go check on her if you want, in the evenings."

He looked up and I saw the redness rimming his eyes. "Would you do that?"

"It would be my pleasure." I patted his arm again. "Tell me about Meriam. Were you really having an affair with her? I mean, that is what they said was your motive."

"Meriam and I were not having an affair," he said in a tone that suggested his words were only truthful to a point. He looked at me. "We are in love. But we didn't do anything about it because of Frank. We both loved him and couldn't hurt him." He sipped his tea and I noticed a small tremor in his hand. "Besides, the boys needed their father."

I sat back. "That is sad. But it's still a motive because now that Frank is gone, Meriam is free to be with you."

Michael swallowed hard. "Except she hates me right now."

"Why?"

"Now she thinks I killed the father of her children. She won't have anything to do with me. She told me herself that she won't bring a murderer into her house." He put his head in his hands. "I've lost everything—my friend, my love, my godchildren, my job, my reputation. I wish I had died instead of Frank."

This time I took his hand and squeezed it. "Please don't say that."

"Why not? Everyone thinks I'm a killer. Who cares if I live or die? With me out of the way, life can go on for Meriam, for the kids, and even for you."

I let go of his hand and sat back, stunned.

"I heard you interviewed four people for my replacement today."

"I interviewed four people to try to replace Frank," I said. "Miss Jones said she would stay on until you got through this. Your job with me is still waiting for you. I want you to know that."

"I highly doubt I'll pass the security briefing after this incident. They can't have a person of interest, even an innocent one, working in the kitchen of the future king."

"But that's not right."

"Life has its ups and downs." He wrapped his hands around the white mug filled with warm tea. "If I'm lucky enough to be found innocent, then they will be kind and offer me a severance package and good reference. But either way, my life at the palace is over."

"It's just not fair," I said. "You did nothing wrong."

"You are the only one who believes that."

"I happen to know your sister Rosemary believes it as well. I spoke to her on the phone this morning. She was adamant that you couldn't have done this."

His mouth lifted in a half smile. "She's my sister. Family always takes care of its own."

"So there's no way I will get you back in my kitchen?"

"No."

I blew out a deep breath. "I guess that means I need to hire two new assistants."

"That would be for the best." He stood and picked up the tea mugs. "Also, you shouldn't come around to see me anymore. It looks bad for your reputation. You just got this job as the family's personal chef. I'm pretty sure you want to keep it."

"I do," I said as I stood up.

"Then do yourself a favor and stay away from me and this mess. Okay?"

"I just . . ."

"What?"

"Want to help."

His mouth tightened into a straight line. "You can't."

I bit my bottom lip and pulled my spring coat off the back of the kitchen chair where I hung it. "Can I ask you one more thing?"

"Sure."

"I saw you in the alley when I left Mr. Deems's wake. There were two pretty scary men with you. It looked like they were going to harm you."

He straightened in shock and surprise. "Was anyone else there with you?"

"No." I shook my head. "Only me. I heard them demand money from you. Can you tell me what that's about? Did you owe them money? Did they kill Frank as a warning?"

"Don't be ridiculous," he said and walked toward me. There was a sternness to his walk and I backed up out of the kitchen. "What you saw was nothing. Do you understand?" He practically pushed me toward the door. "You saw nothing. Promise me you'll never mention this again. Not to me or anyone."

"I can't promise that," I said as we stopped near the door. "You're my friend. If those men are threatening you or your sister . . ."

He grabbed my arm and gave it a little shake. "If anyone knew you saw that, you could be in a lot of danger. I'm not kidding, Chef. Those men can and will hurt you. Stay out of it."

"But if you need help . . ."

"Stay out of it. I'm serious. Go back to the kitchen and make happy meals for the happy little family. You barely know me. Trust me, it's not worth dying over."

"Are you threatening me?"

"No," he said and opened the door. "Look,

you're a nice lady. I appreciate all you did. Now go and don't come back." He gently but firmly pushed me out the door.

"But—" I turned around only to have the door shut and locked in my face. It seemed to me that Mr. Haregrove was in a lot more trouble than he would like to admit. I glanced up at the house. A curtain in the upstairs windows moved shut as if someone had been watching me.

Maybe Rosemary could help me. I made a mental note to call her in the morning. It had grown dark outside and a fog wisped down the streets. I shook off a chill and headed back to the relative safety of the tube and the recorded voice telling me to mind the gap.

Chapter 12

The four interviews had gone fairly well the day before. But now that I knew for certain I would have to replace Michael as well as Frank, I had to really look at the applicants with fresh eyes.

Their résumés were all equally good. Of the four applicants, two had two years of experience and the other two had five years of experience. One worked for one of the other royal families.

It was intimidating to think that I was going to hire people who most likely had more experience with royalty and with British dishes than I did. But that is precisely what I needed. I took a breath and made two phone calls.

"Hello?"

"Hi, is this Phoebe Montgomery?" I asked.

"Yes."

"This is Chef Cole. We met today for the interview."

"Yes, Chef, I remember," Phoebe said.

"I would like you to come in again and cook your best dish for me. Can you do that?"

"Yes, Chef." She sounded excited.

"Come in tomorrow afternoon. I'd like to see how you work in my kitchen."

"Is there a menu planned?"

"I'll take care of the menu," I said. "What I want is for you to create your best dish, whatever that is—appetizer, entrée, or dessert. I'm looking for locally sourced and fresh flavors."

"Got it."

"Good," I said. "I'll give your name to security. Go to the guard hut like you did today and sign in with a visitor badge. Have them call me and I'll send someone to get you. Shall we say two PM? It shouldn't take more than forty minutes."

"Sounds perfect," Phoebe said. "I'll be there."

I hung up and then dialed George Rabe. He also agreed that he could be there at two PM the next day to be part of the cooking challenge.

Phoebe had very little experience but had attended a good school. While George had more experience, he had gone to a less prestigious school. My hope was that they would complement each other and work well with me as a team.

With lunch complete, I went back to my room to freshen up. To be more exact, I went straight to my bed and laid down face first. The bed was freshly made and my room smelled of cleaning products. My chambermaid must have come in already for the day to make the bed and clean. I made my own bed out of habit and I didn't have much time to spend in my rooms, so it seemed like a luxury to have someone freshen the room daily.

There was a small, stackable washer and dryer

in the cupboard in my bathroom. I usually washed my own clothes, but today I found them freshly folded and put away. It was so strange to have someone else do the laundry—especially someone I had yet to meet. It was like having quiet little elves that come in and work while you sleep.

I had washed my own clothes from the time I was eight or nine when my mother showed me how to do it. After that I was on my own when it came to having clean clothes.

My mom was a hands-off parent. She was a modern-day hippie who lived by the motto "Teach a man to fish, and you feed him for a lifetime." It's why I learned to cook when I was five years old. My mother had meetings and protests and other important matters to worry about.

That's why it sat funny with me to have some-one else washing my delicates. Don't get me wrong, it was nice to have clean clothes. I needed them and had no idea when I would have the time to do them myself. It seemed that my entire life revolved around the kitchen these days.

Mrs. Worth had told me my job was to con-centrate on the cooking. I was to let the others do their own jobs. I wondered what the chamber-maid was like. I don't think she had been at the pub the other night with the others, and I made my mind up to ask Penny about her. I imagined her as a grandmotherly type.

My cell phone rang and I snagged it out of my

pocket. It was John. "Hello," I said and rolled over on my back. The ceiling was painted a soft, blue-toned white.

"Carrie Ann, baby, the celebration was fantastic. The reviews were phenomenal. Things are looking great for me."

"Hi, John," I said. "Congrats."

"You sound tired. What time is it there?"

I glanced at my watch. "It's two fifteen PM. What time is it there?"

"Nine fifteen AM," he replied. "Too early for you to sound so tired."

"I'm a little stressed."

"What's going on?"

"I found one of my staff members dead in the greenhouse that's attached to my kitchen."

"That's horrible, babe! Why didn't you call me?"

"It's been a whirlwind." Why hadn't I called him? We are on a break. Should I have called him anyway? I'd have to think about that later. "They arrested my second assistant, but I think he's innocent."

"You've only been there a few days. How could you possibly know someone well enough to know if they are guilty or innocent of murder?"

I frowned at the tone in his voice. He sounded so . . . reasonable. I didn't like it. It made me feel *un*reasonable. "Juries decide if a man is innocent or guilty all the time without even talking to him one-on-one."

"I can't fault you there," John said. "Listen, I didn't call to fight. I called because I wondered if you read the review. I e-mailed it to you. It was fantastic. He says—and I quote—'Chef John Sheridan is well on his way to superstardom. Matt's is the place to go to discover the next culinary superstar.' He called me a culinary superstar!"

Now I felt guilty. "Wow, John, that's fantastic. I'm sorry I didn't read it right away. I told you things are crazy here. Today I have to make three meals and interview and hire two new assistants."

"I know I said we should be on a break, but are you thinking of me?"

"I think about you," I said and a pang of homesickness filled me. "Do you miss me?"

"I do," he said. "You should be here to share in the celebrations. He said my Korean fusion was magic . . . magic! The restaurant is booked for the next six months. They've started the paperwork to evaluate me for a Michelin star."

"John, that's fantastic. It sounds like your dreams are all coming true." While John was super ambitious, I preferred to cook to help others live better lives. John's ambition was more important than me every time. It was like a mistress that I lived with. John loved me, but he loved his career more.

"No, not all my dreams," he said. "At least not yet."

"There's plenty of time," I said.

"Seriously, though," he said, "I need to tell you. I've gotten an offer from a venture capitalist. He wants to help me start my own restaurant in California. He has the perfect building in downtown San Francisco. Babe, my own restaurant! My own concept."

"You're moving to California?" Why did that bother me? After all, I was in London for the next year at the very least.

"It's the chance of a lifetime," he said. "What's the matter? Are you jealous?"

"Yes, that's it," I replied. "I want to leave the royal family to hang out in wine country with you."

He laughed. "That definitely didn't sound sincere."

"Hmm, London, San Fran . . . which would you pick given the choice?"

"I would pick the best thing for us, babe." His tone got suddenly serious. "You should come. You can be my sous chef."

"Please," I teased. "You will be so engrossed with your concept and menu that you won't even miss me. You know how time flies when you are concentrating on your work."

"That doesn't mean I don't miss you," he said.

"I know." I gave him the benefit of the doubt. When John focused on me, I felt like the queen of the world. If only he would focus on me more often. It was something I accepted because I was in love with the guy. But it was also something I wasn't sure I wanted for the rest of my life.

He broke the silence. "So two assistants, wow. You must be in heaven. I know you're used to working alone. Will you hire another American?"

"I know two assistants seems a bit much, but it's nice to have help. I'm looking at two Brits. It's good to have people who know the area, the culture, and the traditions. That way I don't have to worry too much about making blunders. I'd hate to be the classic stupid American."

"Honey, you worry too much about what people think of you. They wouldn't have hired you if you weren't perfect for them."

"I know," I said, "but I can't help my worries." It was an argument we had a lot. John's ambition and confidence were so high that he couldn't understand why I second guessed myself. He thought that life was best lived in the moment, and it seemed that no matter what he did, he came up smelling like a rose. I was the type of person who had goals and plans and worked to ensure that there were as few surprises as possible in my life. While John had luck, I had pluck.

They say opposites attract, and I think they're right. John's boyish good looks still made my heart beat faster. He could get lost in cooking and creating for days, but when he came out of a job, he was spontaneous and fun, while I hated anything that wasn't planned out in detail.

That's why it was so odd for us that this time, I had been spontaneous and left the country to do something only a handful of people get to do. Meanwhile, John's career was taking off because he stayed.

I did miss him. But I wasn't sure if it was just homesickness or if I actually missed *him*. Everything was so new and different in London. With this murder, I craved stability and something, anything, that seemed normal. "Can you come for a visit before you go out to California?"

"There's no way, sweetheart. The restaurant is fully booked. If I'm going to move to San Francisco, I need to train the new cooks. And I need to work on my concept and menus."

"You can't work on menus from London?"

"No, my investor is here. He wants to be involved every step of the way."

"Is this investor real?" I had to ask. "Did you do your research on him?"

"I did my research," he said, sounding insulted. "This guy started some of the biggest names in the Bay Area."

"Then congrats as long as it's legitimate," I barreled on, ignoring his tone.

"It's legitimate. What's wrong with you—are you not happy for me?"

"I'm happy for you."

"Good, because I didn't call to argue," he said.

"How're your parents? Have you heard anything from them?"

"My dad is in the Bahamas with his new wife," I said. "They seem to be having a grand time. He sent me a text and a picture of them on the beach."

"And your mom?"

"She's in Guatemala still teaching local women skills that allow them to make and sell things."

"Your folks always have something new and different going on," he said. "You know, you're a lot like them."

I gasped at the thought. "I am not," I said. Growing up, I was always the responsible one. Meanwhile my father was always off with a new woman on one tropical island or another, and my mother was a hippie who didn't believe in schedules or working for "the man." She would sing or dance for tips. When she wasn't doing that, she was making belts, leather goods, and chain mail for people to sell at Renaissance festivals.

I was an only child and more of an afterthought in my parents' lives. That's why I was so attracted to John. He had ambition and that felt safe.

"How is your family?" I asked.

"Abby's good," he said. "The twins are nearly out of diapers. She and Tim are thinking about having another."

"Wow, that's brave," I said. The last time I had visited John's sister's house, the twins were like wild animals, running around and screaming bloody murder.

John laughed. "Abby always loved a lot of energy and chaos."

"How're your mom and dad?" Unlike mine, John's parents were still together after forty years.

"Mom's got Dad helping her to create the garden of her dreams. They're turning the backyard into a royal garden complete with raised beds, curving walkways, and little nooks for seating. She wants us to come for a dinner party in July. She'll have the garden finished by then and wants to show it off. She even has a Chicago magazine interested in doing a shoot."

"Your mom has the most amazing green thumb," I said. "Who's doing the cooking?"

"She's hiring your friend Carol."

"I'm sure it'll be a lot of fun," I said. "Send her my thanks, but I won't be able to come. I don't get vacation until I've been here six months. Then I earn a full week. That's why I was hoping you'd come out here. But now you have the California thing." I paused. "Are we breaking up for good?"

"No," he said. "It's going to be okay. You'll see, we'll be fine. I know I said I wanted a break, but once we're back together in the United States, we'll be fine."

"I wish I could be as sure as you are," I said and stared at my perfect ceiling.

"That's why you have me, babe," he replied. "To be sure for the both of us."

A pang of guilt hit me. It felt as if the two of us drifting apart would be mostly my fault. I was the one who chose a job opportunity over my relationship. But then again, John hadn't made much effort to change my mind. He was the one to suggest a break in the first place. Now he wanted me to quit my dream job and go to California. Either he really was confident we would make it on his dreams alone or he, too, had doubts that I was the one he wanted for life. Meanwhile all I wanted was for my dreams to be as important to him as his were. Maybe that was an unrealistic dream.

Chapter 13

The next afternoon, both of my interviewees were in my kitchen wearing chef jackets and black aprons. Phoebe Montgomery was short and blonde with a round face and a curvy figure. Her green eyes shone with intelligence and determination. Standing at the island next to her, George Rabe looked to be nearly six feet tall with swarthy skin and dark-black hair.

"I thought it was best to face your competition," I said. "You have one hour to create your favorite British dish out of the available ingredients. I will be watching the way you cook and taking notes. You will be judged based on how you work around each other, the way you prep, the way you plate, and how you clean up. These are all tasks that will have to be done in the kitchen if you get this job. Your time starts now."

They both chose to create a main dish. George made smoked haddock kedgeree with shredded leeks, creamed spinach, and quail eggs. Phoebe made a potato and sage torte with lamb and apricot ragout.

I was impressed by the choices. Both were more winter than spring dishes, but in early May we were still at a time when the weather could be cool enough for a savory winter dish.

I watched as they chopped and simmered and braised. The pair worked well together in the close quarters of the family kitchen. I could see where their skills were in need of coaching and made a comment or two.

"If you put the browned lamb in a fine colander, it will drain off the excess fat," I pointed out to Phoebe as she struggled to drain the fat from the lamb for her ragout.

"Thank you, Chef," she replied and reached for the fine sieve.

I watched George carefully. "If you wash the greens in one part vinegar to two parts water, it will ensure that all bacteria are safely cleaned off. This is important for spinach in particular, as the nooks and crannies in the leaves can harbor salmonella."

"Thank you, Chef." He pulled out a bowl and mixed vinegar in water and washed the greens in the mixture before draining and drying and then chopping them.

The hour flew by. At the end, I called time. They put their plated dishes in front of me.

"The presentation on both plates is good," I said. "Mr. Rabe, your plate could use some touching up—see how the quail egg is leaning?"

"Yes, Chef."

"Miss Montgomery, no matter how quickly we must work, we must always ensure the moisture is wiped from the outer edges of the plate." I pointed to the dampness that sat on the flat white edge of the plate.

"Yes, Chef."

I studied them both. The kitchen behind them was spotless and the dishwashers hummed. They had done everything I asked: prepped, cooked, plated, and cleaned up. All in an hour. George had sweat pooling on the edges of his hat. Phoebe had a cotton wrap on her head that was also damp from her exertion.

"I'm pleased with the way you left the kitchen," I said.

"Thank you, Chef," they both replied.

I picked up a fork and scooped up the potato torte and lamb ragout. It was flavorful with a good chew. The lamb was tender and mild in flavor.

I took a drink of water to cleanse my palate and then took a bite of the kedgeree. I understood why George chose it as his signature dish. The saffron accented the haddock perfectly. It was a tasty dish indeed.

I put down my fork and took another sip of water. "Please relax," I said and pointed toward the empty chairs at the table. "Grab a fork and taste how good these dishes are."

They glanced at each other, and then Phoebe grabbed two forks from the silverware drawer and two small plates from the open shelf. George pulled two glasses from the cupboard and brought over a pitcher of fresh ice water. They both sat down, and I put the dishes in the center of the table. We each had a small plate and split the meal.

"This is very good," I said.

"Thank you, Chef," they both said at once and grinned.

"I would like to hire you both in my kitchen," I said. "Phoebe, I understand that you are talented at breads and pastries."

"Yes, ma'am." She scooped up a forkful of the lamb ragout.

"Why did you choose an entrée to make for me today?"

"I know Mr. Rabe is excellent at handling fish and meats," she replied. "I wanted to prove that I could do the same."

"I see." I turned to George. "Meanwhile, you chose an entrée that I understand is your specialty."

"You asked us to choose our best dish," he said with a shrug. "This is mine."

"The fish is excellent," I said. "There is nothing worse than poorly cooked fish. Good job."

"Thank you, Chef," he said with a nod.

"I am going to recommend that they hire you both for my kitchen. Miss Montgomery, I need a pastry expert who can concentrate on rolls and dough. Mr. Rabe, I want someone who can step up on the entrée portion and ensure that the proteins are always well-cooked and the dishes are plated to the highest order. We are cooking for the future kings of England. Everything must be of the highest quality."

"Yes, Chef," he said.

"People will be watching you both very closely," I added. "It will not be due to anything you do, but it is due to the fact that I am an American and I recently discovered one of my last assistants dead in a pool of his own blood. Do either of you have a problem with that?"

"No, Chef," they both said. But I swear I saw hesitation in Miss Montgomery's gaze.

"Are you available to begin tomorrow?"

They both nodded.

"Perfect, I'll take you to the human resources department where you can finish filling out paperwork. I expect you here tomorrow morning at six AM."

I walked them out, wondering what had caused Phoebe's hesitation. Was it because I was an American or because she would be working a few feet from a crime scene?

After I left my new employees to their orientation, I stopped by Ian's office. "Hello?"

He sat at his desk working on his computer. Turning to look at me, he replied, "Chef Cole, what brings you to my door?"

"I was wondering about Mr. Haregrove," I said. "Do you know how he's doing?"

"Come in and have a seat." Ian waved me inside.

I took a seat across from the big wooden desk where he worked. His office was orderly, and I imagined that discipline might have come from his military background. Penny had told me Ian had served in the Iraq War. "Mrs. Worth had me hire two new assistants. But I like Mr. Haregrove. I can't imagine what he and his family are going through right now."

"He has a preliminary hearing tomorrow," Ian said. He folded his hands on his desk. "After that, he and his defense team will work to set up his trial date."

"So it will be a while before he can work for me again."

Ian lowered his head and looked at me. "Mr. Haregrove will never work in the palace again. There are too many important people who live here and depend on me for their safety."

"But what if he's innocent?" I said and leaned toward Ian. "Are you saying that an innocent man can't get his job back because he was once suspected of a crime he didn't commit?"

"What makes you so sure he didn't commit the crime?"

I sat back and tried not to sigh. "Instinct," I finally said. "I've only known Mr. Haregrove a few days, but I've seen nothing sinister in his behavior at all. In fact, all he's done is his best work with me and then taken care of his dead friend's family."

"You mean his mistress and her children," Ian said.

"Is that the only motive?" I asked. "We both know people have affairs every day and don't kill each other."

"Why are you defending him?"

I swallowed. "I don't know. A hunch maybe," I admitted. It sounded lame even to my own ears, but I just knew he was innocent.

"What aren't you telling me?" Ian's piercing gaze brought a flush to my cheeks.

"The night of the wake, before you walked me home, I saw Mr. Haregrove speaking to two very threatening men in the alley behind the pub. He seemed scared. Hardly the behavior of a killer."

"Maybe he had a reason to be scared."

"What do you mean?"

"Maybe they were the killers and they are after Mr. Haregrove."

"What?"

Ian chuckled. "You have the most amazing imagination. If they wanted Haregrove killed, they would have done it before he was being watched twenty-four-seven by police."

I frowned. "I suppose you're right. Unless the killers are connected to the police, they can't get to him, can they?" I realized I was wringing my hands. "What if they have connections in the prison? What if Mr. Haregrove dies an innocent man?"

This time Ian's laugh was deep. "Chef Cole," he said, "you should have been a writer."

I felt a bit foolish. "If I can prove Mr. Haregrove is innocent, would I be able to hire him back?" I moved to the edge of my seat. "Would you condemn an innocent man?"

It was Ian's turn to frown. "Fine. If Haregrove is found innocent—and that means he had absolutely nothing to do with Mr. Deems's death—then I would consider letting you rehire him."

"Thank you." I stood and smiled.

"But, Chef Cole, he must be innocent of everything. If he's hiding anything, I will see that he doesn't ever step foot in the palace again."

"I understand."

I left Ian's office buoyed with hope. If I could prove Mr. Haregrove's innocence, I could have him back. He could continue to support Mr. Deems's family. And I would get to have one of the best meat men in England working for me. It seemed like a win-win situation.

Chapter 14

Dinner for the family was a light affair of chicken soup, fresh spring salad, cheesy bread bites, and roast beef with mushy peas and roasted potatoes. Dessert was tiny meringue cups with chocolate chips and fresh mint.

I was in the kitchen cleaning up when Penny stopped by to see me.

"There you are," Penny said and flopped down in one of the chairs tucked next to the small table. "I haven't seen you in ages."

"It's only been two days since the wake," I pointed out and hit the start button on the stainless steel dishwasher. "Tea?"

"Yes, please," she said. "Do you have any chocolate biscuits?"

"I do." I put the tea kettle on to boil and rummaged through the cupboards, pulling out teacups, spoons, a pair of small plates, and the black-and-white cookies I had baked today. It was late, close to ten PM. I'd spent some time trying a new cookie recipe. The black-and-white cookies looked good arranged on a white plate.

"I heard about Michael," Penny said and shook her head. "He doesn't seem the killer type if you ask me. But that's typical. I mean, you're always hearing stories about people living next door to killers. They say things like, 'He seemed so quiet and nice.'"

"Michael didn't do it," I said with certainty as I placed everything on the small table. "I'm a good judge of people, and he really isn't the killer type."

"But he's on house arrest as we speak."

"I think he's protecting someone." I put the creamer and sugar bowl on the table.

"That's an interesting idea," Penny said. "Who do you think he's protecting?"

"I don't know, but I plan on finding out."

"Really? Why?"

"Why what?" I asked, startled by the question.

"Why on earth would you bother investigating a murder?"

The tea kettle whistled, cutting through my thoughts. I pulled it from the burner and went through the motions of making tea. "Did you know that Ian won't let Michael come back to work here? The only way is if he is proven innocent, which I fully intend to ensure happens."

"That does make sense," Penny said. "They have to be extremely picky about who works around the family. They can't have an accused killer in the palace."

I brought the pot of tea to the table and sat down. "What if I can't prove he's innocent?" I asked. "It hardly seems fair. Poor Michael lost his best friend and his career all in one fell swoop—pardon my pun."

"That's a risk he took when he decided to protect whoever he's protecting," Penny said as she poured the tea.

"There's no justice in it." I frowned. "Who will hire him if he has no references for the last five years? He might as well have died with Frank."

"I hadn't quite thought it through that way," Penny said and snagged two of the black-and-white cookies. "It does seem unfair."

"I got Ian to agree to consider rehiring Michael if I could prove his innocence before he went to trial."

"Well, that's awfully kind of you," Penny said. "When are you going to have time to do that? Don't you have a family to feed?"

"I hired two new assistants," I said. "They start tomorrow."

"That's something good," Penny said. "Who are they? Are they cute?"

"You are always thinking of your love life," I teased her and then sipped my tea. It was a floral herbal tea due to the late hour. I needed to get some sleep if I was going to be back in the kitchen before my new crew came in at six AM.

"Well, at least I have a love life." She eyed me. "How's that boyfriend of yours? Are you two still on a break or have you convinced him to come for a visit so that I can meet him?"

"He's getting great reviews, and now I guess

some venture capitalist wants to back him in his own restaurant."

"He's talking to you?"

"Yes."

"That's great news."

"But there's no time for a quick visit."

"Sad." Penny shook her head. "I know you hoped he would miss you enough to get on a plane."

"I'm sure we will be fine," I said, although I wasn't sure if I was trying to convince her or myself. "For two people on a break, we talk almost every day, so it's really more like a long-distance relationship. Besides, we can video chat, too."

"Video is not the same as skin-to-skin contact," Penny said. "I don't know what I'd do if I didn't have regular hugs and kisses."

"It really is temporary," I replied. "John will fly out as soon as he can get away."

She put her elbows on the table and rested her chin in her hands. "I think you really want to date other people."

"What? No."

"Yes." She wagged her finger at me. "No one certain of a relationship moves to a different country for a year. Since he wants to be on a break, you should look around. We do have some prime specimens in England."

"John hasn't mentioned wanting to see other people," I said. "I'm busy with this job and now with helping Michael. I don't have time to worry about dating." It's one of the things I did like about having John as my boyfriend; I didn't have to worry about dating and all the complications that came with it. As for physical contact, well, as soon as I hit my six months of employment, I could take a vacation and fly out to see John.

"So back to my earlier question," Penny said. "Did you hire anyone cute?"

"I hired a woman named Phoebe Montgomery. She's cute, I suppose."

"Oh." Penny slumped her shoulders. "I was hoping for the male variety."

"I also hired George Rabe," I said with a sly smile. "I knew what you meant. He seems like a nice guy."

"You are mean," she teased me back. "When can I meet this Rabe person?"

"He starts work in the morning." I got up and put my cup in the sink. "I'm terrible at match-making, so please don't expect much from me when it comes to meeting cute guys."

"That's right." She stood and snagged the last cookie off the plate. "You're practically a nun, long-distance dating a rising star of a chef who only notices you when he needs someone to stroke his ego."

"John isn't that bad."

"He let you move to London without a single protest, didn't he?"

"Yes," I said and cleared the rest of the table.

"But that's because he respects my wish to advance my career."

"I call rubbish on that," Penny said. "Any guy who's in love won't like it when his girl goes away for a weekend, let alone a whole year."

"Maybe in England," I retorted. "In America, a guy who loves his girl gives her the freedom to do what makes her happy."

"Still rubbish," she said as we stepped out of the kitchen. "Haven't you ever been madly, passionately in love with someone? You know, the kind of love where you hurt every minute you are apart from them?"

"You mean have I ever stalked anyone? The answer is no."

She bumped me with her hip. "You are such a kidder. I still say you haven't loved until you've been in a crushing relationship where you can't keep your hands off each other."

"I certainly hope I never have one of those," I said. "I like to keep my sanity. My parents are enough crazy for one person's lifetime. I don't need to join them."

"You are hopeless," she said as we stopped near her door. "But I still like you." She gave me a hug. "Thanks for the cookies, and don't be surprised if I happen to drop by the kitchen while your new assistant is working. I want to judge for myself on the cuteness factor."

"I told you that Phoebe is cute . . ."

"Good night, Carrie Ann," Penny said and waved me along.

"Good night." I went back to my room and tried not to think about what it meant that John and I could manage a long-distance relationship for more than a year. I knew it would be hard work, but I was beginning to have my doubts about it being a relationship at all.

Chapter 15

The next morning, breakfast and lunch work went smoothly. I was surprised how much having two extra pairs of hands helped move things along. Dinner was slow-roasted lamb and was already in the ovens. Phoebe had whole-grain bread rising in the proofing oven while George went to the market for fresh vegetables.

I was making cookies for tea when there was a sudden racket from the greenhouse area. Both Phoebe and I were startled. I rushed to the door to look into the greenhouse. Workmen had taken the roof and one wall out. The noise was coming from a small forklift smashing through the remaining greenhouse walls.

"What is going on?" I asked after yanking the door open.

"Stand back!" demanded a tall man with broad shoulders, a narrow waist, and a square jaw. He was tan, which made his blue eyes look almost electric blue. He had thick blond hair pulled back into a low ponytail underneath a white hard hat that looked as if it was used regularly.

I took an instinctive step back so that I stood in the doorway between my kitchen and the green-house. "I asked what you were doing," I said, facing him and putting my hands on my hips. "We're trying to get some work done in the

182

kitchen, and it sounds as if you are bringing the entire building down on top of us." I waved toward the forklift and the knocked-over beds. "And you are."

"This is my greenhouse," he stated as he stepped toward me, trying to intimidate me with his height and manly chest. He wore a black T-shirt stretched over that chest and sizeable biceps. "You need to stay out until I say you can come in."

I stood my ground and raised my chin, glaring back at him. "You need to give us warning before you start to bulldoze your way into my kitchen. If I had a cake or soufflé in the oven, it could have flopped."

"Did you?"

"Did I what?"

"Have a cake or soufflé in the oven?"

"No, but that is not the point . . ."

"Then no harm, no foul. Now this is a hard hat area and you aren't wearing one, so I suggest you go back into your kitchen and let me get on with my work."

"Who are you?" I asked and mirrored his crossed arms with my own, even though I had a fairly good idea to whom I was talking.

"I'm Jasper Fedman, head greenhouse gardener. Look, lady, I'm trying to do my job. You need to let me do it and go on about your business."

"I'm Chef Cole," I said and did my best imitation of Chef Butterbottom. "I need to know in advance of anything, I mean anything, that you intend to do that will cause dirt, destruction, dust, mold, insects, or oven movement in my kitchen." I ticked each item off on my fingers. "I cannot feed the family food that is ravaged by construction. Is that clear?"

"Very," he said, his mouth thinning into a tight smile. "I intend to do renovations on this area for the next two weeks. That means we will be removing all the beds, steaming the remaining floors and walls, and building new ones. So I suggest you take any cakes or soufflés off the menu until my work is complete."

"Fine."

"Good."

"On one condition."

"No."

"I'm not leaving until you hear me out."

"I'd be happy to pick you up and toss you out."

Now, I thought of myself as a sizeable woman, but he looked as if he could easily make good on his threat. I raised my chin. "I want to have some say in what gets planted in the new beds," I said. "It only makes sense, since the greenhouse is the family's biggest resource for fresh vege-tables."

"The duchess has already given me a list of what she wants grown," he said and took a step closer to me. We were about an inch apart, and I was fully aware of the heat radiating off his body.

He smelled good, like spicy cologne, warm male, and garden soil.

"I want some say as well," I demanded stubbornly.

"Get inside your kitchen, Chef," he said and pushed the door open behind me. "Leave me to my work and I'll leave you to yours."

"I want—"

"Don't care," he said and took my right elbow in his hand and nudged me to the other side of the open door. Then he closed it.

I glared at him through the door. He simply nodded and went back to work. So I threw the bolt on the door, locking him out. It was a small gesture of defiance and not worth the effort really. That entire wall between the kitchen and the greenhouse was glass. There wasn't a whole lot of soundproofing or privacy.

"Wow, that's the head greenhouse gardener?" Phoebe asked. She stared at him like a hungry person looked at a cinnamon bun through a bakery window.

"Apparently," I said, still miffed by the way he treated me. What was it with everyone around the palace? They all acted as if they were the king or queen of their own space. Why was it when I tried to throw my weight around, I got picked up and pushed back in my place?

I'd have to go see Mrs. Worth and protest that I should have a say as to what went into the garden.

It probably would be smart to see what the duchess had already requested first. With my luck, I'd go see Mrs. Worth all upset only to find out that the duchess's list matched my own.

"Check the lamb," I said to Phoebe. "I'll finish the cookies."

"You're going to just keep working while that is out there? You're stronger than I am," Phoebe said. She fanned herself with her hand. The whole time, she didn't take her eyes off the eye candy that continued to create earth-shattering noise outside.

"What's going on?" George asked as he came in with a cloth bag filled with fresh root veggies to roast with the lamb and kale, spinach, and chard that we would wilt and serve as a side dish.

"Mr. Hotness is tearing down the greenhouse with his little forklift," Phoebe said.

"We're stuck with the noise for two weeks," I grumbled. "So we can't plan to cook anything that is fragile in the oven."

George put the bag on the counter. "So spinach soufflé?"

"No," I said and frowned. The noise grew even louder. I turned to see Jasper deliberately smash through three beds, pushing them through to the outside edge of the parking area. I gritted my teeth. "No soufflé until he is done making as much noise and dust as possible."

"There is some dust coming through," George pointed out.

"Go get some plastic. We've got to trap some air between us and the windows to collect the dust or we'll be spending all our time cleaning, not cooking."

"I'll get some from the hardware store," George replied.

"I'll need to requisition it first," I said. "Phoebe, finish the cookies. George, start the veggies and keep an eye on the lamb. I'm going to see Mrs. Worth."

"Good luck, Chef," Phoebe said.

I pulled out my phone and made a short video of the noise and destruction along with the dust gathering on the windows. "I won't need luck when she sees this."

I made the trip to Mrs. Worth's offices quickly, fueled by my indignation. I flung the door open and came face-to-face with her secretary. "Chef Cole," Mrs. Perkins greeted me. "What brings you into our offices today? Do you have an appointment?"

"No," I said. "I have an immediate issue that needs her attention."

"She's in a meeting right now," Mrs. Perkins stated. "I can make an appointment for next week."

"I need her now," I said. "I have an issue in my kitchen that will affect the family's meals."

Mrs. Perkins studied me for a moment. "I'll see if she can squeeze you in between appointments."

I paced in front of her desk as she dialed a number and spoke softly into the phone. I thought I heard her say something derogatory about me, but I couldn't be sure. I glared at her, but she refused to make eye contact. Finally, she said, "Yes, ma'am, I'll do that." She hung up.

"Well?" I stopped in front of her desk.

"She can see you for five minutes. I certainly hope your issue is important or I may lose my job. Do you understand?"

"Yes, ma'am," I said. "I fully understand."

She rose. "Follow me. She said I could let you wait in her office."

"Thank you."

"Don't thank me yet," she said. "If Mrs. Worth deems your 'need,' " she said, using air quotes, "as frivolous, you will lose your job, too."

"Thank you for the concern," I said as I entered the quiet office. "I'm certain she'll be happy you squeezed me in."

Mrs. Perkins flattened her mouth. "I hope you are right." She closed the door behind me.

Mrs. Worth's office was cool and modern. Her desk was sleek Scandinavian; I would say mid-century modern. Two modern chairs made of light wood with metal legs stood in front of the desk.

On the desk was a framed picture of two adults hugging each other. They looked like Mrs. Worth, likely her adult children. It was odd for me to imagine prim, proper, and in-charge Mrs.

Worth having children. Grown children to boot. I wondered if she had grandkids as well. I wondered what her children thought about her running the royal family's household.

I noticed a bookshelf on the far wall and went over to view the titles. They were all leather-bound classics. It made sense, I supposed. Mrs. Worth must have been well read to get and keep a job as important as hers.

The door opened. "Chef Cole," Mrs. Worth said as she stepped inside. Her tone was brisk. "You have two minutes."

"I need to requisition heavy duty construction plastic to seal off the kitchen windows from the greenhouse while it is under construction."

"Why? You have windows. Keep them closed."

"Because the dirt is coming in through the windows." I opened up my phone and showed her the video. "I refuse to feed the family food that is prepared under such circumstances."

"I see," she said and took my phone to play the video again. "This won't do. It won't do at all."

I felt my heart lift for the first time. "So I'll get my plastic?"

"No," she said and handed me my phone back.

"But the food . . ."

She raised her hand to hush me and grabbed her own phone, dialing quickly. "Chef Butterbottom," she said. "You must make room for Chef Cole and her assistants for the next two weeks."

I could hear the protests on the other side of the phone. Mrs. Worth's expression and tone did not waver. "The greenhouse repairs are making the family kitchen impossible to work in. I suggest you clear out a corner of your kitchen. Chef Cole and her crew will be cooking there starting with dinner this evening." She paused while he said something. I couldn't hear the words, but I could hear his tone. "It is your kitchen, Chef," she said, and my heart sank. I didn't want to work under Chef Butterbottom for two full weeks. The man did not like me. Not one bit. The only reason I could figure is because I was American. Or maybe he thought the family should be served by the main kitchen. Was I some kind of threat to him? I couldn't see how, though chefs are notoriously insecure. I knew, not only because I was one, but because John was too.

"But the corner you give her will be *her* kitchen," Mrs. Worth continued. "If I need to put down tape to section off the space, I will, but I hope that you will have a more mature attitude regarding this matter." She glanced at me. "Chef Cole will give you your space. I suggest you give her hers. This is about the family's health and well-being, not your little fiefdom. Am I clear?" she asked, looking at me.

"Yes, ma'am," I said and heard muttered agreement on the other side of the phone.

"Good. Problem solved." She hung up the

phone and eyed me. "I will have Mr. Fedman inform me when the greenhouse is ready. Then we will move you back to your kitchen. In the meantime, I expect you to work well within Chef Butterbottom's parameters. I don't want to see you back in my office for any other emergencies. Is that clear?"

"Yes, ma'am," I said. "Thank you, ma'am." I turned and left, closing the door behind me. Mrs. Perkins stood when I came out. "She understood the emergency," I said. "So you can breathe now. Thank you for trusting me."

"Good day, Chef Cole," Mrs. Perkins said with a nod. "And please don't make a habit out of this."

"Trust me, it's not my intention to," I said and left the offices.

Having to move my dinner and all my things from my cozy kitchen to the stainless steel, industrial city that was the big kitchen was not something I looked forward to. Chef Butterbottom made no qualms out of the fact that he didn't like me. That was fine. I would just keep my head down and do my job.

I just hoped the corner he gave me would be enough room to get what I needed to do done.

I ran into Ian Gordon on the way back to my kitchen.

"Where are you going in such a hurry?" he asked.

"I need to move my kitchen up to Chef Butterbottom's," I said and tried not to sound exasperated. "Mr. Jasper Fedman is making a mess of the greenhouse, and it's affecting my cooking space. So Mrs. Worth has assigned me a corner of the big kitchen."

"I see," Ian said and held the elevator door open for me. "Well, good luck with that situation. How long will you be upstairs?"

"Mr. Fedman said two weeks."

Ian grinned. "It's going to be an interesting two weeks," he said. "I won't be surprised if you or Butterbottom end up on the wrong side of Mrs. Worth. I'd be very careful if I were you."

"I know how much Chef Butterbottom resents me," I said. "If ever there was a make-it-work moment, this is it."

"And you think you will still have time to prove Mr. Haregrove's innocence?"

"Well, let's say I'm going to try," I said, sticking my chin up in the air yet again. "Who needs to sleep, anyway?"

Ian chuckled. "Best of luck to you."

"Thanks," I said and hit the button to the floor I wanted. I watched as the door closed between us and then rested my forehead on the cool steel of the elevator door. My life had just gone from bad to worse.

Was it possible to get into any more trouble? I certainly hoped not.

Chapter 16

We need to pull the lamb out of the oven and move everything up to the big kitchen now," I said as I entered my own kitchen. One of my staff had taken towels and hung them in front of the greenhouse windows to attempt to prevent the thick layer of dust from entering the kitchen further.

"Wait, what? I thought you were going to get plastic," Phoebe said. She had been peering behind the towel-curtain when I came in.

"We're being moved upstairs instead," I said. "Grab a cart each. George, you take the vegetables and everything you need to make them for the evening meal. Phoebe, take the bread and the lamb and prep it for moving. The main kitchen is an elevator ride away."

"Yes, Chef," they both replied.

I filled my cart with the dishes I needed along with my menus, notes, and computer tablet that I used to communicate with the rest of the staff regarding the meals for the week.

George and Phoebe hurried out and up the elevator. I took one last look around, grabbed my extra chef coats, and scowled at the noise and dust behind the wall. Because of Jasper Fedman, I was going to have to spend the next two weeks in Chef Butterbottom's horrible kitchen.

I hurried out, pushing my cart and barely making the elevator in time. We pushed down the hall and stopped in front of the doors to the big, bright, spotless, stainless steel kitchen.

"Stay here a moment," I said and left them in the hallway. I wasn't about to assume which corner he would give us, and I needed to get that lamb back in an oven with as little fuss as possible. I pushed the door open to see the kitchen staff bustling. It seemed there was to be an event at the palace that night.

The kitchen was up to full steam. There must have been ten staff members chopping and cooking away. The scents of fresh herbs, spices, and sweet cakes filled the air. I made a beeline for the back office. I gave one knock and a slight pause before I entered the lion's den.

"Which corner do you want us in?" I blurted out. "I have lamb roasting, and it needs to go back into the oven as soon as possible."

"There is a test kitchen on the other side of this office," Chef Butterbottom said without looking up from his paperwork. "It is yours for the duration."

"Okay," I said. "How do we get to it?"

He looked up. "Through my office." He pointed at a door on the far side of his office.

"You want us coming and going through your office every day for two weeks?"

"I want you out of my kitchen," he grumbled. "Since that is not possible, you are to use the test kitchen. It has everything you'll need."

"Fine," I said. "Your hospitality knows no bounds." I walked to the door and opened it. The door squeaked on its hinges. I hoped the sound grated on his nerves because he was going to be hearing it a lot. I opened the door to find what must have been a large walk-in closet at one time. It was small, with a double oven, a single stovetop with four burners, a sink, a small refrigerator, a work table, and fluorescent lights. Not a window in sight.

"This will do," I said and turned on the bottom oven to preheat for the lamb. I wasn't about to show him any sort of emotion. Let him think what he would. I walked through his office and out into the busy kitchen with large strides and grabbed my crew and carts in the hallway. "Follow me," I said.

Taking my cart in hand, I pushed it through the kitchen. "Coming through," I announced as we dodged chefs. The noise died down as we paraded through the large, open, airy kitchen and into Chef Butterbottom's office without knocking. My staff members were quiet as I pushed the cart past the big chef sitting at his desk and into the tiny closet space.

The door closed behind us and we barely had room to maneuver with the carts taking up what floor space was left.

"This is it?" George asked.

"This is it," I said. "Phoebe, put the lamb in the bottom oven. I've already set it to preheat. The top oven will be ready for the bread. George, use the worktable for the vegetables. We're going to have to stack the carts if we hope to have any room to maneuver. So let's get them emptied now."

"This is ridiculous," Phoebe muttered. "Why couldn't they simply requisition us plastic?"

"You just miss the view," George joked as he helped her move the pan of lamb into the bottom oven. We all had to do a small bit of adjusting so that she could open the oven door and slide the pan inside.

"There's not even a dishwasher in here," Phoebe said.

"We'll do them the old fashioned way," I said. "I'm sure there are rubber gloves around."

"I didn't sign up for this," George said as he stacked the emptied carts and turned to see we only had ten inches to maneuver around from one work space to the other.

"It's only for a couple of weeks until they finish construction on the greenhouse," I said and did my best to corral the things needed for tea, which was to be served in thirty minutes. "Thank goodness we finished the cookies."

"Can we at least keep the serving carts somewhere else when we're not using them?" George asked.

"I'll take care of it," I said. "In the meantime,

George, start the vegetables roasting, and Phoebe, set up the tray for tea." The children participated in tea time to practice the tradition. Their tea was usually more milk than tea and the duchess only allowed them a pinch of sugar.

The cookies today were whole wheat, coconut, peanut butter, and chocolate drops. Along with the cookies, we served vegetable and tiny cucumber finger sandwiches. The goal was to provide a healthy snack and keep tradition alive.

When Phoebe left with one of the carts, I took the other two, still stacked, out through the office, looking for a place to stow them. Luckily Chef Butterbottom was not in his office when I pushed through. I might have run a cart into a thing or two, but I was sure it wouldn't bother him.

That's what I told myself, anyway.

I pushed the stacked carts out into the open, airy kitchen. The kitchen was still very busy, but less so since the tea service had gone out. The sun came through the wall of windows, and I tried not to be envious. I looked around for a closet or area where Chef Butterbottom kept his carts. I didn't see any place.

"Excuse me," I asked a man doing dishes. "Where do you put your serving carts?"

"There's storage out in the hallway. Two doors across the hall." He pointed to the door and then to the left.

"Thanks." I pushed the carts through the kitchen

doors and into the hall. There were two doors marked "Storage." I opened one to find a huge pantry with anything a cook could want in order to feed hundreds of people at a time. There was one cart in between the racks and shelves of foodstuffs. I sighed. I couldn't use this closet.

Onward, I thought, and pushed the carts out of that closet and back into the hall. The serving carts were stainless steel and heavier than they looked. This time I parked them out in the hall and pulled open the second door. The room was surprisingly deep and there were shelves of pots and pans and cooking utensils. One wall was all serving carts. I went back out and pushed our carts from the hall into the room. I didn't want to keep ours with the others or I might not get them back, so I found a small space in the opposite corner to leave them behind a large shelving unit filled with tablecloths and linens. I got some tape and a permanent marker and labeled them as "Family" carts.

I smiled when I was done. That solved that little problem. Suddenly the door to the storage unit opened and I heard someone walk in. I froze at the sound of his voice. I recognized it immediately. It was one of the thugs in the alley who had threatened Michael.

"I swear he will do anything to avoid paying the debt," the man said. "Even go to prison for the rest of his life."

"We both know he didn't do it. Haregrove doesn't have the guts," said a second man whose voice I didn't recognize. Two voices surprised me. I thought I only heard one person enter the room.

"That's what I'm saying. He's hiding behind this murder thing to keep from paying us. Well, it won't work. Anton's got people in prison. They'll beat it out of him just as quickly as you and I would."

My nose had a sudden tickly sensation and fear spiked down my spine. I put my finger under my nostrils to try to keep as quiet as possible.

"Dead or not, Deems owed Anton too much money. If we can't beat it out of Haregrove, we're going to have to go after the family."

"Now you know I don't go for that kind of thing," the man whose voice I recognized said. I peered around the shelf to see his large back. He held up his cell phone in his hand, and I could tell he was using the speaker option. It was why I heard two voices but only saw one man. He wore a white T-shirt and black slacks. I could see apron strings around his thick waist. The man clearly worked in the palace kitchen.

"I'm not the one pushing this," the second man said. I couldn't see him so I had no idea who he might be. "It's Anton. Deems knew this when he got involved."

"But he didn't kill himself," the big guy said. "So how can we take it out on his family?"

"Look, I heard they got a nice insurance

settlement. That's just about what Anton needs to cover the debt. If we can't shake down Haregrove, then we shake down the wife. Either way, he's going to get his money."

I took a step back when my nose tickle flared up again. I held my nostrils closed and looked up. I heard somewhere if you look up you can prevent a sneeze. My heart raced as the tickle continued. I held my breath so as not to give in and then—*achoo!*

Crap.

I froze, but couldn't stop the next sneeze. *Achoo, achoo, achoo!*

Great, I thought as the world tilted under my sneezing fit. *I'm going to die from sneezing.*

I grabbed a clean tissue out of my pocket and wiped my nose. My eyes watered, and I awaited my fate at the hands of the enforcer. But nothing happened. I held my breath and listened. No one was talking, but he wasn't walking this way, either. I peered around the corner. He was gone.

Swallowing hard, I chewed on my bottom lip and tiptoed toward the door. He hadn't come running toward me. Was he lying in wait to see who I was? The door didn't have a window so I couldn't tell. I considered hiding in the room for the next hour, but I knew I had to get back to the test kitchen to make dinner. Clearly no one would harm me in such a public place. Would they?

Then I remembered that Mr. Deems had been murdered on the premises, which meant that, public or not, if someone wanted me dead, I would be dead.

Not a happy thought.

I blew out a long breath and lifted my chin. *Well, here goes nothing.* I pushed the door open and walked quickly and confidently to the kitchen door across the hall. The man wasn't there. No one noticed that I left the room.

What did that mean? Did my sneezing spook him? Or was I lucky enough that he left before I started?

I crumpled the tissue into my pocket and hurried straight to the safety of my new kitchen to wash my hands. It occurred to me that there were cameras in the hallways. I wondered if the man could check the cameras and discover me walking out of the closet. Was I still in danger?

My next thought was that the man worked inside Chef Butterbottom's kitchen. Hadn't Frank worked in Chef Butterbottom's kitchen before he came to work for me? Did Chef Butterbottom have anything to do with Frank's death? Was there somehow a connection? Who was Anton? What kind of money had gone missing?

If Mr. Deems was killed by the man from the kitchen, or even Chef Butterbottom, then Ian needed to know. The family needed to be safe. *I* needed to be safe.

Chapter 17

It was after the dinner cleanup, close to eleven PM, when I finally stopped by Ian's office. I wasn't surprised to find him still at work. This time he was at his desk doing paperwork instead of roaming the halls as he usually was when I saw him at night. I knocked on his doorjamb.

"Come in," he said and looked up. We locked gazes for a moment, and I felt a zing of attraction run down my back. It was disconcerting and my hands trembled. I swallowed and ignored the feeling, all the while praying I didn't blush.

"Hi. I was wondering if I could talk with you about something I heard today."

He leaned back in his chair. It gave a solid creak. "Sure, have a seat." He waved toward the two chairs in front of his desk. "What's troubling you?"

"You know I got moved to the test kitchen until the greenhouse is righted," I said.

"I do. How's old Butterbottom treating you?"

I shrugged. "He's fine as long as we don't talk to him or his staff and stay out of his way."

"So it's détente in the kitchens now?" He raised an eyebrow.

"For now," I said and scooted to the edge of my seat. "But that's not why I stopped by. You see, the test kitchen is too small to store our serving carts, so I had to find a place to put them."

"I'm sure Chef had a suggestion."

"I didn't ask him," I said and waved the thought away. "It didn't matter. Someone pointed me toward the storage rooms. Here's the thing: I was in the storage room toward the back putting away our serving carts when I heard a man talking. I'm pretty sure he didn't know I was there since I was out of sight. I recognized the voice."

"And?"

"He was one of the two men who accosted Mr. Haregrove in the alley after the wake."

"Two men accosted Mr. Haregrove in the alley after the wake?"

"I told you about that," I said. "I suspect they have something to do with Mr. Deems's murder. They were threatening Mr. Haregrove and telling him that, dead or not, Mr. Deems owed them money, and they expected Mr. Haregrove to pay them back."

"I see, and one of these men was in the storage room across from the kitchen?"

"Yes," I said. "He was talking to someone on the phone. He talked about the money that is owed to them. He said that he believes he—Mr. Haregrove—got arrested so that he didn't have to pay them back."

"I didn't think Haregrove was a big gambler," Ian said and rubbed his chin.

"I don't think he is," I said and leaned closer. "The guy on the phone said that with Mr. Haregrove in jail, they would have to go after the family. Michael told me he didn't have a family, but Mr. Deems has two sons, who are Mr. Haregrove's godchildren. I'm afraid they were talking about going after Mr. Deems's family."

"Why?"

"He said something about Mr. Deems having enough insurance to pay off the debt. If they can't squeeze it out of Mr. Haregrove, then they will squeeze it out of the family."

"That sounds serious," Ian said. "I don't like the idea that there are people working in the palace who would talk like that, let alone take such actions. Could this have been staged?"

I frowned. "Why would he stage such a scary conversation?"

"Because you're new and an American. He might want to haze you a bit."

"Well, hazing me by intimidating Mr. Haregrove in the alley seems out of place. I know they didn't see me that night. Why would they make up something like this now?"

Ian shrugged. "Either way, I don't like it. If you can identify the man whose voice you heard in both places, I'll question him."

"What about the inspector? Will you let him know? Maybe Mr. Deems wasn't killed over his bad relationship with his wife. Maybe he had a

204

gambling problem. Maybe he owed people a lot of money and couldn't pay them back."

"I'm sure the inspector will be looking into the Deems accounts," Ian said. "If there is a hint of trouble, he'll sniff it out."

"So you'll look into this other man? The one trying to intimidate Mr. Haregrove? I don't like the idea of working around such a person."

"Can you describe him for me?"

"Well, he is big and bald, and he was wearing kitchen staff clothes, a white T-shirt with black pants. I saw apron strings, so that means he works in the kitchen. And if he works in the kitchen, Chef Butterbottom could also be a suspect. He could have used the man as an enforcer."

"That sounds like a ridiculous theory."

"Which one?"

"The one where Butterbottom is the killer. He has no motive."

"What about the other guy? Do you know who he is?"

"A big, bald man who works in the kitchen." Ian frowned.

"Yes, does anyone come to mind?"

"One or two," Ian said. "Are you certain they didn't know you were in the storage room?"

"Pretty certain," I said. He studied me, and I felt a blush rush over my cheeks. "I had to sneeze and couldn't stop it. I thought maybe he would rush to discover me after the sound, but he didn't.

In fact, he was gone when I left the room. I didn't see the big guy in the kitchen after that. I'm hoping he left before I sneezed."

"But if he didn't, it would be easy to figure out you were the person eavesdropping." Ian's scowl deepened. "If he is indeed an enforcer for a bookie, then you might be in danger. You should have brought this to me straight away."

"I couldn't," I said. "I had to get dinner for the family completed and the kitchen cleaned before Chef Butterbottom had a fit."

Ian shook his head. "You should have called me. I would have come to the kitchen and made a show of seeing you. That way, if they thought about harming you, they would know that I was protecting you."

"I'm sorry," I said and swallowed. "I'm new at this intrigue business. My cooking comes first."

"I'll walk you to your room," he said and rose.

"I really don't think you have to do that," I protested as I got to my feet. "If they were going to harm me, they would have already done it. Don't you think?"

"I think it's better to be safe than sorry. I'll put an extra guard on your hallway. Tomorrow I'm going to call in the men from the kitchen who fit the description. I want you here to see if you can identify the man you saw in the alley."

"Okay," I said. "After breakfast, right?"

"After breakfast." He held the door to his

office open and I stepped out. "I don't understand why you are so interested in Mr. Deems's murder."

"Well, I was the one who found him, and I feel a connection to him. Like I owe his family an explanation for what happened in my kitchen."

"It happened in Head Greenhouse Gardener Fedman's area, not your kitchen," he reminded me as he held open the elevator door for me. "And unless I'm mistaken, and you had something to do with Deems's murder—"

I gasped and whirled around to face him. "No!"

"Then there is no reason for you to worry about what happened."

"Except that I'm convinced Michael isn't the real killer, and that means someone else may die. Don't you think it's important to ensure the safety of everyone else here?"

He gave me a sharp look. "My job is to ensure the safety of everyone here." The elevator opened onto my kitchen floor. He held it and I stepped out. We walked in silence up the steps, past Penny's door, until we reached mine. I was suddenly exhausted. The days at the palace were long, and I'd been truly scared of what I had overheard. It was a relief to share it with Ian, even if I had the distinct impression he didn't quite believe me. We stopped at my door and I turned to him. He was close, and I could feel the confident heat radiating off of him. It seeped into my worried soul, and I was attracted to the safety he represented.

I could smell the starch in his white dress shirt and the undertones of spicy cologne and warm male. "Look, I get that it's your job to keep us safe. It's why I came to you with this information. I don't think it's a coincidence that I keep running into that man talking about money and Mr. Haregrove. I trust you'll look into it. I'm not trying to do your job or the inspector's job; I don't have time for that. I simply want to help. Mr. Haregrove is a good man. He doesn't deserve to lose his best friend, his job, and possibly spend the rest of his life in prison. Especially if someone else killed Mr. Deems. Someone who perhaps also worked with Mr. Deems and Mr. Haregrove when they were still working for Chef Butterbottom."

"You still think Butterbottom is involved in this?" He crossed his arms over his chest, essentially putting a barrier between us.

"No, no, I don't know," I said wearily and ran my hands over my face. "But it's clear someone in the kitchens knows something that can crack the case."

"I'll send a text when I have my suspects in my conference room," he said. "When I do, go to my office. You can view them through the two-way mirror and let me know if you recognize anything about them."

"Thank you for believing me," I said.

"Good night, Chef Cole," he said. "Get some rest. You've earned it."

"Good night." I closed and locked my door behind me and leaned against it. It felt cool and smooth against my heated skin. I created a mental picture of John in my mind. John was who I wanted. John was home.

Then why did my body tell me I was lying?

Chapter 18

The next morning, George Rabe never showed. I called him but only got his voicemail. Worry filled me. Did another one of my assistants go missing? Or was he dead?

I texted security to keep an eye out for him. A few minutes later, I got a call.

"Chef Cole?"

"Yes?"

"George Rabe," he said. "Listen, I can't work in that tiny hellhole of a kitchen. I'm not coming back. You and Phoebe will do just fine. I'm taking a position with another restaurant."

"But—"

"Good-bye, Chef Cole, and good luck to you." He hung up. I stared at my phone, flabbergasted.

"What's wrong?" Phoebe asked. "Was that George? Is he okay?"

"He's quit on us," I said and looked at her. "He didn't like the test kitchen."

"His loss, I say," Phoebe said. "We don't need him. Right?"

"Apparently not," I said and was about to put my phone down when I got another text. This one was from Ian. It read, *Something's come up. Can't meet today. Will contact you tomorrow about your concerns.*

I blew out a long breath, trying to hide my sigh. So he had thought about my story all night and must have decided that I was wrong. That the threatening men didn't need investigating after all. I chewed on my inner lip and stuffed my phone in my pocket.

It was going to be one of those days. I guess I'd just have to investigate myself.

"Phoebe, take the breakfast up now," I said, my tone hurried. We were running out of time. The main kitchen was farther away from the family's apartment, and we had to put in extra time and thought to get the food there on time and still warm.

"I have to admit, I'm glad George isn't coming," Phoebe said as she put platters of eggs, sausages, potatoes, and fresh fruits on the cart. "There's barely room for two of us in here. If George were here, we'd be walking all over each other."

"I suppose you're right." I added breads of all types, including cinnamon buns and banana bread, on trays to the cart. Finally, Phoebe placed carafes of hot tea, coffee, milk, and orange juice.

"Until they finish the construction in the green-house," I said, "I hope you're okay with it being just the two of us."

"Oh, I'm fine with it."

"Good," I said with relief. "Today's lunch is just for the children. We'll make the organic tomato cream soup and cheesy teddy bear toasted sandwiches."

"Sounds perfect," she said.

"Now go. When you get back, start on lunch. I have to go run an errand. I'll be back in time to make the tea menu. Dinner will be creamy mushroom chicken, fresh steamed vegetables, homemade bread, and poached pears for dessert."

"Sounds grand," Phoebe said.

"The duke and duchess have a state dinner later this evening, but the duchess said she wants to eat dinner with the children. We'll make a third plate for her, but I don't expect her to eat much."

"Three plates it is," Phoebe said as she pushed the cart through the door.

"Great." I took my apron off and placed it on a hook on the backside of the door, grabbed a basket of food, and followed her out. "You have my phone number. If you need anything, text me. I'll be running to market to get the freshest chicken."

I left the kitchen in my assistant's hands. Meanwhile, the main kitchen was slowly filling with workers. Chef Butterbottom was cooking for the state dinner. Beef was on the menu, which is why I chose chicken for the children. If the duchess wanted to eat with them, I wanted to give her a bit of variety.

I reminded myself that I wasn't competing with Chef Butterbottom, but I still believed my dinner would be the tastiest of the two. Mostly because I could cook in small batches and add homey touches.

I pulled my purse strap over my shoulder and stepped outside into the rather bright sunlight of a spring day in London. I had yet to see the man who was talking in the closet. Perhaps he worked only during certain engagements. It didn't matter; if I didn't see him, that meant that I was safe.

The basket in my arms was full of cookies, a fresh berry pie, and cinnamon rolls. I was on my way to see Mrs. Deems. Perhaps she could help me understand what was going on with the money and why Frank might have been killed for it. At the very least, she needed to know that she and her boys might be in danger. It suddenly occurred to me that Meriam Deems had every reason to kill her husband. Especially if he had gambling problems. Now she had an insurance settlement and was free of him and his bad habits.

That thought made me wonder if I should ask her straight out if she was the killer. No, maybe it would be better to take a more roundabout tact. I got to the Deemses' house unscathed, certain that no one had followed me. I guess it was paranoia that made me constantly look over my shoulder, but I didn't feel as if it was a coincidence that I had heard the big man talking about Mr. Deems two times now.

I walked up the short concrete steps to the door of the row house and knocked.

Mrs. Perkins swung the door open. "Hello," she said. "What are you doing here?"

"Hello," I replied. "Is Mrs. Deems home? I brought her and the boys some treats." I lifted the basket in my hand.

"Meriam is here," Mrs. Perkins said, "though I'm not certain she's taking visitors. Please come in. I'll go upstairs and see."

She waved me into the small foyer and closed the door behind me. The house was suffocating. The air barely moved. All the curtains were pulled and there was black everywhere. This time the boys didn't come down to see me. I glanced at my watch. It was just before noon. Perhaps they were back in school.

"She'll be right down," Mrs. Perkins said as she came down the stairs. "Do go into the parlor and have a seat." She took the basket from me. "I'll get some tea. You do drink tea, don't you?"

"Yes," I replied and stepped into the parlor as she headed down the small hallway to the back kitchen. The parlor had an old sofa, two small round occasional tables that were topped with white doilies, and ceramic lamps with matching shades. I sat down on the edge of the couch. The room felt cozy with its rugs on top of carpet and two small wingback chairs flanking the fireplace.

"Hello," Mrs. Deems said from the doorway. "Have we met?" She stepped in and held out her hand.

I stood and shook it. "Carrie Ann Cole," I said. "We met at the wake in the pub the other night.

There were a lot of people there, so I wouldn't be surprised if you don't remember."

"Yes," she said. She spoke softly and slowly as if she had taken something to calm her nerves. "Yes, I do remember now. Please have a seat." She sat in one of the wingback chairs opposite the couch. "I'm sorry I didn't see you when you stopped by the other day. Things have been a bit crazy."

"I imagine they have," I said with sympathy. "I brought you a basket of cookies and breads. It's what I do in this kind of situation. Feed people."

"You're a chef," she stated. "I imagine you always feed people. I know Frank did."

"It's a thing in my family. If someone dies, we bring food. If a baby is born, we bring food. If it's your birthday, we bring food. If someone gets a raise—"

"You bring food." She lifted the corner of her mouth in a half smile. "Please forgive me if I don't eat. It's the chemotherapy. It makes me nauseous."

I blinked. She was small and thin with a thick blonde bob that only now did I realize was a wig. She had taken the time to put on baby-pink lipstick and some blush, but her eyelashes were gone. Her eyebrows were drawn on with a light-brown pencil.

"Don't be embarrassed," she said and touched my knee in kindness. "I don't tell people about the cancer. It's breast cancer. They tell me it's curable, but this is my second go-around. The first time, I had a lumpectomy. Two months ago, I found another lump. This time in the other breast. So I had them both removed."

"It's been a struggle keeping up her strength," Mrs. Perkins said as she entered with tea and a plate of the cookies I made on a tray.

"I'm so sorry," I said and put my hand over Meriam's. "You're right, I didn't realize. What an awful time to lose your husband."

"It's the boys that I'm worried about," Meriam said and took the cup of tea that her mother gave her. "With Frank gone, I was counting on Michael to see to the boys' welfare should the cancer progress too far."

"I told her I can raise them," Mrs. Perkins said and handed me a cup of tea with no sugar. "But she won't let me."

"My mother is sixty-five years old. The last thing she needs is to raise teenage boys in her seventies."

"With Michael on trial, I am your only option," Mrs. Perkins said. "Drink some tea, dear."

Meriam pretended to take a sip and put the cup down. "The boys are a handful. I've been sick for the last three years. They've quite gotten used to running wild, I'm afraid."

"I can handle them," Mrs. Perkins said. "I always wanted a boy."

"Boys are much different than girls," Meriam

said. "They need a strong hand and a good male role model."

"We'll get your Uncle Henry to come over every now and again. My brother is good with boys," Mrs. Perkins said to me.

"He's also seventy-five years old," Meriam lamented. "The boys are full of mischief, and I'm afraid Uncle Henry will just encourage it." She turned to me. "They are bright boys. Too bright for their own good. That's what the teachers tell me anyway." She leaned back against her chair and closed her eyes for a moment.

"If it helps, I don't think Mr. Haregrove killed your husband," I said. "And I intend to prove it."

"What on earth makes you think that?" Mrs. Perkins asked. "Are you an inspector? A private detective? Do you have credentials to examine these things better than the inspector on the case?"

"No," I said softly. "I have no credentials. But I've met Mr. Haregrove. He doesn't seem like the type who would do such a thing. Besides, I think he's protecting whoever did."

"Why would he do that?" Mrs. Perkins asked me.

"I have no idea," I said. "I think it has something to do with money. You see, when I walked back to the palace after attending the wake, I saw two men accosting Mr. Haregrove in the alley. They said that, dead or not, there was a debt to be paid. Did Mr. Deems owe anyone money?"

217

"Not that I'm aware of," Meriam said. "But it's possible. You see, I've been out of work for years. The hospital bills are covered, but with two growing boys, we really needed two incomes."

"I moved in as soon as Meriam left her job," Mrs. Perkins said. "I help with the bills and Meriam's care. There was no reason for Frank to owe anyone money. Are you sure it wasn't Michael who owed the money?"

"No, I'm not sure," I said with a shake of my head. "But what I heard made it sound as if Mr. Deems's death was only the beginning of what would happen if the money wasn't paid."

"Well, that certainly sounds worrisome," Mrs. Perkins said and rose. "You are wearing Meriam down. Perhaps you should go."

"Mother, I'm fine." Meriam closed her eyes, but I noted that she had gone pale, and tiny beads of sweat dotted her upper lip. Was it the chemo or was my suspicion that she knew something about the murder causing her to be upset? Did she know about her husband's gambling? If so, Meriam had access to the palace. She could have confronted him.

I looked at her closely. Yes, she was recovering from chemo, but she might not be as frail as she looked. If Michael was a suspect, then I also couldn't rule out Meriam. After all, the last thing she needed was a husband who gambled away her children's future.

"I'm so sorry, how rude of me. I didn't mean to add worry to your illness and loss." I stood and gathered my purse. "Thank you for seeing me and telling me about your illness. I want you to know that I intend to help Mr. Haregrove prove his innocence. Then you won't have to worry about your boys. You will get well, and they will have you, your mother, and Mr. Haregrove in their lives. They will be lucky boys."

A half smile moved slowly across her face. "Thank you for the visit and the food."

"One more question," I said, growing brave. "When was the last time you were at the palace?"

"A few days before Frank died. I took Michael his cell phone. He left it on our table. Why?"

"Just curious if you had seen Michael and Frank working together."

"I did."

"Was there any animosity between the two?"

"No, they seemed fine."

"Thanks."

"I think you should go now." Mrs. Perkins hustled me toward the door.

"I'm so sorry," I said. "You should have told me about her illness."

"Meriam doesn't like to worry people."

"I'll bring more food by. I cook only organic, and I'll wash and peel all the vegetables and fruits. It's best if she can eat during chemotherapy. What does she like?"

"She likes oxtail barley soup."

"Good, then I'll make sure she has a pot of it once a week. I heard if you can get her to keep eating, it helps in the healing."

"Thank you," Mrs. Perkins said. "I may have misjudged you."

"I doubt it was misjudgment," I said and pressed her hands between mine. "You simply didn't know me, and I didn't know about your daughter. Don't worry. Things will work out for the best."

"They always do," Mrs. Perkins said. "They always do."

"Question before I go. Does Meriam come to the palace often?"

"She comes to have lunch with me once a week. Why?"

"I wasn't sure family was allowed inside."

"They ran a background check on Meriam, if that's what has you worried."

"No, no worries. Just curious."

"Huh. All right, now off you go. I know you have dinner to make for the children. Make it spectacular. Sunday dinner is important family time for the duchess."

"I'll do my best," I said. Then I huddled into my coat and walked down the busy street toward the tube station. It was May and, although the temperatures were in the sixty-degree range, London had a dampness that made me shiver.

Chapter 19

Early afternoon in London wasn't as crowded as the beginning and end of the day. Rush hour is what we called it back home; crush hour is what I would describe it here in England. Of course it being Sunday meant that mostly tourists or service workers rode today.

It was nice to walk through the tube station with room to swing my purse if I so desired. I didn't, of course, as that would be rude. I think I was halfway to the platform when I realized that I was being followed.

It started off as a creepy sensation at the back of my neck. I tried to brush it off by telling myself it was the damp that made me shiver. But it was warmer in the station than outside. The elevators and hallways were tiled and smelled old and well used. Ahead of me, someone was playing the guitar and singing. I reached into my purse and pulled out some change to drop into her case. She was a young woman and her voice filled the space with a sweet melody. It should have been comforting, but the sensation of being watched stayed with me. I glanced back and saw a man walking behind me. He wore a trench coat and carried a briefcase. He was blond and looked to be in his midthirties. A plain man in a nondescript outfit. Why, then, was he giving me the willies?

I sped up my pace as the hallway opened up to the platform. The announcement said there were still four minutes until the train arrived and to mind the gap.

The platform was deserted. A lot could happen in four minutes, so I turned on my heel and headed back into the hall, only to run right into the man.

"I beg your pardon," he said and put both of his hands on me to steady me from the brunt of his body weight. It seems he had sped up when I did.

I stepped back out of his reach. "My mistake," I said and sent him an insecure smile. "I just realized I forgot something." I shrugged. "I guess I'll catch the next train."

"You have four minutes," he said without looking at his watch. "Time enough to get back and make this train."

I tried to get around him, but he seemed to take up all the room. Which was a silly thought; the hallways could fit four to six people across. "I'll have to hurry then," I said and ducked around him.

"You do that," he said. There was something familiar in his voice. I couldn't place it. I don't know why I was so paranoid, but I had learned to trust my gut. It had never steered me wrong.

I hurried back through the halls and up into the

damp street air. When I got around the corner from the station, I finally stopped and took a deep breath. The humidity was climbing with the temperature. I felt sweat break out on my forehead and although I was no longer near the tube station, I still felt watched.

A cab turned the corner and I held out my hand to flag it. Taking a cab to Kensington Palace would be expensive, but at least I would make it back safely in time for tea.

"Ian Gordon was looking for you," Phoebe said when I arrived back at the kitchen. "He said to have you go see him the moment you came back."

"Oh," I said as I tied on my apron. "Well, he will have to wait. It's time for dinner prep."

Today's dinner was comfort food and mostly served in the winter, but I felt the need to create something soothing.

Dessert was poached pears. I poached the pears while Phoebe made the crusty artisan bread that would be served with the chicken. It was a casserole, really, but sometimes simple and homey were the perfect fit for a day of revelations.

Not that the duke and duchess had any knowledge of what I learned. But the dish was on the approved list and so it seemed to serve me at the moment.

I got lost in cooking. It was a way for me to soothe myself. I kept thinking about how horrible it was that Mrs. Deems had cancer. That Mr. Deems was murdered and her boys may soon be without any family except for Mrs. Perkins, who wasn't the most comforting of personalities.

If Michael was trying to protect someone from being blamed for Mr. Deems's murder, it wasn't obvious who. I frowned. Unless it was Meriam herself. It seemed that he would have been less likely to take the fall for someone else knowing that Mrs. Deems and his godsons needed him.

Unless he was more than protecting Meriam. What if Michael was a willing accomplice? Then my theory of his innocence was wrong.

That made me scowl harder.

"The chicken is already dead," Ian said. "No need to keep stabbing it."

I looked up to see him leaning against the doorjamb. The door swung closed behind him. "What brings you to my closet?" I asked as I put down the knife and picked up a spoon. What I had meant to do was ladle the stew into a serving taurine.

"You weren't here earlier," he said, and it sounded more like an accusation than a comment.

"I went to take food to Mrs. Deems," I said. "If that is any of your business."

"We were supposed to meet."

"I don't have time to wait around for you to get to me," I said and arranged the taurine on the serving cart along with the rest of the meal under silver domes to keep it warm. "Phoebe, take this up to the family."

She added a plate of butter and salt and pepper shakers and then excused herself to push the cart through the doorway. In doing so, she had to push Ian out into Chef Butterbottom's office.

"Good God," Butterbottom blustered. "It would be nice to have my space back."

I stuck my head out. "You could have given us a corner of the main kitchen."

"There's no free corner in my kitchen," he glared. "And there's no free corner in my office. Close the door. I can't get any work done."

Ian and I exchanged a glance and stepped back into the test kitchen. I looked at the mess that needed cleaning.

"Maybe now isn't a good time," I suggested.

"Fine, come to my office in an hour," he stated. "We need to talk." It sounded very serious.

"Do I need to bring a lawyer?" I asked.

He sent me a look.

"Kidding," I said and raised my hands. "I'll be there as soon as we finish up here."

"Good," he said. "Don't make me hunt you down again."

"I didn't realize I was making you hunt me down now," I muttered as the door swung shut behind him. I heard muffled voices as Ian talked to Chef Butterbottom about something.

"Maybe it's good news." Phoebe had come back while I washed dishes. "Maybe we'll have our kitchen back sooner than they thought."

"I think Mrs. Worth would be the one to tell me that sort of news, not the head of security."

Phoebe shrugged as she put on gloves and took over scrubbing a copper-bottom pot. "A girl can dream."

An hour and a half later, I knocked on Ian's office door.

"Enter."

I opened it. He sat at his desk writing with a pen. It was so odd to see someone use a pen and not a computer keyboard. "Are you signing autographs?"

"Paperwork," he said and put down the pen, slid the papers into a folder, and waved at the chair in front of his desk. "Have a seat."

"Did you figure out who the guy is who wants money from Michael?"

"I spoke to the inspector today," Ian said. "They have done some digging into the Deemses' finances and found some things that may make a difference in the case."

"What things?"

"I can't tell you for privacy reasons, but I wanted to thank you for pointing us in the right direction for the investigation."

"What about the threats inside the palace?"

"I'm looking into that," he said. "You don't have to worry about it."

"I don't know," I shook my head. "I'm not comfortable working around men who threaten families and neither should you be."

That made him sit up. "I take my job here very seriously, Chef Cole. Any man or woman who poses a threat will no longer be allowed on the premises. Is that clear?"

"But how will you know if you don't let me identify the guy?"

"The inspector is looking into it. I have started the proper procedures to fire any person or persons involved."

"What you're telling me is that you don't need me to identify anyone."

"That's correct," he said. "We have the matter well in hand."

"Okay, then," I said and stood. "I won't bother you with this again."

"Chef Cole." He blew out a long breath. "You're new here, and you are not aware of how things are done."

"That's correct," I said. "I'm not aware. I wasn't aware that someone could be murdered in my new workplace. I wasn't aware that a second person, who I came to like, would be unduly accused of that murder."

"The reasons for Mr. Haregrove's arrest still stand," Ian said.

"Did you know that Mrs. Deems has cancer and may die? Did you know that Mr. Haregrove is the only other male role model her boys have now that their father is dead?"

His jaw clenched. "I am aware of the situation. Don't classify me as unfeeling, Chef Cole."

"I see, then you simply have a stiff upper lip about it." I walked to the door. "I thought better of you."

"If by that you thought we were somehow more than colleagues at the palace, then your thinking is wrong. I'm doing my job, Chef Cole. Why don't you concentrate on doing yours?"

I walked out of his office and let the door slam behind me. Fuming, I stormed down to the privacy of my kitchen. Not the test kitchen, but the family kitchen where I was supposed to be working. I hit the lights and slumped against the door in sadness.

The entire space was covered with a light dusting of dirt and sawdust. It would take a lot of work to get it back to usable. After the day I had, I felt horrible and slowly slid to the ground to rest my head in my hands.

Maybe it was all a big mistake. Maybe I should have never come to London to cook for the family. Someone else could have handled this better. *Right?*

"I didn't leave this light on," said a male voice I recognized. I lifted my head to see the handsome gardener standing just inside the kitchen door. His thick blond hair was pulled back into a ponytail, but he wasn't wearing a helmet this time.

"No, you didn't," I replied and stood, brushing the dust off my backside.

He paused and studied me. "You look different when you're not angry and flying at me like a harpy."

"Excuse me?"

"No, that came out wrong." He stepped into the room. "I would like to apologize."

"What for?" For the life of me, I couldn't figure out whether he meant for ruining my garden, forcing me to work in a closet, or calling me a harpy.

"For the mess," Jasper said and stepped closer, "and for the harpy comment, although you were a little crazed when we first met." He reached out and gently lifted my face into the light. "I would have been more careful if I knew my actions would upset you so."

I gave a short laugh and blinked back tears as I stepped away from him. "I probably resemble a harpy right now." I rubbed away the mascara that was running down my cheeks.

"No, you don't."

"Don't what?"

"Look like a harpy." His eyes narrowed. "You look upset." He stuck his hand in the back pocket of his well-worn jeans. "I can't stand to see a beautiful woman so upset. Especially if I might have caused it."

I hugged myself, trying to figure out how to get out of this rather awkward conversation. "It's been a long day," I said. "Why are you down here? Isn't it too dark to demolish anything more?"

"I was walking by on my way home when I saw the light. What brought you down? Isn't the big kitchen comfortable?"

"Have you met Chef Butterbottom?" I had to laugh at the ridiculousness of the question.

"Yes, he seems as if he has things well in hand."

"I guess that's the nice way to say it," I said.

"What, you don't like the man?"

I thought I spied a quick smirk quiver across his mouth. "Let's say he hasn't endeared himself to me," I said. "Right now he has me and my staff in the test kitchen."

"The test kitchen?" Jasper drew his eyebrows together.

"It's a broom closet with an oven and a sink. I had a new staffer quit today over how awful the working conditions are."

"You should say something to Chef Butterbottom."

"The last time I did, things didn't go so well. I am convinced he doesn't think having an American chef feeding the family is right."

"Oh, so a French chef would be better?"

I liked the twinkle in his blue eyes. The man really was shockingly handsome. "Oh, no, not better," I said. "But perhaps more tolerable. I believe Chef Butterbottom thinks only good British chefs should cook for the future kings."

"Ha! As if old Bottom would let them pay him your salary."

"Aha, so I do get paid quite a bit less than the master chef." I acted as if I were surprised.

"Oh, no, did I just let the cat out of the bag?"

Shaking my head, I smiled. "Of course he's paid more. I cook for a family of four and sometimes for their guests when they have private dinner parties. He cooks for state dinners and larger events."

"So you are not envious of his position?"

"No, oh, no," I said. "I am envious of his space, though. As you can see, I had a very nice kitchen, but then a man died and you came to destroy and rebuild the crime scene."

"And you got stuck in a closet."

"I have to go through Butterbottom's office every time I go into or leave my kitchen."

"Ouch," he said and made a face. "I think I owe you a drink for that."

I tilted my head. "Yes, I think you do owe me at least a drink."

"Shall we go?"

"After the day I had, I think we should." I felt as if I needed to forget about everything for a while. It wasn't very often in my life that a handsome man asked me to go for a drink. He did owe me for the state of my kitchen.

"Have you had dinner?" he asked. "There's a pub around the corner that makes fantastic fish and chips."

"I could eat," I said. "I need to get my jacket."

"Just use mine," He offered me the jean jacket that he had folded over his arm.

"But you'll be cold," I protested.

"A few drinks and I'll be fine," he said and helped me into his jacket. It smelled like his aftershave. "Come on then," he said and put his hand on the small of my back to steer me out of the kitchen. "Let's leave the dust behind."

We left the palace via the parking area. Two blocks away was a bustling pub called the Kissing Canary. It was not far from the pub where the wake was held, but it was clearly not as well known to the palace staff.

There was music playing when we walked in, and people greeted Jasper from behind the bar as if they were family.

"Who's this with you, Jasper?" an older bald man said.

"This is Chef Cole," Jasper said. "She cooks for the family."

"Call me Carrie Ann," I said.

"Bob Westin," he said. "It's a pleasure to meet you."

"If I buy you a drink, can I call you Carrie Ann?" Jasper asked.

I felt the heat of a blush rush over my face. "Well, now, it depends on the drink."

The old man grinned. "A woman after my own heart, this one, Jasper."

"We'll take two of your finest whiskey," Jasper said. "And two fish and chips."

"You have the family chef with you and you're ordering food?" Bob asked.

"He owes me," I said.

"How's that?"

"He's destroying my kitchen with dust and dirt. They've got me working in a broom closet until this one finishes with the greenhouse."

"Ah, that's right, that's where Mr. Deems went toes up," Bob said. "Sorry to hear about that mess."

"Who do we have here?" an older woman asked as she came around to Bob's side. She was as short as Bob, with a round face that was flushed from the heat in the bar. She wore a stylish shirt, slacks, and a green apron. Her hair was gray and curled into a bob.

"Jasper has brought us Chef Cole, the new royal family chef," Bob said. "This is my better half, Amy."

"A pleasure to meet you," I said and shook her hand. "Please call me Carrie Ann."

"Jasper's ordered our finest whiskey," Bob

explained as he got a dusty bottle off the shelf behind the bar.

"Oh, boy, what did you do?" Amy asked.

"He kicked her out of her kitchen," Bob said, his dark gaze twinkling. "Now he is going to ply her with whiskey and fish and chips."

"Amy makes the best fish and chips in all of London," Jasper said and took the shots that Bob poured. "Come on, let's get a table before they're all gone."

I wound my way through the crowd of people who looked like regulars. They dressed like people who needed a drink after a long day of work. There were very few suits here. Mostly the men wore jeans and tees and the women jeans and blouses. The crowd was older and the music, while happy, was not as loud as at the other pub.

I followed Jasper over to a corner high-top table with two tall chairs. The windows to the street were behind the table, and he offered me the seat so that I could see the city. I noticed that Jasper had nodded at a few people as we wound our way to the table.

I climbed up on my seat. "You come here a lot."

He shrugged. "I know a few people, if that's what you mean." He pushed a shot glass toward me. "Cheers."

"Cheers," I said. We touched glasses and then tossed the whiskey down. It went down smooth and oaky with just enough heat to take the chill out of my bones from the walk over.

"So may I call you Carrie Ann now?"

"Yes," I said. "The whiskey was exactly what I needed."

"Then we'll have another." He raised his hand and waved Bob over. The bartender grinned and poured us a second round. When he turned to leave, Jasper stopped him and took the bottle.

"The man has deep pockets," Bob said and wiggled his thick gray eyebrows.

"Only for special women," Jasper said. He raised his glass. "To us."

"The best people we know," I finished. It was a common toast I made with my friends, and I'd said it without thinking. He paused for a moment then laughed and tossed down his second shot. I followed with mine. My face warmed and my muscles finally relaxed. "Thank you for this. I didn't know how badly I needed it."

"We all need a night out now and again. How long have you been here? Four days? Five?"

"Six," I said. "Tomorrow's my day off."

"Then it's your Friday night," he said.

"But it's your Sunday night," I pointed out. "What were you doing working on Sunday?"

"A gardener's work is never done."

"Did you know Francis Deems well?"

"Well enough," Jasper's face darkened. "We went to elementary school together."

"I heard you were best friends then."

"Who told you that?" There was surprise in his voice.

"A friend," I said carefully. "I noticed you weren't at the wake in the pub."

"Meriam doesn't like me much," he said, poured another drink, and tossed it down. "I didn't want to cause a fuss."

"What happened to break you two up?"

"It was a stupid thing," he said. He poured himself a fresh shot. "We live in a small world. I dated Meriam before they got together. Then I broke up with her to date Susan Finch. That's all it took to set Frank against me for good once he took up with her."

"It would seem that breaking up with Meriam was a good thing," I said. "Or she may not have ever married Mr. Deems."

"Well, I was a bit of a cad in those days," he said with a sideways grin. "She's never forgiven me and so Frank never forgave me."

"Did that make you angry? If I remember right, you and Mr. Deems had an argument the night he was murdered."

That made him pause and look at me. "You think I might have killed Frank over the way he manhandled lettuce?"

"Is that what you had words about?"

"Yeah, the guy wasn't careful with the produce. I always had to replant after he went through and ripped everything out." He paused. "But I would never kill him over it."

"I'm sorry, I didn't mean to suggest you would. It's so strange to be so new and involved in such a sad thing," I said. "I went to visit Mrs. Deems today. I know she doesn't want people to worry over her, and it's probably the whiskey talking, but . . . Did you know that she has cancer?"

"Oh, God, no. What a bit of bad luck for her. To have cancer and to lose her husband."

"I know," I said. "It broke my heart. I just had to tell someone. She's so brave, but it's clear that it's getting to her. Having Michael arrested for the crime has practically knocked her to her knees. She was counting on him to help her with the boys."

"I heard they were having an affair, and that is why the cops think that Mike killed Frank."

"I don't think he did it," I said.

Just then Amy showed up with two plates filled with freshly fried fish and chips. There was salt and vinegar on the table. "Wow, that smells good," I said.

"Enjoy," she said with a smile. "I'd love to hear what the family cook thinks. A good review is great for business." She winked at me.

I forked up some of the flaky fish. It melted in my mouth with the right crunch of crust, the tang of vinegar, and the perfect flake of white fish. "This is fantastic," I said.

"I told you," Jasper said.

"Thank you," Amy said and left us to our bottle of whiskey and dinners.

"So I hear you have a boyfriend back in the states," Jasper said. "Is it serious?"

"We've been living together for three years," I said. "So it's pretty serious."

"And yet he let you jet off to London to be the royal family's cook."

"He didn't have much say," I said. "Besides, he was proud of me."

Jasper poured me another shot of whiskey. "Sounds more like a brother than a lover. Cheers."

"Cheers," I said and downed my third shot. I was feeling the happiest I'd been since I arrived. The food was good and the man across from me was just as delectable.

We chatted about any number of things. I learned that Jasper had grown up in London but taken a liking to the parks and went to school to be a gardener. It was quite rigorous to become a palace gardener. Jasper had a master's degree, had spent three years as an apprentice and three years as a journeyman, and now he was a master gardener. He was doing well at Kensington but had his eye on Buckingham.

"Hello." A man about our age grabbed a chair and pulled it up to our table. "Who's this?"

Jasper didn't seem the least bit put out by the

interruption. "Calvin, this is Chef Cole, the new family chef at the palace. Carrie Ann, this is my brother, Calvin."

"Hello." I shook hands with the man. It was hard to tell who was the younger brother and who was the older, but I could see the resemblance. They both had thick blond hair, although Calvin kept his cut short like a businessman. He wore a button-down shirt and jeans with a crisp seam down the leg.

"Well, well, my baby brother brings a beautiful woman to the family pub. That's cause for celebration." He snagged Jasper's shot glass and poured himself a shot. "Cheers," he said with a slight lift of the glass toward me and then downed it in one swallow.

"Family pub?" I asked Jasper. He had mentioned it was a family place, but he didn't mention it was *his* family's.

"Amy and Bob are my aunt and uncle," Jasper said with a shrug. "That's why they saved me the good stuff." He winked at me and poured us both another shot.

By this time, I was feeling very mellow and not sure if another shot was a good idea.

"Go on," Jasper said with a nod toward the glass. "If you don't drink it, Calvin will, and I'd hate to waste the good stuff on my older brother."

"Last one," I said. "Tomorrow might be my day

off, but I do have things I want to accomplish." I tossed down the shot.

"I heard a rumor that you were the one who found the dead Mr. Deems in my brother's greenhouse," Calvin said.

"I did find Mr. Deems," I said with a nod. "He was quite dead, but it is my greenhouse as it's attached to my kitchen and is there for the express purpose of my use to feed the family."

Both men chuckled.

"Well, we'll have to agree to disagree on whose greenhouse it is," Jasper said warmly.

"But it must have been terrible to find him there," Calvin said. "Were you alone?"

"I was," I said. "It was my second day at work, and I wasn't sure what to do. Protocol is everything at the palace."

"But you managed brilliantly," Calvin said and grabbed my shot glass to pour what was left of the bottle into the glass and toss it back. "I understand they have the guy who did it."

"Oh, no." I shook my head. "I don't think Mr. Haregrove did it at all."

"Why not? The inspector seems to have enough evidence to arrest him."

"The motive is not strong," I said. "I'm told they think he killed Mr. Deems because *he* was in love with Mrs. Deems."

"Love is a strong motive," Jasper said with a twinkle in his blue eyes.

"But I don't think Mr. Deems was murdered for love," I said. "You see, Mrs. Deems has cancer. Mr. Haregrove loves and cares for her, yes, but he would never leave her alone to battle cancer and grieve over her husband like this. He also loves those boys. It was the first thing he said to me the day I discovered Mr. Deems. He said he had to go check on the boys. They are his godsons."

"We all know what a beauty Meriam is. If you don't think love was the motive, what was?" Calvin asked. He had blue-gray eyes set off by the light-gray dress shirt he wore.

"Money," I said. "I overheard two men trying to get money out of Mr. Haregrove. I heard them threaten the family next."

"Why would they kill Deems over money that Haregrove owes?"

"Because it was not Mr. Haregrove who owed the money, but Mr. Deems. You see, cancer has caused Mrs. Deems to have to stop working for the last four years. Bills add up. I'm guessing Mr. Deems was borrowing money from someone shady, and when they demanded repayment, he didn't have it."

"So why kill him?" Calvin asked. "How do you get money out of a dead man?"

"Insurance," I said. "Mr. Deems had a substantial life insurance policy."

"You know there were rumors that Deems had

a gambling problem," Jasper said. He drew his thick eyebrows together. "They're old rumors. But I remember once seeing Haregrove giving Deems money to play the ponies so he could pay off his bookie."

"That's horrible," I said. "He had a wife and kids to think about."

"I heard stress can cause addictions to manifest," Calvin said. When I looked at him oddly he shrugged. "I took Psychology 101 in college."

"Calvin is a businessman," Jasper said. "They study human psychology to help sell things to unsuspecting people like you and me."

We all laughed.

"But seriously," Calvin said, "if Deems had a gambling problem, it still doesn't get Haregrove off the hook. Think about it. He knew Deems was gambling away money that the woman he loved and his godsons needed to survive. That's a big enough motive."

I suddenly felt defeated. "Oh, I didn't think| of it that way. No wonder Ian said that my investigation was helpful but that Mr. Haregrove was not going anywhere anytime soon."

"You really like Haregrove," Jasper pointed out.

"I barely know him," I said. "But he seems like such a decent guy. You didn't see his eyes. He was truly crushed at the death of his friend. There is no way he murdered anyone." I put my elbow on the table and rested my cheek in my hand. "Now I've gone and made things worse for the poor guy."

"Maybe not," Jasper said. "If he didn't do it, he didn't do it. That means someone else had to have a motive and the means to kill Deems."

"Whoever it was must be angry about the money and have access to the greenhouse," I said. "That really narrows down the field."

"I might know a thing or two about employees gambling in the palace," Jasper said. "Not that I have a gambling problem, but I know where to place a bet or two."

"Then you might know who is threatening Mrs. Deems. I overheard a very large, bald man in a kitchen staff uniform talking on the phone about threatening the family if they didn't get their money back."

"That doesn't sound good," Calvin said. "Does he know you overheard him?"

"I'm not sure," I said. "I went to see Ian, and he said he'll have security do some extra rounds to ensure my safety. This whole thing has me spooked."

"And it should," Calvin said.

"Gordon will ensure your safety," Jasper said. "He's a man the queen has entrusted with the safety of her grandchildren."

"I can imagine Mr. Deems going toes up on the palace grounds really shook Gordon up. He has a reputation, and this just shot a big hole in it," said Calvin.

"I think that's why he's so ready to blame Mr. Haregrove," I said. "The sooner this is solved, the better for everyone."

"I think we have England's finest on the case," Jasper said and patted my hand. "But I'll walk you to your door to be certain you are safe."

"Probably a good idea," I said. My face felt a little numb. "So when will I get my kitchen back? The big guy talking about hurting Mrs. Deems works in the big kitchen."

"I've got all the old beds demolished," Jasper said and stood. He helped me climb out of my tall bar chair and slide my arms into his jean jacket. "I'll manage the cleanup in the next forty-eight hours. With any luck, the new beds will be built and in place in four days. Can you handle four days in the closet?"

"She's working in a closet?" Calvin asked.

I nodded vigorously. "Yes, a very small closet. Butterbottom calls it a test kitchen, but I think it's just his storage space."

"And why are you cooking in Chef Butterbottom's storage space?" Calvin asked.

"Because your brother here has ongoing demolition to the greenhouse and it turned my kitchen into a dirt farm."

"The walls between the greenhouse and the

family kitchen are glass and should probably be resealed," Jasper explained.

"I went to Mrs. Worth and asked for plastic to cover them, but instead she sent me up to the big kitchen."

"And Chef Butterbottom put her and her staff to work in the storage closet," Jasper said.

"So you, my dear brother, are responsible for ruining this beautiful woman's work space."

"It's why he took me out to dinner," I said, and the three of us headed toward the door. The pub was bustling now with neighbors gathering and talking. I waved good-bye to Bob and Amy.

"Hmmm, yes," Calvin said. "I can see that ruining your work space would be the only reason my brother would take you out and ply you with thirty-year-old scotch."

"And fish and chips," I said. "We did eat dinner."

"Next time, have him take you to Antonio's. The tiramisu is to die for, and the place is a bit more romantic than this one."

"Oh, I have a boyfriend," I said as he held the door open for us.

"Really? And where is he on this fine night?" Calvin asked.

"In Chicago," I said. I glanced at my watch. "Most likely working on a new recipe."

"How did he let you go?" Calvin asked.

"After six years, we're taking a short break," I

said. "He's giving me space to follow my dream. But I'm hoping he'll come to London for a visit. He might even love it enough to stay."

Calvin glanced at Jasper. I looked from one brother to the other. "What?"

"Nothing," Calvin said. "It was nice to meet you, Carrie Ann." He took my hand and kissed the back of it. It sent a warm shiver up my arm.

"It was nice to meet you as well," I said. "Have a good night."

Jasper and I walked the couple blocks back to the palace in silence, listening to the bustle of the city as nighttime arrived, and with it, a cold fog that had me shivering. The whiskey warmed me, but only for a little while.

"Thank you for dinner," I said as we approached the palace gate and showed our security badges. "I'm good from here. I'm certain Ian has security well in hand."

"I'd still feel better walking you to your door," Jasper said. He had his hand on the small of my back as if to guide me. It felt nice there. As if all those muscles would keep me safe. I was a little drunk, so I let him walk me into the palace and down the hallway past the kitchen and up the flight of stairs.

"My room is just through here," I said.

He stopped me at my door. I took off his coat and gave it to him.

"Thank you for being so kind to me. I know I

must seem like some silly American all worried about a man I barely know."

"I find it endearing," Jasper said. He reached down to take my chin gently into his hand and tilted my face up. "I find you beautiful."

He kissed me.

It was warm and wonderful, and I might have put my hands around his neck and leaned into it a bit. It had been a tough week. John and I were on a break. I told myself I was far from home and was only taking a small comfort where I could get it.

The door to my rooms opened behind me and, startled, I broke off the kiss.

"Carrie Ann?" John asked. "What's going on?"

Chapter 20

John?" I said, confused. "How are you here?"

"You asked me to come for your day off," he said. His dark eyebrows drew together as he looked from me to Jasper and back. "Have you been drinking?"

"Just a little scotch," Jasper said. "To take the chill off."

"To take something off," John muttered. "Who in the heck are you?"

"John, this is Jasper Fedman. Jasper is the head greenhouse gardener. Jasper, this is John. John's a chef for Matt's in Chicago."

"I'm her boyfriend," John said. "Something I think she's forgotten."

"I didn't forget," I said and blinked as the hallway started to spin. "You're in Chicago. I asked you to come visit and you couldn't. And you didn't want to be my boyfriend."

"I wanted to surprise you," he said. "Looks like I did." He gave Jasper the evil eye.

"What are you doing here?" I asked. "How'd you get inside the palace?"

"Mr. Gordon let me in after much interrogation," John said. "I've been working on this surprise for a week."

"You should have told me," I said weakly.

"Well, I'm here now," John took a hold of my arm and pulled me gently into my rooms. "I've got you." He slammed the door in Jasper's face.

"Hey," I said. "He was just being nice."

"I don't like his kind of nice," John said.

"Sorry, Jasper," I shouted toward the door. "Thank you for seeing me safely home."

John had set a duffle bag on the couch in my living room. The light was on in my bedroom. Flabbergasted at John's presence in my rooms in Kensington Palace and more than a little drunk on whiskey, I looked at him in bewilderment.

"When did you get here?" I asked. "I was only gone a couple of hours."

"I've been here about thirty minutes," he said. "I wish I had gotten here a couple hours earlier."

"Me, too," I said and sat down on my bed. He was mad at me, and I didn't blame him. Neither one of us had expected me to kiss Jasper. It was even worse that John witnessed it.

He paced in front of me. He was a tall, skinny guy in glasses, his dark-blond hair falling into his eyes in a way that made my heart melt. Today he wore his old jeans and a T-shirt with a *Star Wars* logo on it. He looked exactly like he always did only tired and, well, hopping mad.

"I can't believe I spent the money to come all the way across the Atlantic to surprise you only to find you in the arms of some gardener."

"It didn't mean anything, and you said you

wanted to be on a break anyway," I said and laid back on the bed to stare up at the ceiling. I couldn't bear to watch him pace anymore. Besides, the room had begun to spin again. "I had a bad day, heck, a bad week, and you were in Chicago telling me all about your plans to go to San Francisco. I had no idea if I'd ever see you again. Then I'm stuck cooking in a closet on the opposite side of the office of this chef who controls his kitchen with an iron fist."

I paused a moment to try to catch my whirling thoughts. "The room is spinning," I said. "That's not a good sign."

"Finding you in the arms of another man is not a good sign, Carrie Ann." John yelled and finally sat down on the bed, rocking it just enough to set my stomach off. I popped out of the bed and ran to the bathroom, where I tossed up the whiskey and the fish and chips. I hated being sick. I hated drinking, and I hated the fact that I had let some guy kiss me. Most of all I wanted to curl up on the bathroom floor and forget this day ever happened.

"Here," John said and handed me a cool, damp washcloth. "Wipe your face." John's concern for my well-being barely masked his anger. "What did you eat?"

"I think it was the whiskey," I said and took the damp cloth in my trembling hands. I wiped the cold sweat from my face.

"Whiskey? Carrie Ann, you don't drink. I mean

a half a glass of wine gets you tipsy. What were you doing drinking whiskey?"

"Jasper's uncle offered it to me," I said weakly. "He said anyone who found a body at their workplace needed a good stiff drink."

"But you found that body days ago. I've been planning this trip for a while. I wanted to surprise you. I had no idea I'd be walking into this. I think you need to pack up your things and come home."

"What?" I looked at him from my position on the bathroom floor next to the commode.

He squatted down and handed me a glass of cool water. "Drink this slowly."

I took a couple of sips. It soothed my ravaged throat. "Thank you."

"Let's get you showered and in bed," he said with a sigh. "Then we can talk." He took the glass and helped me to my feet.

I stripped as he got the shower warmed up. I stepped in the soothing warmth and let it beat on my body. My thoughts were scattered. I tried not to think about how soft Jasper's mouth was on mine. How nice he smelled, like man and earth and herbs. Why, oh why, had I let him kiss me? And now here was John, just like I'd dreamed about ever since he'd told me he wanted to go on a break as I left for the airport. Hadn't I wanted him to come to London to beg me to be with him again? So why wasn't I feeling overjoyed at his arrival?

I put on my robe and slippers after I finished my shower and went out to the living room to find John sitting at the kitchen island holding a teacup. I didn't want to have this conversation. I wanted to crawl into my bed and close my eyes and pretend my life wasn't a big mess. "Thank you." Leaning against the doorjamb, I was uncertain about moving toward him. "I wish you had told me you were coming. Things could have been so different."

"Come over here and have a seat." He patted the barstool next to him.

I did as he asked and climbed up on the stool. He had a pot of tea waiting and filled my cup. I left it plain because my stomach still wasn't doing so hot. I wrapped my hands around the warm cup.

"I didn't tell you I was coming because it was going to be a surprise," he said. His brown eyes were troubled. "We were together for six years."

"I know," I said.

"And you had this opportunity of a lifetime . . ."

"And you told me to follow my dream," I reminded him. "But you also said you wouldn't move to London and you wouldn't try a long-distance relationship."

"My work is in the states. I love it. I don't want to give it up."

"And now you have this new opportunity in San Francisco." I blew out a long breath. "That's even farther away."

"I know. That's why I decided to surprise you. You see, based on how the next couple of days went, I was going to talk to you about getting married."

The spit in my mouth dried up. "You want to marry me?"

"I realized how crazy it was to be halfway around the world from the woman I want to be my wife."

"You could always come here and work," I pointed out. "There are a lot of restaurants that could use your skills in London. Having a Michelin star here is a great marketing tool when you go back and open your own place in the states."

"I don't know if the venture capitalist will wait a year. He wants me now. You should come to San Francisco with me," he said. "Everyone will want to hire the duke and duchess of Cambridge's personal cook. It would be great publicity for my restaurant."

"I have to be that cook for the duke and duchess first," I said. "I signed a one-year contract. You can't just pack me up and take me home with you." I covered his hand with mine. "I told you this before I signed the contract."

"That was before the review. Before I had this opportunity," he grumbled and pulled his hand away. "Besides, I didn't expect you to be in London kissing gardeners. I expected you to be here missing me."

"I was missing you," I said. "Our phone conversations aren't enough, and you can't have expected me to just sit here and pine for you while I was away after you told me we should take a break. I wanted to try long-distance and you didn't."

"So you kissed another man. Do you want to date other people?"

"I don't know what I want. I didn't expect to kiss him. It wasn't planned. I told you. He ruined my kitchen and took me to dinner to make up for the bad week I had. That was all."

"But I saw you kissing him," John said and ran a hand through his hair. "I can't unsee that. Now I'll always wonder who else you'll be kissing while I'm working in Chicago or San Fran."

"Ugh, this is a bad time for this conversation," I said and closed my eyes. "I'm not completely sober, and I feel like I should be for this talk."

"I agree you should be sober," he said. "But I don't think there's much to talk about. It's pretty clear we're in two different places."

"London and Chicago?"

"No, I'm ready to commit and you're still playing the field."

"I'm not playing anything," I said. "I committed to you years ago, and I was committed to you until you decided you couldn't commit to me. I can't have this argument. I'm sorry I kissed Jasper. It didn't mean anything."

"Are you sorry you kissed him or are you sorry I saw you kiss him?"

My head pounded. My stomach roiled. I put my hand on my forehead. "Both, I think."

He just shook his head angrily. "You look bad. Go to bed. I'll bunk on the couch. We'll talk again in the morning."

"Fine," I said and climbed off the stool, leaving the tea on the counter. "I wish you had told me you were coming."

"So do I," he said and sighed. "Go to bed, Carrie Ann."

There was nothing left to do but climb into bed and hope and pray things would work themselves out in the morning.

Chapter 21

Monday was my first day off. I woke up with a pounding headache and stumbled to the bathroom to get some water and aspirin. I saw my reflection and winced. I didn't want to see myself looking like this. How could I let John see me like this?

Right, John was here. Surprise! The sick feeling that had finally gone away came back with a vengeance. I pulled on my robe and went out to the kitchen to make coffee.

John was gone. There was no evidence that he'd slept on the couch, and his duffle wasn't lying around. He'd cleaned up last night's tea and left a note that read,

> Carrie Ann, I got a return flight this after-noon. If you want to meet me before I go, text me a time and place. ~John

Not even "Love, John." I glanced at the time. It was nearly noon. I don't know if I had any chance at all of meeting him before he left, but I had to try. I grabbed my phone and texted him.

Can we talk? I wrote.

I waited what seemed like forever before I got a text back. *Meet me in Kensington Park in fifteen minutes. I'll be waiting by Peter Pan.*

Fifteen minutes was barely enough time to get dressed and make it there in time. I dropped the coffee-making and rushed to the bathroom where I brushed my teeth, washed my face, pulled my hair up into a messy bun, and put on enough makeup to look alive.

Then I ran to my closet, pulled out a sun dress, tossed it on, jammed my feet into some ballet flats, grabbed my purse, and was out the door with five minutes to spare. Luckily the palace sat at one end of Kensington Gardens and Hyde Park. The two parks together were quite stately. There were plenty of sidewalks and manicured grounds, flowers, bandstands, and twisted trees.

I hurried past security to the area of the park with the Peter Pan statue. I saw John sitting on a bench there. He had his elbows on his knees and his chin in his hands. His duffle rested at his feet.

"John," I said as I approached. My heart pounded in my chest.

He glanced up and stood.

"Thanks for meeting me," I said and stood awkwardly next to the bench.

"Sit down," he said and pointed to the bench.

I sat and clenched my hands together.

"I've done a lot of soul-searching," he said. "I need you as my sous chef, as my partner. It's why I agreed that you should follow your dream and come to London, because it's important for you to expand your cooking experience." He paced in front of me.

"I thought I was making this noble gesture—letting you go to do your thing. I don't know." He tugged on his hair until it stood up.

"You said you were fine with it." I suddenly realized that ever since I'd met John, I had put my dreams on hold. Instead of actively pursuing my career as a personal chef to the stars, I had let myself drift into supporting his dream of becoming star chef. When he said we needed to take a break in our relationship if I wanted to pursue my own goals, I had thought he would come around to my way of thinking. Now I realized he didn't miss me as a person—he missed me as a supporter of his dreams. But I needed someone who would value my dreams as much as their own.

"I somehow thought you wouldn't go through with it. Or that you would get here and miss me and realize that I was more important than some job you've contracted for only a year," he was saying. "But now I don't know what to think."

"You're going to San Francisco," I said.

"And you aren't."

"I can't." If he wasn't going to support my dreams, that meant I had to take care of myself. And I suddenly realized I could do it.

"Even if I got down on one knee and asked

you to marry me?" he asked and pulled out a ring box. "Would you choose this job where people are suspicious of you and you find your assistant dead? Would you choose to stay even if we were engaged? Would you choose your job over me?"

"I signed a contract," I said. Fear shot through me. This was it. This was the moment I'd waited six years for, and I couldn't give John what he wanted, not without sacrificing myself.

"Unsign it," he said. "If you love me, if you want to marry me, go to Mrs. Worth or whoever and give them your notice. Come to San Fran with me."

Tears welled up in my eyes. "John, that's not fair."

He got up and shoved the ring box in his pocket. "Yeah," he sneered, "I figured. Maybe I should have asked you when you got offered the job." He paused and looked at me. "What would your answer have been then, Carrie Ann?"

"This is a once-in-a-lifetime opportunity," I tried to explain.

"So is marrying me."

"I know. I don't think I am ready to marry you, not anymore. I think I really need to figure what I want from a relationship, not just what you want."

"What I want is to get married."

"So that I will support your career my entire lifetime."

259

"Yes, isn't that what marriage is for?"

"No, it's a two-way street. My dreams deserve as much support as yours."

"Being a personal chef is not the same as being a star chef," he pointed out.

"But it's my dream," I said. "Don't you see? I can't give up my dream for you."

"Fine. I've got a plane to catch," he scoffed. "You packed up most of your stuff when you left. Send one of your friends to come put it all in storage. I'm not renewing the rental contract. I've given them thirty days' notice."

"John, I'm sorry it had to end like this."

He gave me an insincere half smile. "Good-bye, Carrie Ann. I hope this life makes you happy."

I swallowed hard. "Good-bye, John. I'll always love you." But I had to follow my heart, and my heart was telling me I belonged in London.

He gave a derisive snort and walked away. I let him go, watching him cross the park to catch a cab.

I sat down on the bench and put my head in my hands. I had made the right decision, but I was still heartbroken. Tears fell. My head hurt from the drinks the night before.

And I was suddenly very mad at Ian Gordon. How dare he arrange for John to visit me in secret? What right did he have to let John into my rooms without telling me?

Anger pushed me to my feet. I stormed toward the palace with one goal in mind: to tell Head of Security Gordon to stay the heck out of my private life.

Perhaps now was not the best time to run into the big man from the kitchen who had threatened Michael for money. Funny how things work out in the weirdest way.

Here I was—angry, heartbroken, and a touch hungover—storming the halls of the palace looking for Ian when . . . *bam!* There he was. The guy who had answers about Mr. Deems and the money he owed.

I had stopped in one of the servants' hallways around the corner from the bank of elevators. He really was quite large. The hallways were small because the palace was old and people had been smaller when it was built. This meant there was little room to get around him. Did I run? Did I hide? Did I say nothing and move on to Ian?

Nope.

"Excuse me," I said and tapped him on his brawny shoulder. He turned to me. He had small brown eyes and a bulbous nose that looked as if it had been broken a time or two. "You work in the main kitchen, right?"

"Yeah, what of it?" he said in the voice I remembered so well.

"I'm Chef Cole. What's your name?"

"Neville." He eyed me suspiciously. I suddenly realized I might be talking to a murderer. Or, at the very least, someone connected to the person who killed Mr. Deems.

"Well, Neville," I said as bravely as I could, "have you seen Chef Butterbottom?"

"Of course. I work for him."

"Right, let me restate the question: do you happen to know where he is at the moment? I need to speak to him."

"Last I knew he was in his office," Neville said. "Are you that American working in the test kitchen?"

"I am."

"I heard you found Mr. Deems's body."

"I did," I said. "Did you know him well?"

"Well enough, I imagine," Neville said. "He liked to play the ponies and such. The man would bet on anything. Got himself twisted up in something is my guess."

I grew brave. "Do you think that's why he was killed?"

"I don't know why he was killed," Neville said. "But you can't squeeze money out of a dead man, now can ya?"

"No," I said as we got onto the elevator together and he pushed the button to the kitchen floor. "I suppose if he did owe anyone money, his death must have left them quite angry."

"I'd say," Neville said and then looked from

the number at the top of the elevator to me. "Not that I would know anything about that, though."

"Of course not," I said. "But if you died and owed a man money, what would he do? Would he hurt your family?"

"Don't rightly know," Neville said and sucked on his front teeth. "I imagine if I had life insurance, he might go to my widow and ask nicely to be repaid."

"And if she didn't repay you?"

He eyed me again. "A debt's a debt," he said. "In the end, everyone has to pay." The elevator dinged and the doors opened. He held them open for me to exit.

"Thanks. Nice talking to you, Neville," I said.

"Same to you, Chef," he said and opened the door to the main kitchen. The hustle and bustle of prepping for tonight's event filled the air. Neville went off to the meat prep station. I figured he was a butcher, just like Mr. Deems.

I went into my kitchen without saying a word to Chef Butterbottom, who glared at me. The test kitchen was quiet. Monday was my day off and that meant it was my staff's day off. The duchess liked to cook for her family, and Mondays and Wednesdays were her favorite days to do so.

I sat down at the counter as the adrenaline of breaking up with John and confronting Neville ran out. I put my forehead on the counter and closed my eyes, waiting for the shaking to stop.

Talking to Ian about my private life would have to be postponed. After I could muster enough energy to make coffee and eat something, I needed to go see Meriam and warn her that she and her boys might be in for a visit from her dead husband's bookie.

All I could do was hope that Mr. Deems had enough insurance to cover his debts and leave his wife and children able to pay the bills.

Chapter 22

It was tea time when I rang the bell at Meriam Deems's home. One of the boys answered.

"Hello," I said. "Is your mother home?"

"Ma!" he shouted over his shoulder. "It's the lady with food."

I felt the heat of a blush rush over my cheeks. I did indeed have a box in my hands that contained oxtail barley soup and homemade bread.

Meriam came to the door. "Chef Cole, please come inside." She wore a blonde wig that was cut in an asymmetrical bob and had on a T-shirt and flowy yoga pants. She wore makeup to cover her missing eyebrows and eye lashes.

I stepped into her hallway and handed her the box of food. "I brought oxtail barley soup and bread. Your mother told me it was your favorite. I understand that eating is important when you are going through chemo. It's all organic, and I took care to wash everything well before I cooked it."

She took the box from me. "You did research on cancer recovery."

"I did a quick Google check," I said. "The preferred palace grocer has a lot of organic vegetables."

"Please come inside the parlor while I put this

in the refrigerator. I'm not terribly hungry today, but I know the boys will love it."

I watched her walk to the kitchen. "Can I help you get tea? I didn't come to make extra work for you."

"It's okay," she said with a dismissive wave. "I had just made a pot to steep. I've got cancer. I'm not a cripple."

Embarrassed by her words, I stepped into the parlor. There were pictures of her and the boys and Frank on every surface. Someone had taken the time to frame each photo.

I picked up one where Frank was holding Meriam and they were laughing in the sunshine.

"That was the day he asked me to marry him," she said. I turned to see her entering with a tray that contained a teapot, two cups and cream and sugar.

"You both look so happy," I said and put the picture down. There were baby pictures of the boys and one where Frank held one boy in each arm and the boys were showing off their muscles. "These are great."

She set the tray down on the coffee table and sat down. I noticed a tinge of gray around her mouth. "I've been going through the photos," she said. "I thought the boys should be surrounded by pictures of their dad."

"Have you seen the digital frames that scroll

through pictures?" I sat down in the small chair across from her.

"Yes, but I don't like that you can only see one photo at a time. This feels better." She waved to all the frames.

"I understand that." I tilted my head. "How are you doing?"

"I'm okay."

"You look amazing," I lied.

She touched her wig self-consciously. "Frank liked me blonde." Shaking her head, she poured the tea. "We both know that I'm looking a little hollow."

I leaned forward. "How are things with you? Are you feeling okay?"

Her expression tightened. "Today was a bad day, but most of the days are good."

"Have you seen or heard from Michael?"

"He's free on bond, but not to leave his home," Meriam said. "He has strict orders not to come near me or the boys. I didn't ask for it but the prosecutor did. As if Michael would hurt us."

"I have to ask, and please forgive me if this is rude, but I overheard two men approach Michael about money. I understand he and your Frank used to bet on the ponies a bit."

"Frank used to have an addiction to gambling," she said. "But he told me years ago that he'd quit cold turkey. He didn't want to endanger me or the boys."

"I see. So it was just Michael placing bets?"

"Yes. Frank said he was worried about Michael. Do you think he got in over his head?"

"Someone did," I said. "Did Frank leave you any insurance?"

"He had a substantial amount of coverage. We both got covered for a million pounds just before I got sick. We wanted to be sure that should anything happen to either of us, the boys would be okay."

"How are the boys doing?"

"They seem to be absorbing it all pretty well."

"Has anyone threatened them?"

"What? No, why would they?"

"No reason," I said, suddenly unsure about going down this avenue with a sick woman. "I just thought that whoever killed Frank is still out there and may want to harm you or your children."

"I never thought of that," she said as distress crossed her face. "Do you think they would? I mean, should I have someone watching the boys' every move?"

"I'm sure they're fine when they are home with you." I tried to pull back my concerns. "But I would ask you and them to be a bit careful out on the street. There is a killer running loose, and I don't think it is Mr. Haregrove."

"I agree," she said and looked suddenly tired. "I told you from the beginning that Michael wouldn't do anything to hurt Frank. They might have had their differences, but they loved each other almost more than Michael loves me."

"Please take extra care," I said. I leaned forward and put my hand on her hand. "I've tired you out, and that wasn't my intention. I'll go now." I stood. "Thank you for the tea. I can see myself out. Just please take extra care of yourself and the boys. Okay?"

"Okay."

I left her home feeling worried. What if what she said was true? What if it was Michael who owed the money and not Frank? That changed things a bit. It could be that Frank called the bookie out and was killed for it.

There was only one way to know for sure. I had to make a visit to Michael Haregrove's home.

Chapter 23

Chef Cole, come in," Michael said when he opened the door and saw me. "How are things in the kitchen?"

"Not so good," I said and stepped into his townhouse. I realized that the floorplan was an exact match for Meriam's home: a small foyer with stairs leading to the rooms above and a hallway that lead to a parlor, a dining area, and a kitchen at the back.

The parlor walls were painted in a neutral blue that was very pale, almost white. It really emphasized the books and leather chairs. Unlike Meriam's home, which was filled with the chaos of children—toys and game equipment scattered about—Michael's home was serene with a dark, masculine look. This time, I realized there was a huge television on the wall above the fire-place.

"What's going on?" Michael asked as he waved me toward one of the oversized chairs. I sat down into a comfortable cloud of leather.

"I didn't come to tell you about my kitchen troubles, I came to ask how you were doing."

"I've managed to stay alive," he said. He shot to his feet. "Oh, can I get you some tea or a beer or something?"

"No, I'm good," I said. "I just came from seeing Meriam."

Michael sat down and his shoulders slumped. "I'm not allowed to see her," he said, "or the boys, until this thing resolves itself."

"What does your lawyer say?"

"He says the case they have is pretty circumstantial. You know I didn't kill Frank."

"Yes," I agreed. "I know. But I do have a question for you."

"What's that?"

"Who is the gambling addict? You or Frank Deems?"

Michael paused for a moment and then ran his hands through his hair and looked at me. "How did you know?"

"I overheard the two guys accost you in the alley the night of the wake. I didn't realize that at least one of them worked in the palace."

"Neville," he muttered. "How'd you find him?"

"By accident. You see, with the repairs to the greenhouse, the family's kitchen has been moved to the test kitchen. I was in the storage room stowing away our serving carts when I heard Neville and another man talking about how death does not get you out of your obligations."

"Frank had an addiction," Michael said and sat back. "He tried to go clean. But the cancer was a stressor, and I discovered about a month ago that he was deep in debt to the local bookie."

"Neville?"

"No, Neville's just the muscle," Michael said. "It's a side gig for him. He has five kids and being a butcher in the palace doesn't always make ends meet."

"So he threatens people as a part-time job?"

"He's a good negotiator," Michael said. "He looks big and scary, so nine times out of ten, he gets people to cough up the money without so much as twisting their arm."

"Meriam tells me that you're the gambler, not Frank."

He scowled. "That is what Frank told her. I went along with it because she's so sick. I didn't have the heart to tell her differently, and now Frank is gone and she's sick and alone with her boys."

"Could the bookie have killed Frank?" I had to ask. "I mean, it seems like the bookie could have been threatening to expose Frank if he didn't pay. They could have fought, and that's how Frank ended up dead."

"It's a good theory," Michael said with a sigh. "But the bookie is strictly a money man. He never gets his hands dirty. He sends out guys like Neville to do the dirty work."

"Neville has access to the kitchen, and he's a butcher. He could very well be the killer."

"Neville has an alibi for that night. His youngest had the croup, and he and his wife were up all night walking the floor with the kid. Besides, everyone knows that Neville might be an enforcer, but he'd never kill a guy. The bookie wants his money. Dead men don't pay out."

"How much did Frank owe?"

"Nearly a quarter of a million," Michael said. "I gave them all my savings, but it was only about five percent of the debt."

"I overheard Neville talking to someone about the fact that Frank had enough insurance to cover the debt and that he had to squeeze it out of his widow."

"That's not good," Michael said. He leaned his elbows on his jean-clad knees and covered his face. "It means the boys and Meriam are in danger."

"That's why I went to visit her today," I said. "To warn her, but then I found out that she truly believes you are the one with the debt. I didn't have enough information to know what the truth was. Now I do."

"They need protection." He stood and paced. "I can't get within a hundred meters of her or the boys until the trial happens." He looked at me, his expression deadly serious. "Things could go very badly very quickly, especially because Meriam doesn't know the truth."

"What can I do?"

"I don't know. I need to think."

"What about the police? Can we go to them?"

"With what? Hearsay that the bookie wants his men to rough up Meriam? I don't think they'll do anything about it."

"But the police need to know that the real killer is out there and that Meriam and the boys are in danger."

"You can go to the inspector all you want," Michael said. "He won't pursue it until something happens. They believe they got their man, and that is that."

"What about Ian Gordon?" I asked.

"What about him?"

"He is head of security at the palace. He must know the rumors about Neville being an enforcer. Maybe he can talk to the man. I know Neville didn't want to lean on the family in the first place."

"I don't know if he'll go for that. You see, his number-one priority is the palace and the family. Our little worker problems are not really his thing."

"Still, I need to talk with him myself." I frowned. "Is it okay if I mention my concerns for Meriam and the boys? He might put a bug in the inspector's ear about it."

"I can't prevent you from talking to him."

Standing, I reached out to him and gave him an awkward hug. "You need to quit protecting Meriam from the truth," I said. "Losing your job and going to jail for life is not worth it. She will find out, sooner or later."

"It sounds like sooner," he said and sighed. "I'll talk to my lawyer."

"Do that." I sighed. "I hired new staff, but one quit already because we are basically working in a closet until the greenhouse is repaired. That means I still have a slot open for you if you want to come back. Proving your innocence opens you back up to work at the palace. Ian promised me that."

"You talked to Gordon on my behalf?"

"I'm sorry if I crossed a boundary, but yes. I told him I suspected you were protecting someone. He told me that even if the charges were dropped, the chances of you working in the palace again were next to none. He said he couldn't have a suspicious person in his palace."

"True."

"But I argued that he couldn't condemn an innocent man," I said. "So he promised that should you be proven innocent, he would consider your application for a position again."

"That was very nice of you," he said. "But when I get out of this pickle, I'm going to concentrate on helping Meriam and the boys."

"That's it then? I can't persuade you any further?"

"No," he said with a flash of a wry smile. "This has made my priorities perfectly clear. Meriam and the boys must come first. I'll need to get a position that takes their well-being into account."

I squeezed his shoulder. "Best of luck," I said. "I'm glad you are going to tell the truth. I promise to keep pushing until we find Mr. Deems's true killer."

"Just don't lose your job in the process," Michael said. "You're a good chef, Carrie Ann. And an even better friend."

Chapter 24

I always thought it would be fun to say I stormed the castle. But in truth, my anger had died down to a quiet simmer by the time I got to Ian's office. I was smart enough to call ahead and make an appointment. I needed time with the man to express all that had happened in the last twenty-four hours.

Mostly, I planned on telling him to butt out of my private life. Not that it mattered, sinc that was in ruins. But in case I ever got one back, I didn't need him meddling in it.

"Hello?" I knocked on his open door.

"Chef Cole, right on time I see." Ian stood for a moment. "Come in. What can I do for you?"

I closed the door behind me and didn't sit down in one of the chairs. "I want to know by what authority you let John into my rooms Sunday night."

"The man wanted to surprise you," Ian said, drawing his eyebrows together in confusion. "I heard you on the phone asking him to come. I saw your disappointment when he said no. So when he called and asked me to surprise you . . ." He shrugged. "You looked like you needed the visit."

"You overstepped. I would have preferred to

have known. I could have met him at the airport."
My tone was sharp and my anger rose at the
memory.

"He said he was going to propose and asked
me to help surprise you," Ian sat down. "How
could I refuse that?" He waved again to the
chairs. "Please sit."

I struggled to keep my righteous anger. I
mean, how could I be mad at a man who looked
like a Greek god and said he was only looking
out for my best interests? "I need to stand right
now," I said. "I need you to understand that I
do not give my permission for you to allow any
'surprise' visitors again. Am I clear?"

"Perfectly."

"Good." I glared at him for a moment.

"Was there something else, Chef Cole?" This
time he raised one eyebrow.

"Yes," I said and finally took the seat he'd been
offering me. How do you go from scolding
someone to asking them for a favor? "I don't
know how to begin."

"You already made your case for privacy," he
said. "I'm not certain what else you have on your
mind." He glanced at his watch. "But I do have
another five minutes scheduled for you."

I took his hint and got straight to the point.
"Fine. I know Neville is a bookie's enforcer."

"I see."

" 'I see'? Is that all you have to say? The

man may know who really killed Mr. Deems."

"He doesn't," Ian said. "I've already discussed the issue with him."

"So let me get this straight. You will let Neville—a hired enforcer—work in the palace, but not Mr. Haregrove? Really?"

Ian crossed his arms. "Neville passed the background checks. His role as an enforcer is mere rumor until he is proven to have done something illegal. As far as I and anyone I've talked to knows, the man has never done more than talk. The talk might be intimidating, but it's all just talk. Mr. Haregrove, on the other hand, has been arrested for suspicion of murder. There is a big difference."

"Mr. Haregrove didn't do it."

"Neither did Neville. Now, if you are done wasting my time . . ."

"So you agree that Mr. Haregrove didn't kill Mr. Deems." I jumped on his words.

He scowled at me. "Let's say I'm not as convinced as the police are that he did it. But I have my own job to do, as do you."

"But I told you they were talking about strong-arming Mrs. Deems by threatening her children. Is there anything you can do to protect them?"

"It's not my job," he said carefully. "You should take your concerns to the inspector."

"I called him, but he didn't answer. I left a message, but I'm not sure he would be willing to help. I thought perhaps you could talk to Neville and get him to back off."

"What do you want me to say to the man? 'I heard a rumor that you were threatening children and I'd advise against it'?"

"Yes," I said and then frowned. "No, I don't think that would do anything at all. Maybe you could tell him that if anything happens to Mrs. Deems or her children, you would see he loses his job here."

"I can't fire people without evidence of misconduct," he said evenly. "Surely you understand that."

I chewed on my bottom lip. "So there's nothing you will do about this."

"There is nothing to do because nothing has happened. Is that understood?"

"Not really."

"I suggest you stick to cooking and let the professionals do their job."

"I know you know Mr. Haregrove didn't do it. Aren't you looking for the real killer?"

"My job is to ensure the safety of all who live and work at the palace. I won't be satisfied until someone is proven guilty." He stood. "Now, Chef Cole, I suggest for the last time, I hope, that you stay out of things that don't concern you."

I stood as well. "I will if you will," I said and sent him a narrow-eyed look.

"Oh yes, trust me, I won't be meddling in your private affairs ever again."

"Thank you," I said sarcastically.

"I've got to go to a meeting," he said as he escorted me out of his office. "I'd suggest you go enjoy the rest of your day off."

I stood in the hallway and watched him walk away. How could I enjoy anything about this day? My sort-of-boyfriend had asked me to marry him and quit my job, both of which I'd refused to do. Then I'd learned that Mr. Deems was a gambling addict and Michael was taking the blame. There was nothing I could do. I mean, John wouldn't listen and so we were over. My heart squeezed at the thought. Michael wouldn't listen and he might go to jail for life. And Ian didn't seem to truly understand how important all this was.

No one seemed to care that I was right about Michael's innocence and my job. Or that the world was falling apart around me. Emotions swamped me and tears stung my eyes. I dashed them away.

What if they were all right? What if everything I had done was just a huge mistake?

I was headed to my room to have a good cry when I ran into Mrs. Perkins just outside the hallway to my rooms.

"Chef Cole," she said, her tone stern. "I need a word with you."

"Right now isn't the best time," I said. I knew my eyes were red and my nose was starting to run from holding back tears of frustration, anger, and sadness. I sniffed.

"It doesn't matter because this is most important," Mrs. Perkins said. "I understand you went to visit Meriam again today."

"I did," I said.

"Stop."

"Stop what?" I asked, confused.

"I must insist that you stop visiting my daughter. You upset her, and she has enough to deal with."

"I did not upset her," I said. "She was tired when I left, but that was all."

"She called me and told me that you told her that her late husband had a gambling problem." Mrs. Perkins's lips were a firm line, and anger flashed from her eyes. "She wants to go over all the finances with me tonight. She's worried."

"She should be worried. Mr. Deems *was* a gambling addict," I said. "Mr. Haregrove is taking the fall for him."

"It's not your place to meddle," Mrs. Perkins said. "I won't have it. I won't have you upsetting my daughter. Not now. Not when she is fighting so many things."

"She has to know," I said. "I overheard men saying that they were going to get the money one way or the other. They know she has an insurance

282

payment coming. I heard them say they were going to threaten her and the boys."

Mrs. Perkins gasped. "You didn't tell her that, did you?"

"No," I said. "I couldn't. Not after she told me that Frank had told her it was Michael with the problem, not him. In case she was right, I had to be absolutely certain before I said anything further."

"Even then, it's not your place to say anything." Mrs. Perkins's eyes flashed.

"I went to see Michael," I said. "He's out on bond, you know."

"Mr. Haregrove has nothing to do with any of this."

"Oh, he does," I said. "He's trying to protect Meriam from knowing about Frank's problem, but he can't. The bookie knows Meriam is getting an insurance settlement. He's going to try to squeeze the money out of her. You have to tell her. Michael tried to pay them off, but he didn't have enough."

"This is family business, and I will take care of it," she said.

"I asked Mr. Gordon to tell the inspector about Frank's gambling problem."

"Oh, you have meddled far beyond reason," Mrs. Perkins said. Her checks flushed red and her eyes flashed. "Frank did not have a gambling problem. I won't have you telling people that my daughter's husband was an addict. It's unseemly and demoralizing."

"I'm trying to save your grandsons," I said.

"My grandsons don't need your help, Chef Cole," Mrs. Perkins said. "Leave my family alone or I will tell Mrs. Worth that you are too busy meddling to do a proper job as the family's cook. Do you understand me?"

"I understand," I said and raised my hands in surrender. "I won't go near your family again. If anything happens to Meriam or the boys, it's on your hands, not mine."

"Good. I'm perfectly capable of taking care of my own," Mrs. Perkins said. "Please see that you take care of yourself before you find your suitcases out on the lawn and a notice of unemployment in your inbox."

She pushed by me with her nose in the air. I slumped against the wall. Mrs. Perkins had a lot of pull with Mrs. Worth. All I needed was to lose my job to make the day a complete bust.

Chapter 25

I heard through the grapevine that you had a surprise visitor yesterday," Penny said the next morning. "Why didn't you tell me?"

"I didn't see you," I said. "It's probably a good thing, since I wasn't having the best day of my life."

She had found me cleaning the dust- and dirt-covered family kitchen. Breakfast had been served, and I'd escaped from the small test kitchen to take my troubles out on the dirt.

"I also heard through the grapevine that you kissed Jasper Fedman," Penny said. She walked over to the greenhouse windows and wiped a small hole clean in order to peer out. "How was that?"

"How would the grapevine know anything? Besides, don't you have something to do for the duchess?" I asked.

"Uh-oh, someone's not happy," Penny said. She grabbed one of the towels I'd brought in to clean with and wiped off one of the kitchen chairs before sitting down. "There are security cameras in the hallways, you know. And I do get a break. It's not all work, work, work here. Now spill. Tell me everything."

"I had a rough couple of days," I said. "Where were you, by the way?"

"I had Sunday off, and yesterday I was working with Mrs. Worth on the duke and duchess's next trip. They have to go to Australia for a few days next week. We've scheduled the tour down to each hour. Then there's outfits and hair and makeup and accessories. We can't have any bad press like the time her skirt kept blowing up at a solemn ceremony in India. Stupid wind. We've weighted down all her hems on her skirts now. They rather clank about her legs, but the press won't have anything to comment on."

"I can't imagine having that kind of pressure to live up to every day," I said as I wrung out the cleaning cloth I'd used and wiped out the inside of one of the cupboards. I'd taken everything out and piled the lot of pots and pans into the dishwashers to ensure they were cleaned. The dirt had gotten into every crevice of the kitchen.

"It's why she likes her few days at home with the kids. She wants to put her hair in a messy bun, wear jeans, and cook dinner for her family like any normal woman."

"I guess it's not easy being a princess. In the United States, we all grow up thinking it would be great. You get to wear wonderful clothes and jewels and have the love of the prince and everyone in the kingdom. There's always a price for our dreams, isn't there?"

"Are you talking about your boyfriend from back home? The one you broke up with?"

"John," I said, and saying his name filled my heart with sadness. "We weren't exactly broken up. We were on a break," I repeated, not for Penny—since I'd already told her—but for myself. "He realized I wasn't happy with the break and thought he'd surprise me."

"How'd he know you weren't happy here?"

"I practically begged him to come visit," I replied. "I know I've only been working here a week, but I wanted him to see firsthand where I was and what I did. I guess I secretly hoped he'd come to London, fall in love with the place, and want to stay near me."

"I take it that didn't happen."

"No." I wiped my forehead on my sleeve and moved on to clean the next cupboard out. "No, he came to ask me to marry him."

"Oh, my gosh!" Penny squealed and jumped up. "Did you say yes? What was the ring like? Was it romantic?" She paused in her excitement for a brief moment. I watched as she thought things through. "Wait. You kissed Jasper."

"John saw me kiss Jasper," I said.

"Oh, that's not good."

"Not one bit," I said and scrubbed harder. "It turns out that while I was hoping John would want to move here, he was hoping that asking me to marry him would make me move back to Chicago and ultimately to San Francisco with him."

"But you have a contract."

"I told him that. He didn't seem to think my dreams and commitments were as important as his own. So we ended things for good." I sighed. "I also told him that I didn't have any intention to kiss Jasper. It just happened. We'd shared dinner and a bottle of scotch. The dinner was Jasper's way of making up for this." I waved my hand at the giant mess that once was my kitchen.

"You don't have to clean this, you know. We have maids to do that."

"It's my kitchen," I said. "I want it cleaned my way."

"You chefs are so odd," Penny said. "If I can get someone else to do the dirty work, I'm all about that. Now, I take it your John has left."

"Yes, almost as soon as he got here," I said.

"You really did have a bad day."

I slumped down onto the countertop. "Right?"

"Poor thing," she said as her phone dinged from a text message coming through. "Oh, boy," she said, looking at the screen.

"What is it?" I asked.

"Mrs. Worth," Penny said and looked up at me with concern. "She wants to know if I've seen you."

"Well, crap," I said. "Why is she texting you and not me?"

"She did text you. Where is your phone?"

I glanced over to the hook where I'd hung

my chef's coat before pulling on an apron to clean. Hopping down off the counter, I went to the door and fished my phone out of the pocket of my coat. There were three texts from Mrs. Worth, all asking me to stop by her office immediately.

"Are you in trouble?" Penny asked as she came up behind me.

"I certainly hope not." I tugged off the dirty apron and rubber gloves I was wearing. I then texted Mrs. Worth that I'd be right up. "Does she only see people when there's trouble? Because this is the first time she's requested to see me immediately."

Penny winced.

That was answer enough for me. "Great." My thoughts turned to the encounter with Mrs. Perkins last night. Had the old bat taken her complaints to Mrs. Worth?

"Maybe the duchess has decided to take you on the tour with them," Penny said as she followed behind me.

"Would she do that?"

"If she wants to take the children, then yes, you would be expected to go wherever they go."

"Let's hope that's the case," I said as we hurried up the stairs to Mrs. Worth's office.

"What else could be the case?" Penny asked.

"I went to see Meriam Deems yesterday and Mrs. Perkins had a fit over it."

"Mrs. Perkins is trouble walking," Penny said. "But you didn't hear that from me."

We reached the offices. "Text me after and let me know if everything is all right," Penny said and then headed down the hallway.

"I will." I did the last button on my chef's coat and double checked that my security badge was on properly before I knocked on Mrs. Worth's door.

"Come in," she said.

I found her sitting at her desk going over something on the computer. "You wished to see me?"

"Yes, come in, Chef Cole, and close the door behind you."

I did as she asked.

"Have a seat."

I sat down in the hard wooden chair across from her desk and waited as she finished typing.

"Now then, where were you? I thought you would be in the kitchen, but Miss Montgomery said you had left."

"I went to the family kitchen to start cleanup," I said. "Mr. Fedman is done with the demolition and appears to be working on the new raised beds."

"I see," she said and studied me. "How are you fitting in?"

"I'm sorry?"

"I wondered if you feel as if you are fitting in yet," she said and got up to come around her desk.

"I know it's been only a week, but this is usually about the time homesickness sets in."

"I'm fine," I said.

She leaned against her desk. "I understand you had a surprise visitor."

I could feel the heat of a blush rush up my cheeks. "Yes, Mr. Gordon didn't inform me that my boyfriend, John, was coming for a visit. I really wish he had."

"I understand that Gordon made a muck of the whole thing. I assume you didn't say yes to your man's proposal?"

More heat of embarrassment made my fingers tingle. I tried not to squirm under her steady gaze. "You know about that?"

"It's why Gordon allowed your John to surprise you. The man insisted that he wanted to propose. Did he?"

"He did," I said.

"Are you planning on leaving us?" she asked and crossed her arms over her chest. Today she wore a white blouse with a pale-blue cardigan and dark-blue knee-length skirt.

"No." I sat up bolt straight. "No, ma'am. This is my dream job. When I signed the contract, I signed the contract. That means I'm staying for as long as you'll have me."

"I see," she said and walked back around her desk to take a seat. "Even though you found a dead man in your kitchen?"

"Assuming people don't turn up dead on the premises on a regular basis," I said and leaned forward. "I'm not afraid of working here if that \ is what you are asking."

"And if we did have a dead person a week?"

I laughed awkwardly. "I think that would be big news, and I would think that Mr. Gordon would lose his job."

"So you're not going to turn in your notice?"

"No, ma'am," I said. "Are you wishing I would?"

"Why would you say that?"

"Because Mrs. Perkins and I had a run-in last night. She said she was going to complain to you that I was a meddling busybody and not doing my job properly."

"I see."

"Am I doing my job properly?"

"I believe that the duchess is happy with the work you have done so far," Mrs. Worth said. "It is why I'm inquiring about your surprise visitor. We aren't ready to give you up to the states yet."

Relief washed through me. At least for now, my job was safe.

She must have seen the look on my face. "Were you truly worried? Well, you mustn't be. I'm sure you'll discover soon enough that we are a bit like family here. We might squabble from time to time, but we take good care of our own. Now you can go."

I got up to leave.

"Oh, and Chef Cole." She stopped me when I was halfway to the door. "Mr. Fedman tells me the new greenhouse will be done in two days. You may return to your kitchen then. I'll have the maids ensure it is clean before your return so you no longer have to worry about that."

"Thank you," I said.

"You're welcome. Do wash up before your return to the kitchen. You have a bit of dirt on your face. Just there." She pointed to her right cheek.

I rubbed my own cheek with my hand. "Thank you again."

"I'm glad you're still with us," she said.

"So am I."

Chapter 26

As it turned out, the children would not be going on the tour with the duke and duchess. The duchess's mother intended to move into the apartment to oversee the children's care while they were away. I was sent a two-week menu. I noticed that there were more desserts with Grandma. I had to smile. My own Grandma Veronica was the same way. While Mom insisted we eat good healthy meals, Grandma made sure we were slipped sweet treats whenever she was around.

Looking back, I think she did it so that we would look forward to her visits even more. I guess grandmas around the world were just as smart.

It was the end of the day, and I was sipping tea in the test kitchen. Phoebe was gone for the day and from the lack of sound coming from outside the door, the main kitchen was also finished.

Considering all the people I'd had run-ins with the last couple of days, Chef Butterbottom had been notably absent. I had heard that he had been gone for a few days attending a seminar in France. I certainly hoped his return would come after I was back in my own kitchen.

With everyone gone, I wondered what it would be like to be in charge of such a large staff and kitchen. I picked up my teacup, tucked my menus under my arm, and stepped out of the test kitchen.

Chef's office was nearly as large as my kitchen. There were files and bookshelves everywhere filled with cookbooks and folders. I picked up a cookbook, sat in his desk chair, and put my feet up. I bet he had to do quite a bit of research for the state dinners. I'm certain he made an effort to serve dishes that wouldn't offend the guests, dishes made with ingredients from the country of origin.

It's what I would do if I were chef of the main kitchen. Of course, he would take the queen's sensibilities into play, as he served her and her son and his wife quite often. I was glad to be in the duke and duchess's kitchen. They were young and progressive enough to take a chance on a chef from Chicago. I had a full year to not disappoint them.

"What are you doing?"

I turned to find Chef Butterbottom scowling at me from underneath a checked cap. He wore a lightweight jacket, a dress shirt, and slacks. In his hand he held the handle of a rolling suitcase.

Well, there it was. He'd caught me sitting in his office chair daydreaming. I jumped up and spilled tea all over his immaculate desk. "Shoot," I said. "I'm so sorry, I thought you were gone for a few days." I rushed into the test kitchen, put my teacup and the menus down, grabbed paper towels, and went back into the office to wipe down the desk.

"Gone or not, this is my office, and the last thing I expect or want is to find you sitting in my chair as if you owned the place."

"Yes, Chef," I said and mopped up the mess I had made. Thankfully there were no papers on the desktop, only a computer monitor, a big blotter, and a cup full of pens, pencils, and wooden spoons. "I just stepped out of my kitchen with my tea. I guess I got to looking at your cookbooks and sat down." I snagged the cookbook I'd taken from the shelf and wiped it dry with a swipe of the cloth.

"What is it you were reading?" he demanded.

I glanced at the book. "*101 Traditional Spring Dishes*," I read.

"Did you find anything of interest?"

"Oh, it's all interesting," I said and tucked the book back into its place on the shelf.

He blustered a bit as he sat down in his chair and gave me a hard glare. "It's said around the world that British food is dull and uninteresting."

"Well, I certainly disagree," I said. "That book was interesting. I think traditional British food has an earthy quality that speaks to the soul."

His beady eyes lit up. "Are you joking?"

"No," I said. "Why would I work here if I didn't believe in traditional food?"

"Why indeed," he said. "You've come from

the States to teach the new royalty to eat fish sticks, chicken nuggets, hotdogs, and French fries."

I laughed out loud. "No, if they want that they can run down to McDonald's or Taco Bell. You have both here in London. I'm interested in serving fresh, wholesome food and traditional fare to the family. I leave recipes for the duchess to try when she wants to cook for her family. It's why they hired me."

"I'm surprised you're still here, what with Deems going toes up in your greenhouse and all the commotion you're making serving three meals and tea to the family six days a week."

"I'm not making a commotion."

"You are in my kitchen," he said and crossed his arms over his chest. "First you cook in my area, then you move lock, stock, and barrel into my test kitchen, and you and your staffers keep coming and going through my office."

"You put us in the test kitchen," I said. "Which, by the way, caused one of my new staffers to quit. We could have done just as well with a corner of your kitchen where we wouldn't have had to go through your office."

"I need every part of my kitchen," he said. His expression was stubborn with a hint of distrust. "My staff and I couldn't have you running around in any of our corners."

"I'm sorry if Mr. Deems's murder was inconvenient for you," I blurted out. "But never fear, Mrs. Worth assured me today that my kitchen will be usable again in two days. My staff and I will soon be out of your hair."

"Good riddance to bad rubbish," he muttered.

"I could say the same about you," I said. "I'm not the one who hired a bookie's enforcer in my kitchen. I would never hire anyone who would threaten the lives of innocent children."

"What are you talking about?"

"Neville, of course," I said. "You pay him so little he has to work part time for a bookie as his enforcer. I overheard him having a conversation with another man about getting Mr. Deems's widow to pay up from the man's life insurance policy. Did you know that Meriam has cancer? This man you hired would threaten a widow with cancer. Shame on him and shame on you for hiring him."

"Neville is an enforcer for a bookie?"

"Oh, don't act like you didn't know. All the palace staff knows. I've been here a week and I know."

"*I* didn't know," he said and pushed back from his desk. "I will have the man fired at once."

That shut me up. "Instead of firing him, why don't you simply give him a raise so that he can quit his part-time gig?"

"Because I have a budget," he said. "Just like you, I have to take into account the cost of fresh foods, sometimes exotic, and always organic. If he can't take care of his family on his salary, then he needs to find another line of work."

I shook my head. "I don't know what to say."

"You already said it," he replied. "I won't have anyone in my kitchens who threatens people, especially widows and orphans. I'll have you know Deems was a good chap and a bit of a friend of mine as well. Sure, we argued occasionally, but I liked the man well enough. If it's true what you say about Neville threatening Meriam, then the man is gone. This discussion is over. Good night."

I headed for the test kitchen and stopped. "Chef Butterbottom?"

"Yes?"

"Why don't you like me?"

"Excuse me?"

I turned to face him. "You haven't had a nice word to say to me since I arrived."

His bluster calmed for a moment. "It's just a bit of friendly competition. I'm not a fan of Americans."

"Yes, believe me, I got that."

"I don't have to like you for either of us to do our jobs well, now do I?"

"No, I suppose you don't."

"Then why ask the question?"

"Why indeed," I said and turned back to the test kitchen.

As I pushed the door open he said, "For the record, you're not too bad for an American."

"Gee, thanks," I said and went into the test kitchen, grabbed my menus, then went back out through the office without saying another word to Butterbottom. Friendly competition indeed. That man could get me worked up quickly.

At least he took my worries about Neville to heart. I had half wished it was Butterbottom who had killed Mr. Deems. That would not only clear Michael's name but also remove the ornery man from my life. But it was clear he was off my suspect list given his friendship with Mr. Deems. Unlike Ian, Butterbottom was willing to fire a suspicious man working in his kitchen.

All I had to do was hope that Neville didn't learn that I was the one to turn him in. The last thing I needed was a large, angry man knocking down my door.

Two days later, we were finally back in the family's kitchen. Although it was smaller than the main kitchen by a fourth, compared to the test kitchen there was so much space I finally felt like Phoebe and I could breathe a sigh of relief. There would be no more stepping on each other's toes.

I personally felt more in control. The maids had come as promised and cleaned out each cupboard, nook, and cranny. All the dishes were spotless and the pots and pans shone from a good scrubbing. The windows to the greenhouse were washed, and for the first time I noticed they were actually tinted green.

Checking to ensure the door was bolted from my side, I noted that the greenhouse was also put back together. The long rows of beds were waist-high and the dirt was bare but softly wetted by sprinklers. I imagined that seeds were already nestled in the dark, loamy earth and would soon sprout new vegetables for my use.

Not that I minded getting fresh deliveries each day from the grocer, but it would be nice to simply go into the greenhouse and pick the ripe vegetables and nip the herbs and greens.

"What's on the menu for today?" Phoebe asked as she arrived. She took a clean apron off the hook by the door and pulled it over her head, wrapping the strings around her waist twice and tying them tight.

"We are going to start with eggs benedict, fruit slices, sweetbreads, and Canadian bacon. Drinks are milk, tea, coffee, and freshly juiced oranges. For dinner we'll make creamed chicken with morels and bacon. Jasper brought me a handful of the mushrooms this morning."

"Sounds fabulous," she said.

"You can start on the breads," I said. "I'm working on the rest."

She got out a mixing bowl, along with flour,

sugar, and yeast. She glanced at me as I stewed the sweetbreads. "So are you and Jasper a thing now?"

"What? Why would you ask that?"

"The mushrooms." She pointed toward the basket. "Morels take some hunting down."

"We're friends," I said as I gathered the ingredients for Hollandaise sauce.

"More than friends from what I heard," she said at a barely audible level.

"What did you hear?" I put my hands on my hips and raised an eyebrow.

She shrugged. "The usual gossip. It seems that someone saw you kissing in the hallway. I thought you had a boyfriend at home. Not that I'm meddling." She raised both hands in a weak protest of innocence.

"Jasper took me to dinner," I said. "That's all. It was very innocent." I tried not to think about the kiss that had ended my long-term relationship for good. Jasper hadn't mentioned it since that night, and I was rather relieved. Pretending it didn't happen was for the best.

Phoebe let out an inelegant snort. "Nothing about Jasper Fedman is innocent. That man has women swooning at his feet wherever he goes."

I had a sudden picture of Gaston from *Beauty and the Beast*. It made me chuckle. "However true that might be, I'm not swooning."

My phone vibrated in my pocket, and I pulled

it out. It was Ian. Strange for him to call me. My heartbeat sped up. "I've got to take this. Keep an eye on the sweetbreads." I pushed the button on my phone and pulled it toward my ear. "Hello?"

"Hello, Carrie Ann," he said, his tone sincere. "Do you have a moment?"

I walked out into the hallway for some measure of privacy. "Sure, what's up?"

"That's a very odd statement," he said. "It sounds like a cartoon. You know, with the rabbit."

"Bugs Bunny?" I asked.

"Yes, it's a strange saying, don't you think?"

"Why did you call, Ian?" There was an awkward silence for a moment.

"I wanted to apologize for not telling you that John was planning to arrive."

"What?"

"You were correct. I should have let you know he was going to be here."

"Oh," I said. "Thank you."

"Also, due to your recent single status, you need to know that the rules have changed."

"What rules?"

"Males are no longer permitted in your wing, no exceptions. Any further visitors of any gender will be restricted to lobbies and visitor areas. If you have any overnight guests, you must find accommodations outside of the palace."

"It's kind of odd that you make this rule after you allow my ex to surprise me."

303

The hallway I was in was narrow and dreary with dark wood floors and walls painted beige. It was built for a different time, when I supposed people were smaller. And it definitely wasn't ideal for talking on cell phones. I felt as if my words echoed along the hall and into people's rooms.

I moved down the hallway to the door that led out to the parking area on the other side of the greenhouse. "Really, Ian, why change things now?"

I waited for his reply as I stepped out into the early morning gray of spring.

"I was wrong," he said finally. "I admit that, and to prevent future misunderstandings, I am enforcing a rule that I should have kept to in the first place."

"I know," I said. "But now everyone on staff will blame me for the crackdown on their private lives."

"I hardly think you are so important as to take the blame for a new policy put into place by security due to recent events."

"Fine," I said, feeling insulted. "I get it. I'm not important and therefore have nothing to fear from gossips. That doesn't mean they won't know I was the last one to have a guest stay in my quarters overnight."

"Carrie Ann—"

"Don't use that scolding tone with me," I said.

"I'm not the one who screwed up. So I get it. No more guests. End of conversation."

There was a long silence.

"I'll be posting the new policy on the staff intranet."

"Fine," I said.

"Good," he replied.

I listened to him breathe for a moment. Then I said, "Is that all?"

"Yes."

"Okay." I hung up my phone. Feelings of anger and frustration filled me. I wanted to throw my phone against the brick wall beside me. I wanted to kick things. I wanted to let out the anger and grief that filled me. My tears flowed freely. I leaned against the brick and looked up, doing my best to get ahold of myself.

That's when I noticed Mrs. Perkins going into a door on the other side of the greenhouse. I didn't realize that there was anything over there. Seeking distraction from my feelings, I walked over to see a covered walkway between the greenhouse and the neighboring portion of the palace building.

What did that door go to? I walked over and tried to open the door. It was locked. I tried to swipe my ID but nothing happened. *Curious*. I dashed away my tears and looked up to see that there were offices of some sort on the floor above the walkway. I didn't have a good lay of the palace yet. I don't know why I had assumed that the greenhouse ended with the parking lot.

Turning around, I reentered the building through the hallway door that I had left from. I took a moment to blow my nose and wipe my face before entering my kitchen.

"Is everything all right?" Phoebe asked.

"Yes, fine," I said and set about making my eggs benedict.

"I'm going to pretend that I believe you," Phoebe said as she kneaded bread dough. "It is nice to be back in a real kitchen. Don't you think?"

I could tell she was trying to distract me, so I went along with her. "It will be better once the greenhouse is lush again," I said. "Jasper agreed to grow the herbs on my list as well as those on the duchess's list."

"Nothing better than fresh," Phoebe said.

The kitchen door opened and Miss Jones came in pushing our serving trolleys. "I thought you might need these." She paused and studied me. "Is everything all right?"

"I'm fine," I snapped.

"Whoa, I didn't mean any offense."

"None taken," I said and sighed. The breakfast was ready. "Load up the tray and deliver it, quickly," I instructed them both. "We want to show our gratitude for having our space back."

"Yes, Chef," they both said, and soon they were

out the door with the proper dishes well-covered for transport to the family's dining room.

I looked out into the greenhouse. It was quite large really, about ten feet by fifteen feet. I suppose I'd never noticed the walkway on the other side because I'd always been busy looking at the veggies. Or the handsome gardener, if I was going to be honest about it.

I sent a text to Penny: *What offices are on the other side of the greenhouse? And who has access to them?*

I waited for her answer. Hopefully she could give me some insight. It seemed that whoever killed Mr. Deems that night might have come from that part of the palace. It was the only way I could think of that would bypass my kitchen. It would give the killer the element of surprise.

With the parking area so close, it might have been just as easy for someone like the bookie to slip into the greenhouse, kill Mr. Deems, and slip out. Except, of course, no one out of the ordinary could get through the locked doors. Plus, the parking areas all had cameras. Surely Ian would have said something if he'd caught someone suspicious on camera that night. I chewed on my bottom lip and started to make the tea cakes for the children for later that afternoon.

I was still convinced that whoever killed my assistant was a regular at the palace. If not Neville, then who—and why?

Chapter 27

It was well after dinner and Phoebe had gone home before Penny answered my text.

The administration offices are across from the greenhouse, she wrote. *You've been there. You should know.*

I texted back: *I take the second floor hallway, and so I walk through the breezeway. I had no idea the greenhouse was under that. I'm still trying to figure out where everything is.*

Ask Ian for a map of the place, she wrote back. *It will help.*

After I wrote her back *Thanks, but I have a map. I simply didn't put it together,* I put my phone down and poured myself a cup of tea. This was my favorite time of night in the kitchen. It was dark out, so the greenhouse was a black blur of shadow. A soft light crept in through the window above the sink that looked out onto the parking area. The kitchen was thoroughly cleaned and smelled of the ginger cake I'd made for dessert.

A small slice of the cake and a cup of tea would ease me into the end of the day. The door to the greenhouse was still bolted. I was safe from any would-be killers.

I had menus pulled up on my tablet and was

Googling recipes when my mind wandered to John. I needed to lay to rest any lingering feelings for him. We were going in two very different directions.

There was a small hope in my heart that I would stay with the family much longer than my one-year contract. But I had to get through my first ninety days without another incident.

"You're in the kitchen late."

I was startled by Mrs. Perkins's arrival.

"I didn't hear you come in," I said with a nervous laugh. "I'm going to have to put a squeak in the door or something."

She was wearing a smock over her usual sweater set. It was thick and white like a butcher's smock. She had a strange look in her eyes, and the hairs on the back of my neck stood on end.

"Do you need some food for Meriam and the boys?" I asked and stood slowly so as not to upset her. "I have some extra creamed chicken, and Phoebe made dinner rolls. I can put them in Tupperware for you to take home."

"Because of you, Meriam found out about Frank's gambling problem. My poor girl has been devastated yet again. She's taken to her bed. She won't eat. She won't drink."

"I'm so sorry," I said. "But she had to know that she and her boys were being threatened."

"She didn't have to know anything. I was taking care of things. I was taking care of my baby." She raised her right hand and showed me the butcher knife she held. "I refuse to let anything or anybody hurt my baby girl."

I held up my hands and took two steps so that the table was between us. Everything suddenly fell into place. "You killed Frank, didn't you?"

"I could not stand by and watch him devastate her further." She shook her head. "He owed so much money. Too much money. I begged him to stop. I gave him money to pay off his debt and stop gambling."

"But he was an addict and couldn't stop, could he?" I said and slowly reached into my pocket. I hit the send button on my phone twice. It would dial the last person I spoke to—in this case, Ian Gordon. There was no chance he'd pick up after the way our conversation ended, but his voicemail would. The sound might be garbled from the phone being in my pocket, but if Ian didn't pick up and anything happened to me, the voicemail recording should tell the authorities the who and why.

"Instead of paying off the debt, he used it try to win more and put himself even farther behind," she snarled.

"That's when you decided something had to be done."

"He was putting the entire family at risk," she said. "I came here that night to tell him he had to get his stuff and get out of my daughter's house."

"You fought with Frank, didn't you, Mrs. Perkins?" I said. "You didn't mean to kill him."

"He laughed at me. Laughed! Then he told me that I was the intruder in *his* home. If anyone was to leave, it would be me!"

"That must have hurt," I said. "I know how you gave up everything and moved in with Meriam and the boys to take care of them through this health crisis."

"He underestimated me if he thought I would let him push my baby girl into an early grave. He had life insurance on her. He was gambling that the cancer would take her, and he could pay off his bills with her insurance. But Meriam is a fighter."

"He was desperate," I said.

"He should have done what I asked. He should have packed up and left immediately. None of this would have happened if he had just done what I asked."

She looked distracted by the thought, and I took that moment to grab a cast-iron skillet from the pot hanger over the stove top. "Put the knife down, Mrs. Perkins," I said in my best demanding-chef voice. "I don't want to hurt you."

"Oh, no dear," she said, her attention suddenly and terrifyingly back on me. "I won't. You see, I've nothing left to lose. You devastated my baby. She may die. I can't let you live knowing what you've done."

"But I didn't do anything!" I said and kept the skillet raised. It was heavy enough to deflect the knife, and I could use it to knock her sideways if I had to. "All I did was tell her to take care of herself and the boys."

"You asked her about the gambling."

"She said it was Michael who had the problem, and I let her believe that."

"You asked her if she was certain," Mrs. Perkins said and took a menacing step toward me. "That was enough. My Meriam is no dummy. She didn't have to look far to find out how much Michael owed. Now she hasn't eaten all day and is worrying about the finances. You must pay for what you did."

"Mrs. Perkins," I said. "Put the knife down. I don't want to have to hurt you."

"I'm not worried about being hurt," she said and lunged toward me.

I swiped the skillet through the air and caught her wrist, knocking the knife to the floor. The crazy woman was between me and the door. Behind me was the greenhouse, but the door was bolted. There was no easy escape.

She screeched and jumped at me with her bare hands extended. I used the pan again and this time aimed at her shoulder. I purposely didn't aim for her head. She was old. She was crazy. I didn't want to kill her.

The pan knocked her toward the sink, giving

me room to get around her. I rushed to the door, but as I reached for the handle, the door opened and I fell headfirst into the solid form of a man.

Mrs. Perkins made a terrifying sound behind| me and grabbed my hair, snapping my head back as she clawed and yanked. Tears filled my eyes.

"Drop the pan!" Ian ordered.

I did what he said, letting it fall to the floor in a clatter. I used my hands to fight off the witch that tried to dig my eyes out. Suddenly she was lifted away from me. Ian held her around the waist as she struggled against him, kicking and screaming bloody murder.

"Stop!" he shouted, giving her a solid shake. She went limp for a moment. We were all breathing hard. Adrenaline had me rushing back toward the door. "I said stop," Ian growled, and I stopped just outside the kitchen door. "What is going on here?"

"See that knife?" I pointed toward the large butcher knife on the floor. "She tried to kill me. So if you don't mind, I'm not going to stick around."

"Don't you dare move," he said. "What do you mean she tried to kill you?"

"I could never hurt anyone." Mrs. Perkins became strangely docile. "That poor girl is deranged. She attacked me with the frying pan."

"Only after she lunged at me with the knife!"

"Enough!" Ian said. He set Mrs. Perkins down.

"Don't let go of her," I warned. It was too late. The moment he let go, she lurched for the knife,

313

picked it up, and swiped a long and terrible arc toward Ian's gut.

Now I have to admit that I'm not all that brave. He was a big guy, and she was a murderer. I figured getting the heck out of Dodge and calling the cops was my best play.

I ran into the hall and dialed the palace equivalent of 9-1-1.

"Mrs. Perkins is trying to kill Ian Gordon with a knife in the family kitchen," I said in a weird parody of the game Clue.

"Help is on the way," said the operator's voice. "Are you okay?"

I slumped down to the ground and hugged my knees. "I will be," I half-whispered.

The sound of footsteps pounding down the stairs filled my ears, and four men rushed the hallway. "Where?" the first man barked.

I pointed toward the kitchen.

They burst through, and I could see that Ian had Mrs. Perkins subdued.

"He's all right," I said to the operator. I hung up the phone and stared at the kitchen door. The security men came out as Ian pulled Mrs. Perkins out. Her arms were cuffed behind her.

"Are you all right?" one of the security team asked.

"I think so," I said and hugged my waist. "Shook up."

"My name is Alfred, and I'm going to walk you

to your room and sit with you a while. Emerson will stand guard at your door." He pointed to a large red-headed man in a security uniform standing outside the kitchen door.

"Are you here to keep me in or the bad guys out?"

"Whichever we have to do," Alfred said. "Come on, up you go."

He got me to my feet, and I found that I was shaky from adrenaline. The walk to my room took what seemed like an hour. He opened my door with a master key, and we waited while Emerson checked the room.

"All clear," he said and came out to stand by my door.

"Come on, let's put you on your couch. You seem to be a bit in shock." Alfred took my right elbow in his hand and guided me to my couch. When I sat, he elevated my feet and covered me with the thick silver throw I had bought for my couch on my way back to the palace one day.

"Thank you," I said.

"I'm going to make you tea," he said and went to my tiny kitchenette. He filled the tea kettle and put it on to boil. He unwrapped an individual Earl Gray tea bag and poured hot water into the cup. "Do you take cream or sugar?"

"Plain is fine," I said and took the cup from him. A sip of the warm brew soothed my throat. "Is Ian all right?"

"Gordon? Yes, he can hold his own with the ladies," Alfred said with a wink. "Now hush and enjoy your tea. I've been given instructions to keep you quiet until the inspector gets here."

"What about Mrs. Perkins?"

"She'll be taken away to hospital," he said. "She's . . . not quite herself. Now no more talk from you. Sip your tea and try to relax."

He went on to chatter about his dog and the recent trip he took to the beach with the retriever and how the dog loved the water and dragged back his body weight in sand and seaweed.

There was a knock at the door. I looked up to see Ian and Inspector Garrote outside. I was relieved to see Ian all in one piece. Inspector Garrote's eyes were hidden behind thick horn-rimmed glasses. It was hard to tell what he was thinking.

"Chef Cole," he addressed me as he came inside. "No, no, don't get up." He waved me down when I moved to stand. He took the wingback chair across the coffee table from me, opened his little notebook, and clicked his ballpoint pen. "Why don't you tell me what happened?"

"I was in the kitchen after hours. I like to take tea and enjoy the quiet after a long day. Mrs. Perkins appeared. She startled me, actually. I didn't know she was there until she said something."

"Mrs. Perkins entered the kitchen."

"Yes," I said, my gaze going to Ian's. "She wore

that butcher's smock and had her hands behind her back."

"Why did she come to the kitchen?"

"I believe she meant to kill me like she killed Mr. Deems," I said.

"That's a large accusation," Inspector Garrote said. "Do you have any evidence to prove it?"

"Besides the big butcher knife she had?" I asked. Sarcasm was a defense mechanism for me. "Actually, yes," I said, suddenly remembering my phone. "When she started blaming me for Meriam's downturn in health, I hit redial on my phone. My phone should have called Ian's."

"You did?" Ian asked, and he pulled his phone out of his pocket to access his missed calls and voicemail.

As I suspected, the sound was a little garbled, but you could make out most of the words—Mrs. Perkins admitting to murdering Mr. Deems and her desire to be rid of me because I had talked to Meriam. When the sound of the fight began, I covered my ears and closed my eyes. I was not ready to relive that.

After a few minutes, Inspector Garrote touched my shoulder. I opened my eyes and took my hands away from my ears. "It's over," he said gently. "You acted quickly in calling Gordon."

"I thought if she was going to kill me, I wanted someone else to know who did it. She was deranged."

"Good thinking," Ian said from where he stood next to the small breakfast bar. His arms were crossed over his chest.

"What made you come in?" I asked him.

"I was making my rounds and heard the scuffle," he said. "I saw you swing that pan at her and thought I'd better step in."

"You didn't know, did you?"

"Know what?"

"That Mrs. Perkins was bent on killing me. That she had killed Mr. Deems."

"No," Ian said. "I didn't suspect."

"She had access to the greenhouse," I said. "She parks her car very close to it. She must have come in unnoticed, killed Mr. Deems, and went out and back to her car without anyone being the wiser. I mean, if you saw her on the parking video, you would simply think she was going into her offices."

"Exactly," Inspector Garrote said. "Although, Mr. Gordon did put Mrs. Perkins on the suspect list."

"Then why did you settle on Michael?"

"Mrs. Perkins wasn't as strong a candidate as Mr. Haregrove," he said. "A jury would take one look at her and assume she was innocent."

"I think that's what she was counting on," I said. "But the stress of her daughter going through cancer and her son-in-law gambling away any money the family had was too much for her. She snapped." I looked at Ian. "You saw her. She looked insane. I don't think she was faking."

"I agree," he said with a scowl. "Luckily I was able to subdue her. The medics came and gave her a sedative, and they took her off."

"Will she go to jail?" I asked.

"Most likely, although I would vote that they keep her in a ward for the criminally insane," Inspector Garrote said. "Not that she didn't know what she was about, but her reason is clearly off. Now, if you don't mind, I would like to take both of your phones into evidence. We can remove the recording and clean it up."

"Yes, of course," I said and handed the inspector my phone, and Ian did the same.

"You were very smart to make the call since there are no cameras in the kitchen," the inspector said. "Without this voicemail, I would only have your word against hers. Mr. Gordon didn't see enough to determine who was actually at fault."

"Clearly she assaulted me and then Ian," I said.

"With the recording, yes, it is clear," the inspector said. "Without it, I would need to have an in-depth investigation. As far as we can tell, Mrs. Perkins is the only injured party."

"What?"

"She has bruises from where you hit her wrist and shoulder with a frying pan," he said and gave me a steely look. "You did hit her with the frying pan, correct?"

"Yes," I said, "but only after she came at me with a butcher knife. I didn't try to hit her in the head. I only wanted to delay her so that I could get away."

"I can attest to that," Ian said. "When I arrived, Chef Cole was running out the door. Mrs. Perkins leapt on her from behind and dragged her back to the kitchen by her hair. It was clear that Mrs. Perkins was the one committing assault."

"Assault?" I said, my voice rising. "She was trying to kill me! I was only defending myself."

"You seem a little hysterical," the inspector said. "I imagine it's been quite the night."

"I'm not hysterical," I protested, but the rise in my voice made me seem that way. I stopped, took a deep breath, and blew it out slowly. "Mrs. Perkins tried to kill me for the same reason she killed Mr. Deems. She thought she was protecting her child."

"Why would Mrs. Perkins feel that you are a threat to Meriam Deems?" the inspector asked.

"Because I overheard two thugs saying they were going to squeeze the widow to get the insurance money. You see, Mr. Deems had a gambling problem. He had told Meriam that he kicked it, but her cancer was a stressor that made him go back into that world. He owes his bookie a quarter of a million pounds. Mrs. Perkins killed Mr. Deems to prevent him from putting her daughter and grandchildren deeper in debt."

"What you're saying is that Mrs. Deems didn't know her husband was gambling again."

"That's right. She thought it was Mr. Haregrove who had the gambling addiction."

"And you told her the truth? How did you find out?"

"I told you, I overheard the thugs talking. Then I spoke to Neville from the main kitchen, and he told me it was Mr. Deems with the problem. I went to Mrs. Deems to warn her that she and her boys could be in trouble."

"Mrs. Perkins saw that warning as a threat?"

"Yes. You see, she was trying to keep the news of the debt from her daughter. I spilled the beans thinking I was saving Meriam from the thugs. Mrs. Perkins said that now Meriam isn't eating or drinking anything. With her cancer and chemo treatments, she has to keep her strength up."

"And that made you a threat to her daughter," Inspector Garrote said as he wrote notes.

"In her mind, yes," I said. "So she came to do to me what she did to Mr. Deems."

"That's insane," Ian said.

I looked at him with tears in my eyes. "Yes, it is."

"Like I said, it's a good thing you recorded the conversation," the inspector said. He placed my phone in a clear evidence baggie. "Now, you've been through enough for one night." He rose and handed me his card. "Contact me if you remember anything else."

"Okay," I said and slumped into the couch.

"We may need to speak again," the inspector said. "But I suspect what I need is pretty much on this recording."

"What about Mr. Haregrove?" I asked.

"I'll see his lawyer gets a copy of the voice-mail. Then he can put forth a motion to dismiss, and Mr. Haregrove will be free."

"Good," I said. "I'm glad to see justice done."

"Good night, Chef Cole," Inspector Garrote said. "Let's hope I don't see you in any further adventures."

I gave him a short half smile. "I most certainly hope you don't."

Ian walked the inspector out. Alfred and the other guards still stood in the hallway. I clung to my cup of tea and tried not to let the shivers overtake me. There was a knock at the door and I looked up to see Jasper.

"I heard what happened," he said. "Are you okay?"

I sent him a small smile. "I'll be okay."

"Can I come in? I mean, I know I might be on your bad side."

"What do you mean?" I asked and then noticed he waited by the door. "Yes, come in."

"Penny told me that you sent your ex-boyfriend packing. I hope it wasn't because of me," he said and tried to look comfortable as he sat in the flowered chair across from me. Unlike the inspector, who looked at home in the chair, Jasper was muscular enough that he looked like he was wearing it. "I'm sorry. I shouldn't have taken advantage of you like that."

"It was just a kiss," I said and clung to my teacup. "I was a willing participant. Besides, it's not what really broke us up, so you're off the hook."

"I didn't come here to get off the hook, as you say. I came to see if you were all right."

"I will be," I said. "John wanted me to quit this job and go to San Francisco with him."

"And you didn't?"

"It was his dream or mine," I said. "I chose mine."

Jasper leaned toward me. "Smart girl."

I rubbed my eyes. "I don't feel smart right now."

He reached over and patted my knee. "You are, and I admire you for it." There was a knock on the door and Ian stood in the doorway. "I'd better go," Jasper said. "Take care."

"Thank you," I said.

The two men eyed one another as Jasper left and Ian came inside and closed my door. "Are you all right?"

"I'm shaken but not hurt. How about you? I saw her swipe that knife at you," I said.

"I managed to get it away from her pretty easily."

"I don't know how she killed Mr. Deems," I said. "It had to be a surprise attack or he would have fended her off as easily as you did."

"Yes, I imagine she got him from behind," Ian

323

said and leaned against the kitchenette counter. "We'll go over the video from the parking area that night. I remember seeing Mrs. Perkins walk to and from her car, but that is nothing out of the ordinary because she usually enters her workplace through the door on the other side of the greenhouse."

We were both silent, lost in our thoughts for a moment. Finally, I broke the ice. "Thank you for saving me," I said.

"I think you pretty much saved yourself," he answered. "Smart thinking on the frying pan."

"My mind went to the need for a shield. I saw the pan and thought it might be heavy enough to deflect the knife. I really didn't want to hurt her."

"Also, smart thinking to call me. It's lucky I didn't hear the phone ringing and the whole incident was recorded on voicemail."

"I hope it's useful for the inspector." I glanced up at Ian. "I told you Mr. Haregrove was innocent."

"I know," he said. "As promised, I'll give him another chance to work at the palace."

"He won't come back." I hugged my knees. "He told me that he wanted to get a less stressful job so that he can take care of Meriam and the boys."

"What about the debt?" Ian asked.

"There was enough life insurance for Meriam to pay off the debt and still live comfortably."

"I see." Ian sat back. "Listen, I wanted to apologize again for mucking up your personal life."

I put my cheek on my knees and looked at him.

"You're forgiven. I suppose you were only trying to do a nice thing. You didn't know it would end a six-year relationship."

Ian winced. "He didn't get up the nerve to ask you?"

"Oh, he asked, but I said no. He wanted me to quit this job and to move to San Francisco with him. I wanted him to quit his job and move to London with me."

"You are going in opposite directions."

"Yes," I closed my eyes for a second. "We are. It's over."

"Right," Ian said and straightened. "Sorry."

I motioned toward the chair. "Don't go," I said, knowing I sounded pathetic. "Please. I'm afraid."

"All right," he said. "Go take a hot shower. I'll tuck you in bed, and we'll see how you feel after that. Okay?"

"Thanks."

"You're welcome. Now," he pointed to the bathroom, "go take that shower. Trust me, your muscles need the heat to relax."

"Have some tea." I nodded toward the teapot on the kitchen counter. "Your muscles have to be just as full of adrenaline as mine. It's not every day someone tries to kill you with a knife."

"I'll make tea," he agreed.

"Thank you, Ian. I appreciate all you did." I closed my bedroom door behind me, grabbed my robe, and headed toward the shower.

Chapter 28

Right after breakfast the next morning, I was called into Mrs. Worth's office. I went there straight away, leaving Phoebe to make the cookies for tea. Lunch was to be organic tomato soup and little man-shaped cheese toasts.

Mrs. Perkins's desk was empty when I arrived, so I knocked on Mrs. Worth's office door.

"Come in," she said through the closed door. "Ah, Chef Cole," she said once I entered. "Thank you for coming."

"You're welcome," I replied and stood with my hands behind my back.

"Please sit," she said and folded her hands on the desk in front of her. "I understand you've been through quite an ordeal."

"Yes," I said simply. I was tired of telling the story.

"I would have never thought Mrs. Perkins was capable of such a thing. I've known her for thirty years."

"She thought she was protecting her daughter," I said. "The inspector said that she may be put in the hospital for the criminally insane."

"Well, it certainly has been a terrible two weeks." She put her elbows on her desk, rested her chin in her hands, and studied me. "Are you all right?"

"I'm okay," I said.

"I'm glad to hear that. The duchess has made it clear that she's very happy with the meals you've prepared for her and the family. I'm also going to ask you personally to stay. I think you are a good influence on the staff. If you need a few days off, let me know. We can work it out."

"I'm fine," I said. I had a few bruises from my encounter with Mrs. Perkins, but for the most part, I was unharmed. "I'd rather keep working if that's okay."

"That's certainly all right," she said. "The duchess wants to see you. Do you have a moment?"

"Sure," I said and stood. Who turns down an audience with the duchess of Cambridge?

Mrs. Worth stood as well. "Good. Come with me. She's waiting."

I followed Mrs. Worth back through the servants' hallway to the office where I'd first seen the duchess. Mrs. Worth gave a short knock.

Penny opened the door. "Hello," she said with a welcoming smile. Then she turned to the duchess, who sat at her desk perusing paperwork. The children played quietly in the sunlight from the large windows that lined one wall. This time there was only one nanny in attendance. I assumed that meant the duchess planned to play with her children as soon as her duties were done. "It's Mrs. Worth and Chef Cole," Penny announced.

The duchess looked up. Her smile filled the room. Even though she was clearly home for the day—her hair was in a messy bun, her makeup was minimal, and she wore a striped boat-neck T-shirt and dark jeans—she still looked radiant. "Hello, come in. I promise I won't take but a moment of your time."

Mrs. Worth stepped forward, and I caught myself before I curtsied. We walked up to the elegantly appointed desk. "I brought Chef Cole, as you requested," Mrs. Worth said.

"Right," the duchess said. "Please, Chef Cole, have a seat."

I sat down.

"I realize that I haven't had the time to get to know you and to really welcome you to the family," the duchess said. "I try to keep things as normal as possible for the children, but sometimes duties overwhelm."

"I understand."

She placed her folded hands on the top of her desk. "First of all, your meals have been spot-on. I want to thank you for creating such wonderful dishes. As you know, we like to be as careful as possible with the budget. My husband's father believed in using what is available to us, and we agree with and want to continue that tradition. So thank you for adhering to those standards."

I nodded. "You're welcome. I'm glad the food has been satisfactory."

"I also understand that things in the kitchens have been a bit extraordinary lately. Security Chief Gordon has informed me that you have been holding your own through a terrible time. And Mrs. Worth tells me you have been flexible while the facility was cleaned and renovated. For that, I would also like to thank you. It can't be easy being so far from home and thrown not only into the royal palace but into the scene of . . ." She glanced at her children. "Unusual affairs. I wanted to personally thank you and let you know that your dedication has not gone unnoticed. Mrs. Worth tells me that despite all that has happened, you are staying with us for the next year. With all the comings and goings on in our life, it is good for the children to have as much stability as possible."

"Yes, ma'am," I said.

She flashed me a quick smile. "Now I want you to know that you can come to Mrs. Worth or myself with any questions or concerns. My husband and I like everyone to be one big happy family here. Let's hope the last two weeks have been a once-in-a-lifetime event. I've tasked Security Chief Gordon with ensuring that is the case."

"Thank you," I said.

"Do you have any questions for me?"

"No, ma'am," I said.

"Wonderful. I've sent menus for the next two weeks while I'm off on tour. Are they agreeable to you?"

"Yes, ma'am."

"Great. Thank you, Chef Cole, for solving a difficult problem in the kitchen and for continuing to remain loyal to the family. You are appreciated."

With that, I stood and left with Mrs. Worth.

"Well done, Chef Cole," Mrs. Worth said once we were in the hallway. "I think you've proven yourself a fine addition to the family."

"Thank you," I said.

"Now back to work." She pointed toward the kitchen. I walked back by myself and thought about all that had happened in the last two weeks. A new home, an errant kiss, breaking up with John, and finally, a murder solved. It was enough to make my head spin.

The best part was that I still had a job. Chef Butterbottom might even have been showing signs of begrudging respect. My new life was filled with possibilities.

I entered the kitchen, put on a clean apron, and went to work on the tea cakes for tea. I might be a fish out of water, but I was quickly learning to swim with the current.

Queen of Puddings

Queen of Puddings is a classic bread pudding dish with the twist of jam and meringue. I was attracted to the dish because of the name. Traditionally you use strawberry jam and white bread. When I made it, I used triple-berry jam and pretzel bread crumbs. Pretzel bread gave it a nice chew, and it's fun to chop into chunks. I don't suggest using store-bought bread crumbs because you really want the cubes to soak up the egg mixture.

Ingredients
2⅓ cups milk
1 cup white bread crumbs
1 tbs butter—plus some extra for the dish
2 tbs light brown sugar
1 tsp vanilla
1 tbs orange zest
2 eggs, large
4 tbs strawberry jam
¼ cup extra-fine sugar

Directions
1. Preheat oven to 350 degrees F. Butter sides and bottom of a 4-cup ovenproof dish or roaster pan.
2. In a heavy saucepan, bring milk to a boil.

Remove from heat and add bread crumbs, butter, brown sugar, and vanilla. Finely grate orange zest into the mixture and let stand for 30 minutes to allow the bread crumbs to swell.

3. Separate eggs. Add the yolks to the mixture above and pour into dish. Stand the dish in a cake pan half filled with water. Bake in the center of the oven for 35–40 minutes until set. Remove from water bath.
4. Spread jam on top.
5. Whisk egg whites until stiff, adding all but 1 tbs of the extra-fine sugar until you have a thick, glossy meringue.
6. Pipe or spread the meringue on top of the jam. Sprinkle with remaining sugar. Place dish on a flat cookie sheet and bake for another 15–20 minutes until the meringue is crisp and golden. Serve immediately.

Spring Frittata

To me, there is nothing better than a frittata for breakfast, lunch, dinner, or even a picnic. This dish is the one Carrie Ann wants to make before she finds her assistant dead under the kale bed. The original used spinach, but I made it with kale for a nice texture. Chopped and slightly wilted, kale has a strong flavor and great antioxidants.

Ingredients
  8 green onions
  1½ cups cooked peas (fresh or frozen)
  ½ cup fresh spinach or kale
  24 small new potatoes
  2 tbs butter
  2 tbs olive oil
  2 tbs chopped chives, basil, and parsley (fresh)
  ½ cup finely grated parmesan cheese
  10 eggs, large
  ¾ cup heavy whipping cream
  Salt and pepper to taste
  1 cup feta cheese, crumbled
  3½ oz thinly sliced pancetta or bacon

Directions
  1. Cut new potatoes into quarters and cook until tender. Wash green onions and chop. Wash spinach/kale, drain well, and wilt in a pan with a little olive oil.
  2. Melt butter and olive oil in a large (8 inch) ovenproof frying pan. Cook the onions until soft. Remove the pan from heat and add the peas, wilted spinach/kale, and potatoes. Sprinkle with herbs and parmesan cheese.
  3. Whisk together the eggs and cream. Add salt and pepper. (I use ½ tsp salt and 1 tsp pepper.) Pour into pan over vegetables. Crumble the feta over the top. Add pancetta in small twists.

4. Bake at 350 for 25–30 minutes until set and golden brown.
5. Serve immediately. Also makes great leftovers served cold.

Simple Scones with Vanilla and Lemon Zest

What is a good British book without a classic scone recipe? This simple recipe uses lemon zest to keep the scones light. That way you can serve with any fruit jam or even lemon curd. I like to place the jam in the center and then pipe whipped cream in a circle around the edges. Perfect for afternoon tea.

Ingredients
3¾ cup all-purpose flour
¼ cup light brown sugar
½ tsp salt
3 tsp baking powder
7 tbs butter
¾ cup buttermilk
¼ cup milk
1 egg, large
1 tsp vanilla
Zest of 1 lemon

Directions

1. Preheat oven to 425 degrees F.
2. Sift together flour, sugar, salt, and baking powder into a large mixing bowl. Cut butter into the dry ingredients until pea size.
3. Blend together buttermilk, milk, egg, and vanilla.
4. Make a hollow in the center of the pea-sized mixture. Finely grate lemon zest into it and pour most of the liquid. (Leave out 2–3 tbs to put back in if mixture seems dry.) Mix dough gently. You want a lightly bound dough that is neither sticky nor dry or crumbly. (It should just make a ball.)
5. Lift ball of dough out of bowl and knead on flowered surface just enough to get rid of cracks—overworked dough makes tough scones. Pat dough into ¾-inch-thick slab. Cut out dough with round pastry cutter or biscuit cutter. Place scones on baking tray.
6. Bake 10–12 minutes until well risen and golden.
7. Once cooled, top with jam and piped whipped cream. Serve with tea.

Acknowledgments

It takes a team to bring a book to life. I'd like to thank Matt Martz for believing in me; Heather Boak and Sarah Poppe for all their hard work and support; the editors and copy editors at Crooked Lane for their insightful suggestions; and my agent, Paige Wheeler, for all she does for me. I'd like to thank my family for their love, support, and understanding. And last, but never least, I'd like to acknowledge the readers, without whom books would never be made.

Center Point Large Print
600 Brooks Road / PO Box 1
Thorndike, ME 04986-0001 USA

(207) 568-3717